HOMELESS BONES

INTRODUCING SEAN DOYLE

STEVEN LEWIS

PAYTRAD

FRONT PAGE

HOMELESS
BONES

BOOK ONE
THE HOMECOMING

BY

STEVEN LEWIS

THANK YOUS

A Thank You
Proof reading and support
Jill Peeke - Les Lanfear - Glynis Taylor -
Edward Pearson - Gill Pearson.
A big thank also to Les and Jane Rhind
Cheers to Lewis and Amy

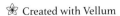 Created with Vellum

WHO AM I?

A judge once likened us to Vikings, using some wise words everyone in court listened. Us lot sat behind a screen, supposedly for our own protection. The articulated sentences he vocalised were a paradox. He asked to see us in his chambers after the verdict had been delivered. The words he chose this time were less official and not so public school, and spoken in a friendlier tone. He removed his robes and wig, moving towards us he shook each of our hands, with what I believed was real genuine respect. But to be honest I couldn't disagree with his description of us. You got in my way you were dead, and I would take what I came for. Whatever opinion any of you formed of me - you didn't want to be with me at the wrong time - in the wrong place!

My relationships lasted around six to twelve hours the longest was provided I slept a while after the main event.

Yet the women never complained, a few begged for me to stay. I didn't. Some felt the same as me -- didn't say a word dressed and left.

We got pissed whenever one of our own was killed. We celebrated their death as if it was his birthday. And your opinion of me doesn't count unless you mixed our DNA the four of us couldn't have been any closer. Every century captured its own history and documented it in books. You had men who didn't / couldn't abide by society's rules or the laws of the land. Why was I different? Different to the likes of Josey Wells, Jessy James, Pablo Escobar and the Kray twins? I believe it was six years, two people and one golden ring.

1

EARLY BIRD

November 18th
Tuesday morning -- two minutes into the day's new dawn

A small round stone tapped against the glass; a sound was heard. A second stone was collected and tossed, this one larger; a louder tap was heard. The thrower cringed and bent over slightly in anticipation of a crack. The moment passed. A third stone was picked up but dropped quickly when the curtain was pulled to one side.

The thrower watched the sash window open. 'Tommy, we're going to the river you coming?'

'I can't ... my mam says - I'm not allowed out. She's gone away with HIM! My nan's here looking after me.' The young lad was half hanging out of the window, excited to see his friend.

'There's gunna be hundreds of Yanks here at weekend, you know for the Queen's birthday. We need to collect coins and other crap off the shore. Tell them all it's linked to Willy.

The Americans love Shakespeare. They'll lap it up and we'll make a fortune - again!' His eyes lit up with the anticipation of further sales.

'My mam'll kill me if I come out when Nan's here. She ain't got all her marbles.' A strange expression appeared on Tommy's face. 'She keeps asking me where Harold is, and will he be back from the shipyard soon? Harold was my grandpa an' he's bin dead 20 year. I only know him from her photos and what mum's said.'

'Can we use your metal detector? I'll make sure you get a share of the finds. You still got your museum T-shirt from last year?' he asked, not knowing how to answer his friend regards granddad Harold.

'Yeah, I have but it's a bit tight. Wait there. I'll fetch my detector but it needs batteries.'

'Oz'll pinch some from the supermarket when he goes for our breakfast.'

Tommy had already disappeared from his window; it was quiet for two minutes. Simo spotted Mr Kumar from next door spying through his curtains, he gave a slight but polite smile the material fell.

'Here you ready? Don't let it drop!!!' And he lowered last year's birthday present down to his best friend. 'Damages and you pay -- deal?'

Simo nodded agreeing to his mate's terms. The pair did a thumbs-up. As good as a handshake for these two. He was happy as his cold fingers untied the cord.

'Ta, Tom, we'll see you later mate. Good luck with your nan,' Simo was off cradling the detector; his arm went up and waved. At that moment Tommy was as happy as any human could be. He couldn't go with them, but he was in a way.

Tommy and Simo had been inseparable since nursery

but a year earlier Tommy's extremely attractive mum re-married a wealthy, older Chinese man. The only drawback was *he* didn't like kids and that included young Tommy.

17 minutes into dawn 0651 hours

It was cold, wet, and still dark; even the resident feathered friends were slow to rise as the heavy drizzle fell.

The small group of cockney treasure hunters left their mate, watching with envy from his window. They set off making their way to the supermarket leaving behind the neighbourhood where the money lived, and the kids wore private school uniforms.

A mile down the road the trio stopped again. 'Don't hang about, Oz get straight in and out don't want a repeat of last time. You fucking listening? And don't provoke anyone.' Simo gave a look, Oz nodded in reply; his funny face always seemed to display the wrong emotion at the wrong time.

'And grab a packet of at least four double A's and plenty of grub. I'm Hank Marvin, mate, fuck all in our larder again, she's pissed it up the wall,' growled Simo, his head shook as he thought of his mum. He took a breath and lit up a smoke to pacify himself.

'Give us a drag before I go then?' begged Oz.

Before Simo could say anything, Jono interrupted, 'Two's up.' But he was ignored.

'Get going, Oz I'll swap you a full stick for the batteries.' Simo waved the box of cigarettes to entice his friend. It was always Oz who was sent to pinch stuff, and it was always from this same Tesco the one on canal street. His mum worked there on the deli counter -- only for the single mother's allowance of 18 hours a week. But the manager of the store was slipping her one. And with him being a married Christian, with seven kids, this news would not have gone down well over at the New Life Church on Abbey Street. Him begging fat Beryl for a blowjob on Friday behind the boxes of salami, her receiving overtime and some damaged goods for the chore. Him preaching to the congregation from behind the lectern telling them to restrain from their sinful wants on a Sunday. This chubby chaser's duplicitous standards ensured that Oz never got more than a warning -- if he did get caught.

Oz set off walking, his cold hands pushed firmly in the pockets of the torn tatty jacket.

'Two's up,' reiterated Jono, well before the ginger-haired Oz was out of sight.

'Fuck sake not had a drag me self yet.' Simo leaned against the graffiti covered wall inhaling the smoke with the experience of an old docker. A satisfied expression displayed on his young face. Daylight breaking behind the formed bricks the smoke floating up in rings. An image the tobacco industry would have loved for an advertising poster! He passed over the fag cupped backwards in his hand Jono eagerly asked if he could finish it.

'And I'll finish you. Couple of drags. Then give it back,' warned Simo, with piercing eyes. Jono was at least a year older than his mate and a lot bigger -- the biggest of all four of them. But no one messed with Simo who was now sat on a discarded milk crate putting on his poor man's wellingtons. The two doubled up Asda carrier bags were pulled over his school shoes and taped tightly around his skinny calves.

33 minutes into dawn 0707 hours

The quiet moment was broken; out of nowhere, loudly

they heard 'RUN! RUN!' Oz came into view legging it, his shoulders moving not his arms as they were carrying two full bags. Out of the back gates of the supermarket he came, being pursued by an overweight security guard. The waiting two lads started laughing and then began baiting the uniformed man as they fled. He stopped and bent over bracing his heavy torso on his knees. Breathing fast and shallow his heart was racing well past any health recommendation. At that moment he wished that he hadn't smoked 20-a-day for the last four decades. The young treasure hunters began to walk again feeling like winners and laughing with their arms around Oz. They knew they were safe: there was no Bradley Walsh left in the red-faced Bob Hoskins lookalike.

Dawn had broken 0717 hours

'Come on we've only got a couple of hours before the tide comes back in,' ordered Simo, finishing his all-day breakfast sandwich and giant Mars bar. He jumped off the old stone steps and landed with a splatter sinking past his ankles into the London silt. Simo who was only months into his 12th year. Had to grow up quicker than most lads his age and this silly pleasure of jumping into puddles was one childish act that had not yet vacated him.

0737 hours

The two other lads finished eating and joined their friend on the shore, but they kept close to the quayside dragging stuff out from the 300-year-old massive oak supports. Simo took the risk and ventured closer to the retreating Thames. Sweeping Tommy's metal detector in front of him. Left, right and back again; this was repeated over and over as he walked towards the water. Several times he bent down and pocketed small items. All three were quiet as they concentrated on discovering some treasure, ensuring they would get a big pay day at the weekend. The good stuff that was found they sold to Knob Feeler. He paid well for it but all the lads from the estate knew what he was really after and they never went to his house alone. The shit stuff that looked old was sold to tourists mainly the Yanks or the Chinese. Any "odd" finds went to fat Fagan over at the pawn shop. The Thames washed the pebbles turning them over as Simo swept away with the metal detector.

0803 hours

Jono, eating his second sarnie, noticed that his friend had been stationary for a while. 'Simo, Simo what yah found?' Getting no reply from his mate he shouted much louder. 'What yah found? Hey!' There was still no answer. He nudged Oz and then walked over to Simo. 'You deaf? What you found -- gold?' Standing next to him Jono saw the expression formed on Simo's face. He followed his mate's stare then became cold and frightened. He threw up as he collapsed to his knees. There were no tears all the emotions had come too quick to process; he froze. Oz ran over to the pair, but he ran off when he saw the same sight as his two mates. Within ten minutes Oz was inside the glass telephone box. With one hand pushing the door tightly shut with the other he tapped the number "nine" three times and began screaming down the public phone.

0814 hours

'Which service do you require?' asked the operator. Unable to get a reply she transferred him through to the police. The screaming continued. The police officer tried to calm the young lad down. He informed him to wait where he was and that he was sending a police officer over to help and right away. He pressed a switch and his computer screen lit up; a colleague appeared. Oz still holding the receiver with both hands drew in a deep breath and slid down the back of the BT phone box. The lad did not move -- his legs outstretched his feet wedging the door shut. Petrified by what was down on the riverbank the same thing now had a place in his mind but in his head 'it grew' he was terrified it was coming for him.

Within minutes as promised two uniformed police officers arrived at Oz's location. They approached the young lad who was pointing and shouting.

'A ... a... a... monster ... c... c... c... coming ... ooout ... the river. He's got my mates. Are they dead? Help my friends, please help them- I don't know where they are?' he cried out, staring hard at the female officer through the glass. Knees came up he quietened down a touch viewing her sweet soft face. 'Hello,' She opened the door knelt to equalize their heights. The other officer had walked off slightly and began talking into his radio. 'We're going to require assistance on, Old Road leading down to the river, over.'

'Roger that can you give any further details, Steve? Over.'

'No, not at the moment. Send us what you can. K9 will be essential, and an ARV are the ambulances on route. We have a very distraught kid here. We may be dealing with a child abduction. Enquire about a helicopter, over.' The officer facing back towards his colleague. Fingers still on the radio.

'They're on route Steve; we'll be standing by for an update, out.' Central ended the conversation. With the mention of child abduction, the chief constable was informed. The police dog and handler arrived first followed shortly by one ambulance and then the armed response vehicle. The female officer approached the ARV.

0849 hours

'Two hundred meters on the shore just past Hangman's Wharf. He's saying that two of his friends have been attacked by a monster?' she told the driver through the window. The BMW's blue lights ignited, and it shot off. The ambulance crew were now talking to the police and trying to persuade the young lad to come out of the phone box and get into the ambulance. 'He's like a limpet stuck on a rock. I can't get a hold,' referenced the medic. 'And I need to treat him, immediately his hearts racing, really racing.'

0857 hours

Two more ambulances and three extra cop cars arrived at the scene plus two plain vehicles with blue flashing lights built into the radiator grills. The area had been cordoned off. Officers were running across roads with reels of tape in their hands. Blue and white cones slid along the kerbs; the armed response team remained on guard. A circling helicopter up above reported in every five minutes.

0900 hours. Everything is under control?

'Can you tell me where you live, please so we can go and collect your parents?' softly asked the uniformed PC.

Simo didn't even acknowledge her presence, let alone answer. He sat on the wheeled stretcher inside the ambulance, shaking whilst holding a plastic cup with both hands. The untouched content was warm sweet tea. He stared with wide eyes down at the non-slip squares pressed into the rubber mat which made up the ambulance floor. The PC painfully watched from the back entrance. Her mind racing trying as fast as possible to piece together enough parts of her police training to be able to deal with the unfolding situation. The lad's feet were crossed; they swung forward and back again and again. For a moment her thoughts stopped as she spotted what remained of the torn Asda shopping bags taped to his legs; she didn't or couldn't comprehend the reasoning but how could she? Their worlds were so apart. Then she was back and watched his legs clattering against the stretcher some more, every clatter loosening the cover from around the lad's shoulders. She moved in and pulled the red blanket tight around him.

'Here clip it with this or it'll just slip again,' said the paramedic as he passed her a large safety pin. Simo didn't move but he had stopped his legs banging.

Scene safe - information gathering begins 0919 hours

A plain-clothed officer appeared at the door. 'Have you had any joy?'

'No, sir he's not spoken a word not even looked at me. He really is scared. I've never seen anyone as frightened as he is right now.' She spoke softly shaking her head. She made her way just outside the ambulance to talk further but out of earshot of the young patient.

'None of the other boys have talked either, not as yet. The small one who called us has had to be sedated. He was petrified when the ambulance arrived at the phone box. Apparently, he kicked and screamed continually. His heart rate was over 200 the medic was that concerned for his life he had no option but to sedate him, poor lad.' The officer stared at young Simo then curled his lips and gave a small of centre smile to Cathy she didn't speak he continued.

'A long time since I have seen such fear myself,' the inspector answered, still looking over Cathy's shoulder at Simo. He watched the medic wrapping a cuff around his thin arm. Without being judgmental he noticed that the lad's arm already had become a canvas for ink. But he knew that on these estates you had to survive.

Cathy was well aware of what state the other lad was in. She was the first officer at the phone box but thought it best not to interrupt her boss.

'Stay with him a little longer. We're trying to get hold of the head-teacher from the local school. Get some IDs. That way we can at least find out where the poor sods live.' He looked away from the crude home done tattoo – a bullet with smoke swirling behind.

'Will do sir,' acknowledged Cathy, feeling like a real police officer for the first time in a year.

'I won't be here for long I have to deal with the questions then I must go over to the hospital. The coroner has finished the autopsy on another case; the old woman at the funeral parlor. She was shot dead then prepared and placed in one of her own boxes? Sad affair and we have very little to go on.' Said the inspector as he turned and walked away, heading straight towards the crowd of vulture-like press. The paparazzi were warmed up and had continued their shouting of questions, pushing in force against the temporary barricade.

Cathy turned and looked at the young teenager covered with the red blanket.

The wet mud from when he had slipped more than once was all over him. He had tried. With every muscle in his body to make his escape from whatever he saw on the riverbank. She instinctively wanted, desperately in fact, to hold him, to hug him, and give him some reassurance. She watched as the young lad stared at the floor harder and harder, never once blinking. All her police training and professionalism told her to remain at a distance, take notes and just keep him safe; humanity begged her to hold the splitting child.

'Everything will be okay.' She sat next to him and pulled him into her. Realising he was still shaking she held him even tighter and reiterated to him that things would be okay.

A minute is a long time when such powerful emotions are at play: that's how long Cathy held the terrified lad for. Her clothes were now as wet as his, she pulled away. He started to swing his legs again. The paramedic smiled as the lad turned towards Cathy.

'Number 17, The Back Gardens just off Parade Square. Get my sister Sarah. My mum'll be pissed or in bed with a hangover shagging a scum bag.' The cup was up to his lips and down, 'My name is Simon Tiler, miss,' he told Cathy. His light blue eyes began blinking and tears started rolling.

'Nice to meet you, Simon Tiler.' Cathy smiled, which he attempted to mirror.

She looked at this young but very streetwise little man, who had probably seen more violence and disarray in his short life than she had in most of her 24 years. What had he seen down by the river to instil so much terrifying fear?

· · ·

Information gathering over - 0930 hours

'Start wrapping it up men. Only another twenty minutes and we'll have to move it,' instructed the police sergeant. The four-strong forensic team heard the warning, but it came a little late as the men were already paddling in water.

Their crisp white suits were no longer white; not even Persil could have removed the stains. Not after crawling around in the mud for an hour gathering shreds of possible evidence. The mighty Thames had begun to return to the shore in waves, each wash extending its cover an inch closer and further up the shoreline. Cathy couldn't hold back her curiosity any longer. Against the advice of her inspector, she placed down her warm coffee and hobbled down to the river's edge, falling into the silt on at least one occasion. Back on her feet, her hand which was so full of mud it started oozing through her fingers as they travelled through her long brown hair. Now minus one police issue shoe she limped several feet closer and looked to where the forensics had been crawling. Able to catch a glimpse her throat dried up; it felt as if it had been disconnected from her stomach. None of the other officers paid any attention to her.

Four hundred metres away from Cathy - 0945 hours.

'Can you confirm that what has been found on the shoreline is an alien creature of some type, inspector?' loudly shouted an overly eager reporter. A second one asked at the same volume. 'We've heard it's actually, ... a prehistoric monster,' the voice squeaked, 'The likes of Nessie up in Scotland. Can this be confirmed, sir? Sir ... Can this be confirmed?' The questions continued to fly at the inspector. No manners displayed from the people who called themselves "professionals". He stood tall remaining quiet and composed while the excitement lowered a little. His clothes said that he'd dressed in somewhat of a hurry but had done enough to pass muster. He waited for a few more minutes knowing from the dozens of speeches he'd done, that it was best to allow the crowd a moment to vent before engaging with them. To be prepared because whatever was said now would be dissected in print and on the internet within hours. Making it un-retractable.

'Members of the press thank you for your interest in this matter. I really do appreciate you all wanting a story for your assigned papers. If you, please allow me to speak I will give you my statement.' The eager crowd softened in their excitement just as he had anticipated, but the cameras continued clicking. The recorders with the big fluffy microphones held steadfast in his direction.

'I am sure that when I ask you all for your cooperation with regard to this sad and as yet unexplained matter, you will be more than willing to give it.' His forehead raised; his eyes scanned the crowd. Judgment and timing were everything.

The inspector turned to a female who had appeared and was now standing to his left. His arm half stretched out to receive some papers. She opened her folder and passed over several sheets of A4. He switched on his politically correct head, took a hidden breath, then counted to three and began reading from the prepared statement.

'Earlier today a 999 call was received by one of our emergency dispatchers this call was from a concerned member of the public. A second call one that I cannot elaborate on was received only minutes later. This particular call increased our response. The call was given preference and checked out by operational staff. Who subsequently visited the scene; these were uniformed armed response officers. Following the results of this action, the call was then immediately upgraded to a major incident on their findings.' Another scan of the crowd. 'The appropriate resources were correctly assigned to the scene. Hence, why we cannot currently allow any members of the public down on to the riverbank.' The inspector placed the front page to the rear and continued to read the pre-arranged text.

'What has been discovered here today,' As good as any newsreader, his eyes went over his glasses, and back down, 'Will not be disclosed at this point in time as we have some evidence to suggest that it may be part of a much larger and ongoing investigation. Of which the Metropolitan Police have been engaged in for some considerable time. Also, we believe it may endanger others if we allow information to freely circulate.' A second sheet of paper was put to the back. The press started to talk amongst themselves as the realisation that they were not going to receive any significant information dawned on them. The inspector continued with the briefing.

'Because of the importance of this case our legal team has applied immediately to the courts for an injunction.' His eyes went to his watch. Hand up he removed his glasses and stared boldly into the crowd, not a single face muscle twinged. Glasses back in place. 'This will ensure no significant details regarding this incident are or could be reported on which may compromise the investigation in such a way. That would prevent any future arrests being made.' Eyes wide and into the herd again, very much aware that what he had just told them – "no reporting of any significant facts related to what was found today" – meant roughly translated that they would not be receiving any type of confirmation.

The press hounds left the barricade and started running

towards the parked ambulances, just as two paramedics guarded by several armed officers pushed a trolley across the road. Secured to this chrome bed on wheels was a zipped-up, shiny black body bag. The police rushed in – at least 20 in numbers – arms linked locking together to form a human wall.

The herd was upon them. Cameras were held in the air some reporters climbing on the shoulders of others just to get a glimpse of what would be, could be, the greatest scoop of the decade. The police officers stood fast holding the Roman barricade together, more officers joined to bolster the ranks. One of the press shouted out loud that the ambulance was about to leave. An elbow then broke the nose of one of the officers. She fell to the floor, the first shot had been fired, in retaliation a baton shot out towards the press. The man's glasses smashed as his nose exploded. Another officer was knocked out. The human wall had been penetrated and it became a free-for-all. In the following hours eleven arrests were made and seven people had been hospitalised.

The ambulance carrying the secret cargo left with an escort that the president of the USA would have been proud of. Simo, Jono and Oz were all taken to the hospital and remained there for several days, up on the top floor in a ward with locked doors. Oz has never since said a word to anyone about the horror he witnessed; Jono received ongoing therapy after developing agoraphobia. Simo left the area and now lives with his older sister in Bridlington, East Yorkshire.

2

SPIES AND LIES

November 14th
'That will do, Garthwaite. Hide the damn camera.'

The Canon was lowered quickly below the height of the windscreen only a couple of seconds before the black Mercedes drove past the Mondeo.

'Plumber,' stated the minister, from the back seat of the Mercedes.

'Sir.'

'Drop me off near the old clock in Fountain Square and don't forget you're to collect my wife and daughter this evening, and please ensure you are punctual. They are to attend an exclusive production of *Havana* at the Theatre Royal. It promises to be a splendid show performed by the travelling Shakespeare Company. Ensure that they have their escorts with them and they are all to be armed!' The minister looked into the rear-view mirror for confirmation from his driver.

'Of course, I'll make it my priority sir. Why armed escorts though? Are we expecting an event?'

'Remember our conversation, Plumber? The one about you asking too many questions regarding situations above your pay grade.'

'I do, sir and I apologise again, sir! I mean no harm, just wondering if I'll need to be packing as well,' he answered, deflecting from yet another of Shoebridge's pointless reprimands. 'Are you not going to the club this evening? Sir.'

'No, well not this evening maybe later tonight around eight and will you refrain from using gangster terminology; bloody "packing", you know how much I dislike brutalising our beautiful language. His eyes found Plumber in the mirror for the second time. 'I have something important to attend to a task that I need to make sure has been completed and fulfil an order for export to Africa. And whilst it is on my mind have you arranged for a courier to pick up the case from the club? After the collection I will proceed to join my family at the theatre. Plenty of prominent people to see me there.' His thin lips exhumed a smile.

'Very good, sir. Shall I pick you up from the Magnolia later?'

'No need you concentrate your time and effort solely on my daughter all evening. There is a good chap. And yes, please have your weapon with you but concealed! I do not want another incident like the one we had in the cafe!' He looked again in the rear-view mirror with an eye-roll then picked up the conversation.

'You are aware of how important my daughter is to me. I will arrange my own transport when I feel comfortable about the order. You will have enough on your plate.' Shoebridge grabbed his monogrammed briefcase, his two thumbs working in unison. The numbers "I 8 7 9" were spun on both the dials, his thumbs pressed inwards and the lid popped up.

Plumber slowed the Mercedes before coming to a complete stop as he obeyed the changing colours.

'Why have we sto ... oh, o... bloody traffic lights ....' The minister returned his attention back to the papers in his briefcase. His solid gold pen began to scribble on the assigned lines until he was interrupted for a second time. On this occasion by a loud wet *slap* and *squash*.

'What the bloody hell?' he cursed looking up witnessing a dirty sponge slide across the brand-new car's windscreen. Shoebridge watched the skinny disfigured fingers which were attached to a heavily tattooed hand. They pushed left and pulled right producing a dirty trail of muddy water. Chinese lettering covered the skin from the tips of the knuckles across the back and travelling up the forearms.

'Is he one of "them" homeless persons, Plumber?' asked Shoebridge with natural upper-class belittlement.

'I believe so. Shall I drive off, sir?'

'No, no, ... let us not be rash. We do not know the man's circumstances, now do we. Give him an invitation for the hostel. We need to start filling that place up and I have still to replenish stock for Benin, at least for the present. But mark my words Plumber if the American contract emerges fully - I WILL bring the mumbo jumbo deal to an end instantly, whatever the bloody consequences!' He spoke out loud, but he was talking to himself, beefing up his own bravado for a showdown that he was well aware was coming. He had been threatened on more than one occasion, by these heathens "godless folks", as he referred to them.

'Yes, sir. Whatever you say, sir.' Plumber pressed the button for the window to come down, letting in November. The cold air and rain droplets began entering the brand-new Mercedes.

'Just a pound please guvnor. But only if you're fully satisfied with my work that is?' requested the surprisingly well-spoken man.

Plumber forced a pseudo smile onto his square face as he passed over a glossy A5 booklet which also contained a crisp £20 note. He pressed the same button the opposite way this time raising the window, without entering into any conversation with the posh homeless boy.

Click - click - click, could be heard in the Mondeo four cars back. At least 30 times the Canon's shutter blinked.

'I got some good shots sir, including a decent one of a booklet being handed out the Merc's window,' reported Garthwaite.

'Did we manage to pick up any audible?'

'Nothing, sir. Their car must be lined or it's a got deflector fitted,' he replied whilst adjusting a switch on the dash. The only sound that came through the speakers was white noise, not the upper-class voice they were both hoping for.

'Let's call it a night. It appears he's going to the club for the remainder of the evening.'

'Yes sir.' Garthwaite clicked the indicator ready for the next left turn.

The lights changed and both cars drove off as the homeless windscreen cleaner returned to the pavement. Letting go of the dirty sponge it fell back into the square bucket. He became excited when he opened the booklet and saw both the money and a fancy invitation with its pages full of pictures of beds, dining areas and even a swimming pool.

'It's for two people, Lou. We can both go for a week it says here. Look!' He passed her the open booklet including the money and invitation. She flicked through the shiny, squeaky pages.

'I don't believe it! I really don't.' She looked up from the booklet; spirits lifted somewhat she carried on. 'This is that new charity, Heno. It is the one that's being set up by a government politician and he's a Sir as well. I think his name is Shawbridge, no ... no ... wait, Sir Shoebridge that's it. He's a big shot minister high up in the government.' Her eyes widened. 'I saw him on breakfast TV just this morning in the launderette. I was with Polish Anna. We were saying it looked like a good thing for us. The people that are accepted in the place pay for the hostel themselves.' Lou was forced to stop talking as the coughing started and so deep to the point of releasing phlegm; she began shaking from the cold, chilled right through to her homeless bones.

Her clothes were drenched by the rain, and she was feeling the effects of a raised temperature the coughing continued. Henry had tried to leave her back at the squat where it was at least dry, but she always insisted that she came with him when he was out earning money. This invitation was a lifeline for her in November.

'Come on sweet cheeks let's get you to this minister's wonderland and into the warmth. You need a hot bath and maybe a doctor, get checked over.' He put his thin arm around her shoulders. Pulling her in close he placed his lips on top of her well-worn woolly hat and kissed.

She smiled out of simple contentment as Henry spoke

more, his well-formed voice putting her at ease. She really did love him, he was her life and future, yet she wasn't aware of his family background or connections. To her Henry was an enigma, but she didn't care all she wanted was to be with him and whatever came with that was fine.

'We'll get a taxi with the money, Lou. Don't you worry we should be there in no time,' Henry reassured her with his words and a further squeeze of his arm.

'Yes, that would be nice. I'm really cold and feel very tired Heno. So, so weak... I feel sick with it and it's been every morning this week. I think I may be coming down with something.' Her head fell to the side resting softly on his shoulder.

After slipping the bucket, mop and sponge behind the advertising board feeling like he had secured his livelihood, the pair walked off, his arm supporting her while he was reading the directions map printed on the back of the booklet. Their lives were on par with our hunter-gatherer ancestor's, up with the light, find money or food, and back to the safety of the cave before dark.

Lou was quietly waffling on, telling Henry about the posh minister she'd seen on TV earlier that day, and that he was very confident, talking animatedly about the prospects the new hostel brought and what it would mean to the London's homeless folk. And, in fact – to the city as a whole, as everyone could benefit.

'You should have seen him, Heno he came across as a really nice man. Honest and with a good heart he was smiling the glint twinkling in his eyes as he explained to the reporter the plans he had for the old Waterfront.' She began to mimic the minister's words in between coughs. 'The homeless community could help people in ways that we don't realise yet. And the day centre, plus the residential places, could be paid for by their own donations and contributions.' Clearing her voice, her coughing subsided somewhat. 'Look! It says that here in the leaflet – page four.' Lou lifted the booklet showing him the page and somehow feeling incredibly special that she had been given this chance. As both her and Anna had said earlier, getting an invitation for the hostel would be like finding a Willy Wonka's golden ticket. The pair stopped for a moment to allow Lou to catch her breath. She pointed to a page and passed the leaflet over.

'This is what excited me.' Her finger guided Henry as his free hand took hold of the booklet.

Page four from the leaflet –

As our new charity begins to expand it is clear that the many talents these people have will need to be built upon and carefully nurtured. Thus allowing these individuals to both grow and flourish in their own right. A period of time would be set aside for the investments made to be repaid back with interest when a person has become financially independent. This in return will produce further funds allowing more expansion to take place and many more discoveries of fresh talent to be uncovered. An X factor for the homeless, if you like. They have what we need and in abundance. So, let them share everything with us. Let stars be created. Artists be discovered. And geniuses be found.

End of page.

She was motivated further to reach the hostel as Lou was a great singer so to her this page wasn't just printed words it was a contract and one that she would love the chance of signing. She was forced to stop for a while longer as the coughing replaced her words for a second time. Sweet Lou bent forwards with the exertion and struggled to straighten back up because of the sharp pains she felt. Henry rubbed her back up and down his palm went attempting to warm her. Feeling powerless and having to watch the one he loved suffer. His arm went out in the direction of a taxi.

'I don't care who pays for it it's free right now and that's all that matters.' He rubbed more and more, trying to ease her breath. 'You need to see a doctor and be in a nice warm bed.' He hurried their pace supporting her as the pair moved along his arm still up. They were forced to fight against the winter elements leaning forward in an attempt to streamline themselves in the wind. The rain continually adding more weight to their load with every step they took.

Four taxis they had approached and so far, all had refused to have them in their cabs. The last one telling them plainly, 'Fuck off! You stink like dog shit! Both of ya are disgusting, ya make me sick! Get a fucking job, pay ya taxes like the rest of us! Scum.'

The pair of hippy lovers ignored what was shouted from the cab. As sadly to them and many more like "them" this abuse was a daily occurrence. The rain came down even heavier as they resigned themselves to going by foot. Henry pulled out a carrier bag from his pocket and ripped it along the side. It was formed over Lou's shoulders tucking it into her collar to ease the penetration of water.

The last abusive cab driver, now several hundred metres further up the road, pulled over and answered his mobile phone. Listening, but never once answering back, he placed it back down on the dash. Remaining quiet for a moment he looked at the blank screen of the phone, shaking his head ever so slightly as it hurt. The man's stubby fingers on his left hand adjusted the rear-view mirror. His fingers on his right hand travelled to the left side of his face. Attentively he stroked the six-inch long blood-stained Band-Aid in place from his earlobe to the bottom of his chin. The voice on the phone had told him to ensure the homeless couple arrived at the hostel. Each of the words he listened to were spoken using perfect English and matched by the accent that delivered them. Injected with fear the cabby checked the traffic and about-turned. Soon pulling alongside the two lovers one eye on the road whilst at the same time trying to catch their attention. 'Hello – you there! Can I apologise? I'm really sorry for what I said just now back there. I'd received some shitty news about my separation and took the frustration out on you two; that was wrong of me. Please, please allow me to take you somewhere?' The cabby tipped his Burberry flat-cap and at the same time flashed his polished pearls at Henry. But Louisa was unable to look up as all her effort had been sustained just moving forward against the driving rain. The driver waited before he gave another glance to Henry and a glance through the windscreen after the wipers had passed.

'That's very good of you and thank you it couldn't have come at a better time. My friend is sick and she needs to see a doctor pretty quickly I fear.' Henry didn't hold back the worry, his eyes squinted for protection from the heavy downpour.

'Again, I feel really bad for my earlier comments so like I said as a recompense allow me to take you on your journey to the hostel. With no charge of course.' His polished teeth were once again displayed in the frame of his lips. 'Come on, the pair of yeh get-in quickly. You must be drenched!'

Henry worried that Lou was freezing to death, she was coughing so hard and much more frequent. Her slim frame forced right over then back up and off to one side with the backstabbing pains; she really looked ill.

'Thank you we do appreciate the lift.' The pair climbed in the back of the black London cab. Lou had gripped the yellow bar, but her fingers were so cold she struggled to let go, Henry from behind, helped prise her digits away from the rail. They were in, the door was pulled too when the driver informed them that he would turn up the heater followed by, 'Are you hungry, luv? I've a couple of sandwiches left over from lunch. Here, help yourself. They're cheese and tomato and fresh – honest! Smell 'em. They're from Lil's, you know, at the end of the market in Kings Square. She does a bloody good roll that woman does.' Rambling on at speed he moved the bag towards them his face closer.

'Thank you, sir, and again very kind of you.' Henry nodded, taking the food. And for the first time he noticed the fresh Band-Aid on the cabby's cheek. No comment made, it wasn't his place to do so but his pupils widened and he thought to himself *nasty gash under there.*

Lou shook her head as she removed her coat then melted into the seat. Henry broke off a quarter of the sandwich then broke that in two again. 'Here eat this tiny bit please for me Lou.' The bread touched her mouth; her lips accepted the nourishment as they subconsciously opened.

The 25-minute taxi journey would shuffle them across London using several roads, over at least two bridges and under one pass, before finally terminating at a massive grain store currently listed under conservation. It was located down by the old docks right at the other side of the city on the waterfront. A colossal 1.2 million pounds so far had been invested in this old Victorian warehouse. It was built originally in 1820 for the storage of Chinese porcelain, a very valuable commodity in its day.

Miraculously and unlike most social projects of this scale, not one single penny had come from the purse of the British taxpayer. This up-market sixty room rehabilitation centre was a listed building. A £200,000 grant for the facade work came in from the London Heritage Society and the National Lottery. The remaining one million was a gift from our American cousins across the pond a large chunk towards the purchase.

Some thought it was crazy to have a homeless project dead centre of the up-and-coming docklands of London, but not Sir Shoebridge. No. He was adamant and spoke passionately during numerous interviews on TV and the same message came across in countless articles written for the white pages.

A Shoebridge quote, taken from *The Guardian* newspaper:

"These people are currently living on the streets of our divine city many of them arriving there through no fault of their own, temporarily down on their luck. However, being homeless will soon be condemned to the history books. If we all embrace the new hostel many more will naturally follow. These undesirable people are worth a lot and deserve the second chance that this hostel would be able to give them. People across the world would also greatly benefit from the latest precious wares stored in the warehouse.

Jonathon Bishop
Investigative journalist

There was no need for any of the hostel's critics to worry. At least not regarding the exterior of the building and the possibility of this lowering the tone of the soon to be posh area; as it would, when finished, be more akin to a luxury hotel rather than a hostel for the city's homeless population.

Everyone who entered through the doors of this one of a kind "second chance" were fumigated, thoroughly cleaned, fed, and given clean clothes. Education was made available in so many forms including all the standard academic classes starting with the ABCs and finishing with the building trades and all the arts. Residents were to be at the beginning of their stay under a very strict regime of monitoring and detoxing so these entrance courses would help relieve the tension.

However, this all came at a high cost as lots couldn't hack this harsh five weeks reprogramming. Some, a good few, of the new residents ran away and a lot were never to be seen or heard from again. The police put the missing people down as relocating to other towns and cities across the country, embarrassed after failing such an opportunity.

The charity named "BONES" had recently spent a small fortune on publicity for the new up and coming hostel. This new charity planned to educate, retrain and set up its own employment agency. All within the walls of the modernised Waterfront warehouse. Their management team had reached out to a lot of the major corporations with the hope of receiving both backing and funding to assist with the educational programmes. The council had given a grant and helped the charity to set up a recycling plant. Paper, glass, metals creating a valued extra funding resource. Then there were the giants of the construction world such as Barratts and Wimpey. All these were approached for help with building trades. The likes of Alan Sugar, Richard Branson, and even rumours of Arnold Schwarzenegger and Tony Robbins were to attend and give motivational talks. Also, a talent school would eventually be in operation. This was to gain extra funding from Simon Cowell who would have the first pick of the stars the school discovered. The profits from all the departments would be pooled and used to both run and expand the hostel. The increase in financies would allow the charity to facilitate residential accommodation for a further 176 homeless folks. Each individual would be assessed before being placed on the one to five tier rehabilitation route, eventually seeing them exit the Waterfront. Even forward-thinking had taken place: an independent financial banking system which was to stand alone from the mainstream lenders. It's prototype complete and was in the process of being rolled out. Given the fact that most people coming off the streets would have no credit rating. Let alone a bank account; once again the interest produced from this could be re-absorbed back into the Waterfront. The money from across the pond was a gift to help Shoebridge purchase the rundown building. This was received from the owners of a charity who have a similar project already well-established and running successfully in the United States. After a lot of ill-feeling at the beginning of the program the American hostel became very successful, and several were now open and welcomed by the communities they had been located in.

Although the British charity had been operating for several months from a separate site, its official opening day for the UK's BONES and the Waterfront was planned to take place in one week's time. Forty residents were already in the new repurposed warehouse! Its latest porcelain – It could be said.

A trip to the States had been arranged to take place two days after the official opening of the site this would see thirty lucky people picked from the hostel's current residents they'd be flown out to America by chartered aircraft no less. The chosen would spend at least a month in one of the American new home communities. Every one of these American places were equal in size to five of the UK hostels each holding a thousand people at any one given time.

Sir Shoebridge's hope was that the success the British homeless people would see and feel whilst over in the United States would rub off on the chosen few, and hopefully be brought back with them on their return. Then the hope was it would be infused within the Waterfront hostel and its new clientele as the staff were to be part paid – part voluntary. This was part of his speech during every interview how much the Americans had helped and inspired whilst seeking no financial reward!

Unlike the rain the black cab stopped, two of its wheels up on the kerb and two remaining on the tarmacked road. 'We're here! This is the new homeless hostel the Waterfront the one on your leaflet,' the cabbie spoke through the rear-view mirror.

Henry touched the leaflet in his back pocket but shook his head and spoke, 'Thank you but are you certain we can't pay something to recognise your good turn?' Henry held out the £20 note.

'No, please, no need, you keep your money. It's my treat and I hope you both have a great time here and I apologise again for my rant earlier,' replied the cabbie, twisting his body and leaning further over the back of his seat. The expression he wore was a mask but one well-worn by a great pretender. The only thing Henry saw was the fresh blood seeping through the long band-Aid.

Henry and Lou were both out of the taxi. They heard the cab's horn sound twice as all four of the vehicle's wheels were back on the road. Henry gave a courteous wave. Standing side by side the pair looked in awe at the partially renovated warehouse. Even with the scaffolding still erected in many parts the building was perfectly illuminated and gave them an instant impression of grandeur.

'We are going to like it here Lou. It's a good place, it feels right. I can see our lives being changed forever – you'll see.' His eyes scanned the building some more as he affirmed, 'Yes I can. I really have a good feeling about this place,' reiterated Henry, squeezing Lou then kissing her wet woolly hat once more.

She was too exhausted to speak. She felt warm inside knowing Heno was pleased and this in return pleased her. He was her whole world. The pair were greeted as they walked under the arch above the steel gates. It displayed one dual word, "Waterfront", the letters spanned equally across the curve. The square heavy letters which had been smithed in a forge were then painted gold to replicate old Victoriana, the era in which this impressive building had been born.

A female wearing a uniform but not a uniform, a navy skirt and light blue blouse came to meet them small strides dictated by the tight skirt. 'Good evening to the both of you and may I ask do you have an invitation to the Waterfront or are you here to make an enquiry?' She waited underneath the umbrella for the couple's reply, her hand on top of her other hand, elbows bent, heels and toes touching, the high heels perking up her backside. The umbrella wedged tight in her arm.

'Yes, yes we do have an invitation... here ... look?' Henry

pulled out the booklet from his back pocket and showed it with determination to the pretty female. So eager as if he were the winner of a competition, but to them this invitation was the golden ticket. Just like Lou and Anna imagined. Henry's eyes were drawn away from the female for a moment – redirected to a black van or minibus parked up at the far end of the building. Several torch beams erratically being waved around to and from the vehicle to the building. Voices could be heard, but they were not clear enough to be understood – not from such a distance. The wind was against him but then switched direction and blew in the undistinguishable sound of a van door being slammed hard. About to ask the attendant for an explanation he was stopped as the painful coughing came again from sweet Lou. His gaze went back to the pretty female who had checked their invite at the same time his arm pulling Lou in tighter to him emphasising to the attendant that she needed some help.

'That's fantastic, ... and everything looks in order in fact, this invite has the signature of Sir Shoebridge?' she looked from the page to the homeless duo. 'Our founder, you two must be very special. So if you would like to accompany me inside the Waterfront we will get you warmed up and fed.' The booklet was closed by the pretty assistant whilst projecting a radiating welcome as if on cue, then she shared the cover of the umbrella with Lou.

The three of them reached the entrance where a very tall medium-set man opened one of the frameless glass doors. 'Good evening to the both of you and may I welcome you here to the Waterfront,' sincerely greeted the man, wearing navy trousers and a pale blue shirt. His smile was also as radiating as his female colleague's.

Through the gigantic doors, the first thing that hit the

homeless couple was that the place was immaculately presented with quality stone tiles laid on the floor. Authentic works of art, displayed tastefully, hung on the smooth plastered walls of which the large centre piece was a Banksy. A gift presented by the unknown artist herself. The far wall was home to a shaded glass counter where again the building's name was displayed, this time in coloured florescent tubes '70s style. Several people were milling about the foyer. It wasn't a quiet place but yet the noise somehow was comforting to Henry. He noticed two of the people were workmen and a couple who were clearly reporters, given the equipment they carried.

The ceiling height of the newly refurbished foyer must have been well over 40 feet before it began to curve into the point. Henry got an ache in his neck looking all the way to the top and out of the glass dome; a sense of his childhood was in the air. However the same experience was, it had become overwhelming and all a bit too much for Lou. As she tried to remove her hat, she came over all faint collapsed and flopped to the floor.

'Lou! Lou!' Henry dropped down beside his girlfriend. 'Help her! Please, can someone help her!' he cried out loud. Stroking the back of her pale hand he looked to her his voice lowered several decibels he began reassuring the love of his life. Telling her over and over again that she would be alright, they had made it, they were here and safe now; everything would now be good for them, the end isn't nigh.

Within less then a hundred seconds she was checked over and fixed to a monitor. The bleeps began. On the count of three Lou was picked up and placed on a wheeled stretcher before being rushed off to the medical centre which occupied a quarter of the space on the ground floor, and one full upper story, of the warehouse. The brochure stated in bold letters "in-house" medical centre but the set-up was better than most NHS hospitals and could attend to any procedure. From an everyday headache to a complete lung transplant. All carried out in its "state of the art" operating theatres and clinic rooms all of these linked directly to the helicopter pad situated at the rear of the building.

'She is going to be fine, sir,' assured the man dressed in two shades of blue.

Ignored at first by Henry partly because of his worry over his girlfriend but also because it had been a long time since he had been intentionally addressed with this or any other positive title especially "sir".

'Follow me, sir and I will give you a quick tour of the ground floor, then we'll begin the process of getting you settled in for your stay with us. How does this sound to you, sir?' spoken with what came across as genuine concern and interest.

Henry stared at the pleasant looking man, making many assumptions, before setting off with him. He had entered a different world here and it had all come about very quickly. Feeling at ease and with no major knots in his gut he followed his host. A silence was in operation, but this was okay with Henry as it allowed him time to have a good look around the place.

Further into the tour, the guide slowed his pace, breaking the silence. 'This is one of our community dayrooms. It has multiple uses as you can see.' Not stopping the guide carried on.

'It's big. And very loud,' Henry stated the obvious. He didn't get a reply; the guide continued on with the tour.

'And through here sir is the first of our four dining areas. We like to call this one the TV lounge. I'm sure you will be able to guess why!' The man sniggered to himself as he watched Henry who was mesmerised by the massive television fully covering one decent sized wall. The guide then pointed to several smaller areas within the large space some with traditional kitchen tables and one with an imitation bar and pool table. **And** last but not least, was the library with more tables complete with green onyx and brass reading lamps. The flooring was the only separation of these areas, yet it somehow appeared to work imagined Henry.

The guide's arm remained in the direction of each area for a few seconds, just as a game show host would show off the prizes to tantalise the contestants with what they could win – If they won?

After viewing several more rooms the staff member spoke further. 'Now sir this next area may at first appear in contrast to what you have seen so far. However, please don't be alarmed as I am very confident that you will warm to it as your stay with us extends.' He cleared his throat but had the decency to cover his mouth with the back of his hand noted Henry. He began again. 'It's more of a clinical therapy area you'll find, but a very important part of our ethos.' He took a short breath and then was off again. 'Here at the Waterfront we try our very best to increase and sadly in some cases instil self-worth in our residents. We here at the Waterfront always encourage all of our guests to involve themselves with our team of both counsellors and life coaches.' Every one of his words was spoken with perfect pitch and delivered with a measured amount of enthusiasm. Certain words would be repeated and emphasised for easy recognition and the implementation of a brand, all without the recipient even realising they'd been sold their ideology.

Henry was indeed surprised when they entered the all-white circular room. The walls had been draped with long very white curtains; these rose into the centre of the vaulted ceiling.

Remaining at the back of the big tent just inside the doors Henry stood as Scrooge did accompanied by the spirit of his past, watching with trepidation and both relief and disbelief as a couple of the patients / participants acted out a scene where a drug dealer was attempting to sell them drugs.

'Strange therapy!'

'Let me explain exactly what you have just witnessed in our paradise room, sir. It is one of the ways in which we at the Waterfront try to prepare our clients to say "NO" to a fix. We are very aware that dealers will be ready to pounce on them the moment they are allowed back outside...' a small cough, 'After their incubation period has finished. Our residents themselves have voiced to us that one of the hardest aspects to overcome is their addiction to drugs. We believe that this form of theatrical therapy has been a highly successful practice with our American cousins. So, it is essential that we use the same format here! Don't you agree with this, sir?' His guide waited for a reply whilst he held open yet another door for Henry to go through but Henry only slightly shook his head as he gave thought to what was being said.

The male continued. 'You see, sir, a lot of our clients have been homeless for such a length of time that they have been unable to fulfil even the most basic of their human needs. Thus, allowing drugs and other mind-numbing substances to become a welcome substitute in place of real life for these forgotten people. Unfortunately they are unable to see a future for themselves and may have no way of believing one could even exist for them. This sad fact may have even begun well before the lack of a roof over their heads was a part of their lives. These individuals may have been abused, manipulated and sadly some kept as slaves and used for a multitude of tasks.' His eyes blinked slowly as he looked away from Henry for a moment. Then he was good again. 'After so long most humans will submit and only strive for the basics of Maslow's triangle.'

Again, this was delivered with perfect pitch from his guide. For a moment Henry imagined his host to be a walking, talking shop mannequin relaying programmed responses read from some invisible autocue that was attached to Wikipedia, maybe. Who actually talks like that in real life? Where do these politically perfect speaking staff come from? Is there a college that half the world's population aren't aware of? The same place where the motivated management get their made-up words and phrases from. "Ability to see the blue sky", "Out the box", "Touch base", "Level set", "Join a tigers team". He smiled to himself, refocused and fired off another question. 'Are we not allowed outside then? Are we kept as prisoners in here! Is that what you're saying?'

'Prisoners? No, no of course not, sir. No one is ever held captive in the Waterfront against their will. For one, that would be unethical. NOT to mention it would also be. Illegal.' He laughed a little but not enough to patronise the questioner, then continued. 'However, as I am sure you will be aware a lot of homeless people do have complex addiction problems. So, we do insist that as part of their new life upgrade they must sign up to take part in our five-week revitalisation programme. The five weeks also allows the individual to take full advantage of our balanced meals and daily injections of vitamins. Thus, ensuring optimisation of the charity's success rate. We all want this exciting opportunity to succeed and grow. Hence we do have a very strong selective induction. Of course, we would love to take in anyone who comes to us off the street but I'm sure you understand, sir, we must ensure our first clients are what we require them to be? For a multitude of reasons and like most successful businesses we have a shopping list to fulfil, a selection process which has to be implemented and adhered to. They must have what we stipulate in the programme! If we need people to swim in the winner's lane, that is. Just like you and your girlfriend were selected.' He then continued lecturing Henry about the benefits of the five-week induction come detox programme even once likening it to being re-born from an "egg".

'I guess it makes sense,' Henry agreed, his head nodded naturally but he was really trying to remember the moment he was given the booklet, because what selection? But quickly thought it best not to say anything in fear of jeopardising this great opportunity especially with his Lou being ill.

Henry had been living on the streets long enough to see a lot of these people that the mannequin was referencing on the whole, the man was sadly correct with what was said. He may have used big flashy strange words – entangled in political phrases. Henry agreed people were, and are, really struggling with life and not just the homeless. Personally, he had known over twenty who had taken their own lives – well over 30 if you added on the accidental drug overdoses and half of these people had roofs over their heads, just no funds left after they'd paid the bills.

'Right, sir I think you have viewed most of the ground floor communal areas so it's time to introduce you to our lovely resident doctor,' said the man in blue, who turned on the spot as he said the word doctor. His unusually long arms pushed a second set of doors and he waited holding the door open for Henry to catch up. Looking at him as he approached without any embarrassment or judgment. Something this homeless posh boy wasn't used to, this whole experience was surreal and had appeared so quickly. Henry was astute and not a daft lad by any meaning of the word. He had taken to living by his wits when on the streets. But inside this lovely hostel he told his protective paranoia to take a holiday. *Not everybody is out to harm you*, his inner voice reassured.

'A doctor?' queried Henry, out of surprise rather than worry as he joined his host at the door.

'Yes, that's right a doctor. Our doctor. We will require you to undergo an examination and some bloods will be taken from you. Think of it as a full MOT, sir followed up by a full-service.' ... a cough into his hand and he was speaking again. 'It's standard practice for every person coming in to join us here at the Waterfront including all the staff. I may add. There really is nothing to fear. This way if you will sir.' ushered the mannequin, giving another little chuckle believing himself to be funny yet again.

Three sets of doors and a change in the flooring later.

'Hello, I am Dr Moe, and this is my assistant Nurse Fuller.' His arm stretched out and pointed to a semi-attractive nurse a few feet to his left.

'Hi!' greeted the nurse, her slight scouse accent emphasising the H.

Henry remained silent; his inner voice may have been reassured but it still was not fully convinced about the situation.

'I will leave you in the capable hands of the doctor, sir. He will call me when you are finished here and it will be my pleasure to take you on your journey. Wherever this may lead.' The man in blue nodded and smiled at the nurse and doctor then he was gone closing the clinic room's door very quietly.

'Please undress and discard all of your clothing into the orange bin – over there,' instructed the doctor pointing to the left wall. No "sir" attached. *Not a welcoming bedside manner*, thought Henry.

'Undress! Take off my clothes?' He glanced at them both. 'What? Everything?' Henry's arms opened to emphasise his question.

'Yes, everything. Your clothes will need to be incinerated unless you have any emotional attachment to them?' The doctor spoke the words but didn't mean them, still detached from any decent emotion, rather than to begin a two-way conversation.

'You may go behind the screen if you would prefer,' added the nurse noticing some apprehension from their patient.

What the hell! Henry shrugged his shoulders and began undressing on the spot. Clothes in hands he walked to the orange container. There was no emotional attachment on Henry's part towards these rags. His left arm went forward to lift the lid, when it automatically raised the clothes were gone; the only thing remaining was a small black notebook tied on a leather cord and hanging around his neck. He was forced to step back as he came about.

'Wow!' he remarked. Nurse Fuller was right there up in his personal space, a foot away if that, her eyes wide open.

'You have a lot of tattoos I see,' she commented but it wasn't the body art that had widened her pupils. She brought her eyes back up and began to tie a tourniquet around his left upper arm.

'Please take a seat and I'll take some bloods for the

doctor who will then carry out the required tests. After I'm finished here you will be required to take a shower and have a cleanse bath.' She was still looking him over. Wishing the doctor wasn't in the room.

'What's a clen...'

'Sheep dip,' she answered with a grin anticipating his question.

She twisted the red top back on the tube it was placed in a see-through bag. Henry's name written on a line, she twisted the lid off another container while still smiling at him, 'Open wide, please?' in went a stick with a swab on the end around and around it was pushed and scrapped along the gum then back in the container and sealed.

'Could I ask how my girlfriend is doing? She collapsed in the foyer on our arrival earlier this evening.' Henry was sitting. He turned away at the last moment when the needle entered. The nurse rubbed the area where she'd injected,

'Ah yes the pretty girl was she with you?' responded the doctor. 'Were you aware that she is pregnant?' His words spoken not so matter of fact.

'Baby! Expecting! No way! A baby - for real?' Henry was astounded at the suggestion of a new life. In this life he was only existing!

'Yes, she's with child. I would estimate three, possibly four months along. We will know more later when her blood results come back,' confirmed the nurse, as she placed a plaster over the injected area.

'No, I wasn't aware at all; although with hindsight she has been sick and tired a lot lately. I thought she had a virus!' Excitement was present in Henry's voice. He had recently turned twenty eight and had been clean from drugs for over two years - since the day he had met Louisa. The same day of the fatal fire. Louisa had gone back to rescue him after the animal rights gang left him to die.

Henry's life early on some would have classed as dreamlike, privileged looking in from the outside that is. On his 18th birthday all that changed. He fell from the great heights of grace he was born into and what followed was a train wreck that would derail him for a long time. Virtually a decade would pass before any form of normal reality would be reinstated. Henry often thought of his mother who he loved dearly, especially over the last two years aided by the clarity of being clean. This child could be the catalyst to take him back home, more so now that his father was dead! Something that didn't upset Henry. His mother would be over the moon with a grandchild as it would continue her family bloodline and this next generation would take her lineage to over a thousand years. And four generations of the family would be under the same roof at once. He was brought from his reminiscing.

'Now come on don't you be worrying about her for the moment young man. She is in very good hands; I can assure you of that. Everything is being done that needs to be done,' said the doctor strangely, his tone slightly warming; he appeared to become excited.

Still in shock but happy about the possibility of being a father he took a deep breath. Henry was given a cup of sweet tea; he had five minutes rest after the phlebotomist had filled the test tube, his gums still a bit sore from the DNA swabbing.

'Have you a pen I could borrow, please?' he asked Nurse Fuller, who quickly obliged looking again to Henry's lower body. He scribbled away then tore the last page out of his notepad. He was dressed in some very light blue scrubs, and after further tests in the clinic, he was told to strip once more and enter the shower room. He was then prompted to stand up against a wall where a red liquid was sprayed all over his front; a further prompt he spun around hands up and flat on the wall, he was sprayed again. His body shook caused by the sudden covering of lots more freezing fluid.

'Open your legs wide! ... Wider?'

Henry obliged. 'Fuuuck!' his buttocks clenched his balls shrinking ten-fold as the red freezing cold liquid entered parts rendered private. Hose switched off for a minute the detergent was washed off with a hosepipe. Goose-pimples appeared everywhere before he entered a warm deep bath and was left alone to wash and rinse at leisure. Relaxing in the warm water he imagined becoming involved with the Waterfront in a big way.

Inside a second clinic room, only five doors down from the bathroom where Henry had been sterilised and was currently relaxing.

'And just roll over for me one last time please, miss,' requested the female doctor. Louisa was still very tired; she obeyed the doctor's command without question, as most would do in the same position as her.

'That's just fine – there thank you.' The medic pulled a nylon tape measure around her calves, thighs, hips, waist, breasts and neck.

'You're a little underweight but not to worry we'll soon put some meat on your bones. There's not a lot we can do with a stick insect is there now?' The medic commented as she wrote down the female's measurements.

'What's that? What's it for? What you trying to do to me?'

asked Lou as another medic approached her bed pushing a wheeled stand from where a fluid bag hung.

The medic didn't answer the anxious female's questions; she came closer. – It was the first medic who spoke to her again. 'We need to get some nutrition into your body as soon as possible because of your baby Louisa. But there's no need to worry you won't feel a thing I promise.' The female doctor turned and told the medic to continue with the drip egging her on with her head.

'BABY! What baby? You're lying! I can't be pregnant...' Lou began to fight but her effort was futile because as the doctor had taken her measurements, she had also secured her patient to the bed at each point of contact.

'It's alright Louisa. Don't be getting stressed. It's not good for our baby. We know it must have come as a shock especially if you did not know you were expecting. So, please just relax and allow us to do our jobs. There's a good girl.'

The skin was punctured the drip line filled with the coloured fluid as Lou struggled and struggled, attempting to break free.

'I'm not pregnant I can'...' she started to shout just as the liquid travelled through the needle and into the cannula; seconds later she was asleep.

Back in the bathroom along the corridor.

'Hello, again Henry,' said Dr Moe, approaching the shower area. Walking slow and carefully placing his feet on the wet tiles anticipating a fall.

'Doctor,' acknowledged Henry, rinsing off the shampoo from his hair. First time in a lot of years he had been so clean and it felt good, really good. Finally, the voice within gave up and started to calm down as the warm soapy water ran down his back.

'We have received your blood results back.' The doctor looked down at a sheet of paper attached to a black clipboard held to his chest height.

'Am I pregnant as well doctor?' laughed the posh speaking homeless boy.

'No, you're not pregnant but you do have hepatitis B... Were you aware of this?' The doctor's tone clearly back to matter of fact.

'Yes, I'm aware. I was diagnosed about three years ago, dirty needles. But it's all under control.., all good.' Henry plunged back under the water to finish off the rinse. Splashing back up he ran his tattooed fingers through his curled, matted hair pushing it backwards. His eyes opened. He heard the doctor talking. But it was a couple of seconds before his vision was there.

'You are no good to us now! You dirty, contaminated animal!' snarled the doctor, seconds before he pulled the Luger's trigger.

The A4 sheet of clean paper developed spotting.

The water dyed red; bits of Henry's brain slowly slid down the white tiles.

An orderly wearing two shades of blue protected by a full-length disposable apron moved in towards the large square bath. Hosepipe in hand, he started washing red fluid from the walls for a second time.

'Remove the rest of his head and the hands then take the carcass over to Mary's parlour, Stewart, with a thousand pounds. Tell her I will pay the remainder on Friday when I collect the proof!' ordered the doctor, as he left the room. Dr Moe was a coward at heart, and inside he was shaking after what he had just done. His self-reasoning which allowed him to continue his endeavours, was that it was ultimately easier to hurt others than to be hurt yourself and so this is what he did, all in the name of science, and to enhance his cloning research. A modern-day Dr Frankenstein.

Two hours later, Barchard and Ward funeral parlour.

'No, I told him we are doing no more. Get the body out of here now before I call the police, yah hear?'

'He wouldn't like it if I have to go back with the body, and if the big man finds out...' The male voice half sounded genuine, but also frightened, not of the doctor, but of the big man.

'I don't care, get the body out of here, this minute!' Mary picked up the phone, stared at him and pushed the phone into the air.

'Ok, ok, I get it, but don't say I didn't warn you.' He pushed the trolley out.

Mary took a deep breath. Should she call Sean and just confess all of what was happening? She was scared, terrified of this big man, but embarrassed about telling Sean what was happening.

Stewart drove away from the parlour and headed for the river. He drove fourteen miles in the hurst before stopping, 'Sunny, you wanna earn a monkey?' asked Stewart, the man pulling on a rope looked at him while his arms still worked. 'I said no more, we nearly got caught, last time? It's not worth the risk!' His arms still working, then they stopped, one broke free and removed the fag from his lips. Stewart said nothing, another fag was lit, the packet offered to Stewart. 'I want six hundred? And you come out with me it'll be quicker!' He offered the lighter to his friend,

'Deal! But we have to do it now? Got the thing in the car, it's freaking me out.' Stewart inhaled, he was relieved. And he'd made four hundred notes, it took the pair less than five minutes to have the black nylon bag crunched up in the boat's cab, 'Puncture the bag... or it'll float, and wrap these around the legs.' informed Sunny, who then took the knife off Stewart and started stabbing the bag, 'You can't hurt him now. He's dead.' The knife was passed back. Stewart didn't look well as he wiped the blood from the blade.

3

SQUEEZE

November 13th

Again, he'd been forced to return to London, but this hadn't been the sole cause of his insomnia; because of his lifestyle he never really sweated the small stuff. Coming to terms a long time ago with the fact he was most likely not going to be around to draw a pension. Physically, his body had already suffered from so much trauma, and he hadn't celebrated his 30th birthday yet. Unable to disperse the weight of the secrets he carried, no one ever told him he looked young for his age.

Added to this, the man's mind had to deal with much more than average Joe. Einstein once said the true sign of intelligence is imagination. So, did this make him a genius, as he lived a life, that most couldn't dream of imagining? But it wasn't a life he'd created for himself.

He looked up, the small gap in the heavy material allowed a tiny amount of light through, this highlighted the well-used paraphernalia, barely visible in the semi darkness of the hotel room. Sitting on the arm of a square sofa next to these items, his fingers removed the foil from the small round tin. This he'd done so many times in his life, at one point two or three times a day, and the outcome he still needed.

An old spoon with the handle curled right over; solid silver, he'd owned it for years. This sat on the table next to a monographed Zippo lighter displaying a couple of wings. His restless fingers took a hold of it and his thumb flicked at the serrated wheel; the flame appeared instantly and licked at the tin. The contents ignited, and in less than a second, blue and yellow flames danced. He picked up the spoon then blew out the fire. The spoon was soon full of a black tarry liquid. Tilting it carefully, he poured the hot polish along the wells of his boots. Silver spoon down, the toothbrush went to work, ensuring the polish was deep into the wells. Next came the well-worn, damp, yellow cloth; this was twisted tight around his thick index finger. It was dipped in the tin's lid before he began the ritual of spinning tiny circles.

Thousands of times, round and round his finger went, stopping only for more spit. Thirty minutes spent concentrating, and both the boots were now immaculate, the man's square face reflected in the toe caps. Boots down, a quick glance at his watch told him he had 34 minutes remaining. Hanging in order on the makeshift washing line was a highly pressed shirt, light brown in colour, followed by a pair of heavy-duty trousers pressed and creased to perfection. In the same condition, the suit jacket came next, then the wide grey braces and tanned tie.

Ten minutes remained when the text came through to his phone.

"Your car has arrived; the driver is waiting outside.
Your vehicle is a silver VW Passat WE15FPF".

Adjustments of the tie were made in the mirror. His

wallet and ring were picked up and securely placed into his pocket. He looked around the room, ensuring nothing had been left. As he wasn't returning, his final act was to switch the light off. In the corridor, the door was pulled to. The receptionist waved goodbye, attempting to secure a tip; he didn't reciprocate and walked straight past. He paused for a couple of seconds before he stepped into one of the segments of the revolving door.

A few metres across the two by two concrete pavers, he was at the VW, he heard the paper seller, "The 13th November see's the Tories battling to keep in power". A quick inspection carried out visually of the taxi's backseat before he entered. The door was opened and closed; it was to his satisfaction.

The driver looked twice over the seat at his passenger's attire. It took a moment before he asked, 'Where to, sir?'

'One Canada Square, Canary Wharf,' replied the passenger, pulling on the seatbelt; the back of his hand kept the belt from rubbing on the jacket.

'The big glass house, sir?' questioned the driver. He got no reply back and somehow the cabbie knew to stop the questions.

A long 20 minutes had ticked past since he had left the small but tidy hotel. Taxi journey over, he paid the man's fare and politely gave thanks, then walked tall through the all-glass doors fronting the skyscraper.

On entry, he received the same looks that the driver had given him earlier, plus a polite professional smile from the cute receptionist who asked for his name.

'That's great, sir, ... sergeant, we have you down here. Please take a seat. Someone will be out to see you,' he said, whilst offering him a badge displaying a number and the temporary title, "VISITOR" all in red capital letters. He accepted the badge and scribbled on the sheet of paper on the line opposite the badge number. And it was a scribble not at all resembling his name or rank. The receptionist saw the squiggly line he'd made. He looked at the man in front of him but said nothing except the words, 'Thank you, sergeant.'

He walked away from the desk but didn't take up the offer to sit. He stood and waited, aware people were staring his way, as if he was a museum exhibit. It wasn't long before his name was called by the familiar voice. He hadn't sat for a reason.

'Please follow me, sergeant. I can see you're struggling, so I'd like to thank you for returning. I know it can't be easy for you.' The woman knew full well he'd been ordered to attend these sessions. Was she just looking for some sort of self-justification of her position, or was she being genuinely polite? A further four minutes in the high-speed elevator when it stopped on the 48th floor, two storeys down from the top of the second tallest building in the United Kingdom. The doors opened and she was out into a large lobby, which replicated the splendour of the reception area. He placed his hand across the door to stop them closing. He joined her, but they quickly moved into one of the side offices, one of many in the giant of a building.

He remained silent, stood in a military pose, but not "at ease", staring out of the massive window. The office was so high up, there wasn't a part of London he couldn't see, including the canal, which he followed with his eyes up to the old funeral parlour. Should he visit or not, or just call Mary and have her meet with him? His demeanour was the same as it had been, the last three times he had attended this place, one three-hour session per week over the last three weeks. Not one word had crept over his lips during any of these sessions. Not even a courteous hello or goodbye. Not bad manners on his part; self-preservation was his reasoning. The familiar voice that brought him to the office had sat down, relaxed partly in the same soft leather chair. A few minutes had passed, and he was still staring out of the floor to ceiling window.

'Would you like a coffee or a cold drink, sergeant?' she politely asked, again and for the fourth time: no answer. She had to do something different if she was going to get through to this man. He was clearly an enigma, but unfortunately, she wasn't Alan Turing.

It wasn't just her curiosity that wanted satisfying, nor was it the title engraved on the brass plaque hung in the centre of her door; it was human decency, pure concern for another person who she saw as suffering.

'How about if I were to read the questions out loud and you give me an answer, yes or no, even a shake or nod of your head, sergeant, whichever you're comfortable with. I feel that I must stress to you that your superiors have given you no more time with me after today's session.' Feelings of melancholy came over her and she was forced to stop talking for a second. Her hands took hold of the coffee cup before she continued. 'And unfortunately, you understand, that I will have to make mention in my report of the continuing silence, which you have upheld throughout our sessions.' She both asked and warned, at the same time, with the hope it would help him finally open up to her.

The recipient of her time came away from the window and sat down opposite her, his large hands placed on the well-worn arms of the leather chair, his fingers wanting to squeeze the soft, supple material, but he wasn't giving anything away. And one thing he wouldn't allow was him to be controlled.

She began reading.

'One: Do you feel that you have recently been through a traumatic experience, and if yes, has this experience affected your mind in any way?' She looked up from the questionnaire.

No reply came her way.

His fingers still did not squeeze.

'Two: Did this experience you endured involve a death or torture to either yourself or anyone close to you, which you witnessed first-hand?' She waited.

No reply came her way.

'Three: How did you feel at the time you were in this situation and after the event was over? Also, if someone close to you died or suffered from serious injury or harm. Could you please express this in another answer?' She looked at him then continued to give three options. 'A = helpless, B = scared, C = combination of both.' She looked up again.

No reply came her way.

She felt as if she were running a marathon and had hit the wall. And not everyone got over the wall. But she ran on. 'Four; Ho...' she started the question then was amazed by the bricks falling.

'D,' the recipient said, fingers still wanting to squeeze.

'Thank you. I know that can't have been easy for you. Would you like to elaborate some more for me, please?' she asked tenderly, not wanting the silence to return. There was something different about this client. She had read the brief, which gave her a detailed account of the incident that had landed him on her caseload, and the synopsis of the last three years in the regiment, but both of these, to her, were only the prologue, and intuition told her that he was a series, not a one-off bestseller. The Sean Doyle Novels, her brain manifested.

He thought her voice sounded perfect, quiet, but still perfectly audible, with no immediate evidence of an accent. He watched her lips as they correctly pronounced the words. The features around the mouth weren't too bad either. He, on the other hand, spoke slowly, with a couple of accents crossing over each other. One with a strong twinge of Irish, enough to be noticed, although he hadn't a clue as to where he was from originally.

His stare remained, the windows of his soul looking right through her. She glanced back at him, then quickly looked down to the floor. A sharp breath in, then her eyes were back up. Rose felt the fear, for sure, not for herself but for him, her client - the enigma. She could see the emotional weight of too many deaths held in him. His saddened blue eyes appeared glazed over. Rose smiled, and this somehow, like witchcraft, released him; his fingers felt the pleasure of the squeeze. He tried to give a smile back but it didn't show, least not on the outside. She wanted to help him, desperate to make him feel at ease. He knew he could never be at rest, and as for the questions she wanted answered, if he told the truth no one would believe what had gone on, to civilians it would be fiction written by the great Lee Child, a Jack Reacher novel.

He spoke again, conscious of his loud voice in the quiet office. 'D, equals energised, a switch being turned on, no going back, whatever we faced? We defeated! We are the last option!'

She scribbled on the question sheet then sat back in the soft chair. Crossing her legs, the hem of the grey cotton skirt rested softly on top of her right knee.

He noticed the same knee had a long thin scar in the

centre - pure white the skin was. She acknowledged his efforts politely as her tongue pressed softly against the inside of her cheek, barely visible but he noticed it. He blinked twice and started his story at the beginning, but he had returned to staring out the window, unable to look at another human.

As the words struggled to come forth for the first time ever, she spoke again not wishing for the silence to re-establish itself. 'I am here to help you. No one can exist as an island, Sergeant Doyle, Sean.' Rose waited with both professional and personal anticipation.

He began at the beginning, the very start of his memory, and the story commenced, he spoke to the whole of London through the glass, but only Rose heard. 'The only skill I had was looking after people, always had from an early age, couldn't help myself. From being a small skinny child to a big man. And a big man I'd turned out to be, but still I wasn't satisfied. I continually pushed myself and pushed my abilities even harder. The SAS I'd reached, a sergeant, and a good one on all accounts. But I nearly died on the last excursion we'd ventured on. I'd been injured before, several times in fact, it came with the territory, yet it was nothing like what happened on this occasion. And it wasn't just the hip - for the first time I could remember it had made me think. Twelve days on the other side of the world, in some godforsaken jungle; the first set of 24 hours, we all spent acclimatising. And don't be getting the image of us lot doing nothing, lying around sunbathing and getting pissed. It was adjusting to the hellish temperature. But to be fair that's what the first day consisted of, lots of nothings one after another. The next three, 24-hour slots consisted of battle PT, is what they called it. "Sweating your fucking bollocks off", us men called it. Making adjustments to one's body scent was its intention. Becoming animals was the aim, and not just by the way of smell. Some people die inside when everything is taken from them and they're forced into a world of difference and full of the unknown. A few people thrive and seek these challenges over and over.

The ninth day saw the end of me. I was flown out by Lynx helicopter to Panama - three broken bones, and all of them in the same leg. My patrol had been ambushed during an intelligence gathering operation (IGO). A tree was felled to block the exit. When it came over, nobody had shouted "TIMBER!". Chalky was in its path. I dived to knock him clear, but my leg was caught, Bagsy let rip with the machine gun - turning the tree into kindling freeing me. We scrapped our way out the ambush. Another one of us had been injured and one sadly left us for good; he was collected by Freja and taken to Valhalla. We discovered later there was a rat in the ranks of the wet backs we were there to train, he's no longer alive. I was given some time to recoup my health and regain fitness and then back to the regiment. I believed I was as fit as ever, could have given a butcher's dog a run, but the x-rays and white coats apparently disagreed with my diagnosis. A few days later, a second incident occurred in Hereford, which meant that I was now on borrowed time, which is also the reason I'm here with you.' He looked to her for a moment.

'Yes, I was made aware of the bar fight,' she acknowledged.

'I didn't start the fight? Well, it wasn't a fight, he wet himself and I did some damage, that sums it up.'

'Again, I am aware of this, but breaking both the man's arms and all his fingers! Some may say that was over the top a little?'

Sean rose and went to the window. 'He offered a bloke

some child porn in front of me! For fuck sake, I should have killed him?' He didn't look at Rose, and carried on with his story. 'No need to worry, I'm experienced enough to be kept around, used for training, planning operations and then the preparation (the six P's). Plus, there's always the admin shit. But being the best in the world, by title alone, means zero to me. I always said that to be the best, whether it be in the army, a boxer, actor, ballerina, even an author, no one could get to the top of their chosen path and achieve the goal, by just wanting only a title. There has to be some inner driven belief. Their brain would need to have a relentless gear, that they could switch on and leave on. People at the top of their game, in a lot of cases, are for sure, paid the lion's share of the money, but they started with nothing except for a handful of dreams and the ability to not quit. Some believe in themselves and have the strength not to listen to the naysayers. For want of an explanation, they are all warriors in my eyes.'

His gaze left the window and city below. He focused upon Rose and re-sat. She smiled softly and crossed her legs the opposite way. He remained sitting but returned his stare back out the glass and picked up his story. 'Then the universe's energy, karma, magic, or the butterfly effect, whatever title you wanna give it, opened another door in my life. Reluctantly, and possibly semi-encouraged by all the pain I was feeling, I stepped through. Never really been part of modern society, never fitted in to what most called "normal". But let's be fair, depending on what you've been through and where you began life, surely this defines your "normal". DON'T let it define your future, that's what I was taught.' He looked from the window back to her. Rose uncrossed her legs leaned forward and placed the writing pad on the small glass table, that divided them. He tried to smile again, but it was still a no show. He continued as he stared at the old funeral parlour.

'Two great people I owe my existence to, and the closest I'd ever come to love and family. Two rules I lived by, the first had become unbreakable: don't trust a soul. And the second, do your best to protect those who can't protect themselves. I had, like most people, trusted unconditionally at one stage of life, but unlike most, mine wasn't from birth. It started at the age of nine or ten, and the two I did worship, well, who were they?' He stopped with the words for a minute, and he thought of the funeral parlour; his fingers felt the squeeze for a second time. 'The skill I was born with, the only thing I was good at would now be back in play. My world of action was to become a world of discovery. Who was I? What was I? Where did I come from? Tired of proving myself, it was time to discover myself, and that's all she ever wanted. She used to tell me, and I didn't really know who "she" was either. But I did have love and understanding in abundance from the dream lady, regardless of who she actually was, and for that, I am who I am today.

My time spent with *"him"* gave me both rules and grit. He also taught me that the only thing you're born and leave this earth with, is your word and reputation, so always keep true, ensure people know that you're trustworthy, and no one is worth any more or any less than you, Tony would tell me again and again, and he was right.' Sean appeared to stop functioning – going quiet in mid-sentence. 'All across the globe people were, and are good, decent, kind, caring folk, just as Tony had said, and most of them would go well out their way to help others. I've travelled the world, but not as a tourist, mostly it would be to sort out the people who weren't mentioned above. Because just like the internet the world has a dark side. You didn't need many of these types to spoil the barrel, the likes of drug barons, people traffickers, would-be Hitlers. People who could, and did kill for pleasure, as well as greed and to increase their personal power, wealth and reputation. My question is, am I any different? I've dispatched plenty of targets in my time, way more than I like to recall when I close my eyes. Some at long distance; centred in cross hairs, several with a cheese wire or knife and one whose head I pounded in with a rock. I've followed orders without question, apart from on one occasion when four of us refused to neutralise a nine-month-old child! The tiny thing had care infused in her light brown eyes, so instead we dropped her at an orphanage in a war-stricken country. We removed her from a life of dark wealth, but she lay on a mattress of daddy's dirty cash when we left her at the old church door. To this day, only three of us now know what really happened to the small angel. Maybe now is the time for me to relocate, just like the little girl - a new start - a new horizon. Find my own old church door.' He turned from the window; Rose had an abundance of tears rolling down her cheeks, a handkerchief collecting each one.'

Sean returned to camp in Hereford the day after. He'd remained in London for the night but didn't call Mary or visit the funeral parlour.

Seven AM, the day he returned.

'Do you have to leave today?'

'It's a long drive, and I have a briefing. I could call in sick.' Her hand reached out for his shoulder. 'Please? One more day? Please Sean.'

He looked at the clock – he'd been there more than 12

hours and she hadn't complained. But nor had he. Her hand fell from his shoulder as he stood. He turned about; she came up on her knees the sheet falling away. He walked to the bed, grabbed her head his hand pulled her over, calling her name as he pulled on her hair.

4

GRUESOME GALLERY

'I can't find the fucking entrance, Donna,' was said with annoyance into the receiver.

'Which street are you on, Carl?' enquired the soft-spoken female.

'Apple Cart Lane, where you said the job was, right near to the middle, I've been up and down twice now, and nothing,' he shouted; this was caused by the external stress in his life, not Donna.

'The customer said to look for a yellow door, mustard like, the entry box code is 34 35... and calm down, please, remember what the doctor said about your blood pressure.' She was calm as always.

'I am calm! Stop telling me about the doctor! The fat twat should take his own advice and there's NO fucking door I'm telling you, never mind a bright yellow one! It's been a windup, luv. I'm leaving!' he stated, his impatience uppermost.

'Wait, Carl, just wait, and please will you calm yourself down. Let me try and call the client. I'll ring you straight back. Stop being so impatient just give me a couple of minutes. Don't go anywhere ... are you listening to me?' she told him, still not riled.

'It's a poxy, 60-quid lock change! I won't wait long. Got two more customers waiting before tea, and I'm out with the lads tonight, remember. It's Alex's birthday, so I can't be late.' He spoke to himself; Donna had already gone.

Two minutes later, the conversation between them was picked back up.

'She re-checked the address. It's off Apple Cart Walk, Carl, not Lane,' she told me there's a little snicket, but it's well overgrown with bush. Turn left there off Apple Cart Lane, and that's the start of Apple Cart Walk. At the end you'll see there is the yellowish door. She also apologised for the misunderstanding and said that she'll pay the extra £30, for going over the hour, as long as the job is completed today.' She placed the piece of paper down.

'I'm here, going down the walkway now, yes, there's the yellow door. It's very secluded, you'd think they didn't want the place to be found. I'll ring you when I've finished the job.' His voice not as angry, his phone about to be switched off he held it there and listened.

'Okay, take care. It will be dark soon, and with all the disappearances of late, I worry about you working alone when you go to these strange places,' said Donna, then she softly replaced the receiver. In her mind she was much more than just a secretary to him, but the feelings weren't reciprocated.

Carl tapped in the numbers, "34 35". The key safe's small door dropped revealing a brass key on a hook. He entered the building and was faced with two safe-like stainless steel doors. To Carl it appeared he was in an electric sub-station. *First or second*, he pondered, trying to recall which lock to swap. The yellow door self-closed behind him. *Fuck, there's no signal now*, he held up the mobile higher, still no bars appeared, the phone went in his pocket, the toolbox lid flipped open. The cordless drill took one hour, twenty minutes and fourteen drill bits until he was able to pull the lock free. He slipped in a wedge at the bottom of the heavy door, securing it and allowing him to carry out his work. *"What is that fucking smell"*? he asked himself.

Torch switched on, when he remembered he wasn't to enter the room under any circumstance. He brushed aside the heavy rubber curtain and only a few feet into the room, his lamp's beam gave him a glimpse of a different reality. His eyes didn't believe what was being visualised, forcing him to stop. The handheld light became useless. A motion detector had picked him up and this switched-on dozens of tube lights, the flickering stopped as all the gases were alight, creating powerful illumination. Carl could now see he was in one row of many, in this spotlessly clean room, a gruesome gallery which had been racked out with floor to ceiling shiny grey shelving. Each of the shelves held dozens of human body parts stored in clear glass jars. As he realised where he was the shock knocked him backwards. This unimaginable sight caused him to vomit, weakened, he fell over. Time stood still for a moment before fear arrived, kicking in the fight or flight response. Trying to scramble onto his feet, he slipped again on his own sick. Up once more, Carl's vision unwillingly locked onto a single jar: this clear vessel contained deformed hands covered with Chinese letters impregnated into the skin with dark blue ink, plus, some crude English letters spelling out the word "LOUISA".

Carl was up and ran out. Finally reaching the end of the snicket and bumping into a man who had turned into Apple Cart Walk. 'Don't go down!' he told him, panting hard, his left hand trying to stop the bleeding on his forehead. He grasped another breath to continue. 'S...s...sir, listen to me ... s...stop! Please! Are you listening to me? Don't go, stay up here. It's fucked-up in there! I'm gunna call the police.' Carl quivered with the aftereffects of the fear, feeling he could in some way relax after escaping and reaching another human.

'Calm down, calm down, man. Pull yourself together. There will be a simple explanation for what has spooked you, I'm sure of it,' spoke the stranger.

'Nooo way! I'm not going back down there, it's fucking Amityville! You didn't see all the bits of bodies, like Frankenstein's lab. I'm telling you, there's eyes, fingers, feet, heads and even cocks.' Carl rested against the fence.

The man produced an ID card, articulating with confident authority, 'Come on, show me these things you think are there. You'll be safe, just stay behind me.' He opened his jacket and showed Carl a wooden handled pistol cradled in a brown leather holster, nestled deep in his jacket.

This gave him confidence, and if the truth be known he wanted another look! Had he really seen what he thought he had?

Carl never called Donna back. He never met the lads that night. He carried out no more lock changes. Going through a messy divorce at the time, which meant he was about to lose a lot of cash and assets, so, when the police investigated his disappearance nothing was found out the ordinary. It was filed as absconding. All his assets had been liquidised in less than a week from the day Donna reported him missing. His body was never found.

On the phone behind the yellow door.

'Angelina, we will still need this lock changing, and make sure this time we have a person on site to show them which door and that they don't enter! I am disappointed, must I always do things myself Angelina?' Shoebridge pressed the red "end call" button. Carl stopped gasping for air as Shoebridge let go of his lifeless body. It slid down his legs as it dropped to the floor.

Shoebridge stepped over his kill and pressed the green "call" button 'Plumber.' Assertively spoke the minister, turning round a specimen jar squaring up the label.

'Yes, sir,' Plumber answered, on the second ring.

'A clean-up team is required at the dispatch room, and make sure to use what you can. Body is clean, apart from a small amount of bleeding from its forehead and bruising around its throat,' informed the minister.

'Roger that, sir. I'll call the night cleaners right away. Martin can put the carcass in the freezer.'

'No, we will be pragmatic, have it transported immediately over to the warehouse. Get that lazy Moe straight on to it. I want it parcelled up tonight, tell him. The police will be informed of his disappearance, let's not be sloppy? I'll give it fresh to the Africans, it should appease them. And who was last here? The covert doors where not in place!'

'Will do, sir. I'll tell Martin it's a straight forensic sweep, Not sure who's been, sir.' Plumber ended the call and entered "N" into the search box in his contacts.

Shoebridge collected several items from the shelf, placed them carefully into steel flasks and then into a tan coloured attaché case. This was subsequently sealed with a British government official tag. The minister put his phone away and pulled across the sliding covert door, a fixed shelf which had working electrical parts adding to the substation story. The heavy steel door was next, and then he replaced the brass key back in the small key safe. At the top of the snicket, his choice was to turn left. He walked off, making his way to some nearby public toilets. During the 500-meter walk, his picture was snapped over 50 times by security cameras, but his identity was not discovered. Inside the public toilets the outer shell of middle-class clothing, plus wig, tash and contact brown lenses were hastily removed then doused with the full contents of a lighter fluid tin. A twenty-second string fuse was ignited and pushed into the pile of clothing. The cubicle door was closed calmly.

Outside, the now impeccably dressed minister walked away from the toilet block and waited in the zoned-off area for a taxi to arrive. All around, people began to panic as the flames grew. Black smoke bellowed out of the doors and windows while the minister sat cross-legged on the red plastic curved bench. *The Times* newspaper, open and kinked in the middle, his attaché case close by his side secured to him via a transparent anti snatch cable.

'FIRE! FIRE! FIRE! THE TOILET'S ON FIRE!' screamed and shouted a number of different people.

As the blue flashing lights came nearer, Shoebridge pulled the taxi door too behind him, his attaché case held tight, his newspaper tucked under his arm as he sat back.

'The Magnolia Club, White Chapel, please, and don't spare the horses my good man.'

'On the way, guv. That's a very exclusive club, sir. Are you a member?' the driver asked and acknowledged, then flicked on the meter. He received no time or any information whatsoever from his passenger. He altered the rear-view mirror.

. . .

The Magnolia Club, Leeman Street, White Chapel, London

'Good evening, sir. Could I relieve you of your case?' asked the awaiting manservant.

'No, you could fetch me my usual immediately,' replied Sir Shoebridge.

$\sim$

Plumbers phone flashed and displayed the words Night cleaner.

'Hi, Martin, Terry, I've a job, just a forensic sweep, shouldn't take long?'

'Not sure what time I'll get there, I've a full scene to alter, these Russians keep me busy, another head blow that I've to change into a suicide.' Martin was holding his phone with his left hand. His right held a foot-long stick, half of which had been inserted into the dead man's forehead, he forced the head back and upwards.

'As long as it's before the morning, mate?'

'Roger that, send me the details,' Martin slipped the phone back into the tool box, and took hold of a test tube full of the victim's blood, this was poured over the man's head so it ran backwards. He began to measure from his head to the wall and also up towards the ceiling. 'Do your bit, Sally?' he stood back.

A second person stood in front of the victim, placed a small pistol in his hand forced it up towards his head, then simultaneously closed her eyes and pressed the trigger. The noise was deafening, ears ringing even with them wearing defenders.

'Perfect, Sally, right, finish the carpets and pack up, I have another job, I'll go alone.'

'Ok, boss, we'll see you back at base, yeh?' said the female wearing glasses, mask and full forensic suit and two pair of gloves.

Kensington Apartments, number 19
1630 hours

WPC Cathy O'Conner had been given a couple of days down time after the Thames incident. The 24-year-old graduate copper was fresh from Oxford University. She had not been at all prepared to stare at a headless corpse: the body had its chest off the floor, ghoulishly perched up on its elbows. The hands had been removed, its knees bent, arse in the air. The corpse appeared to be crawling out of the water, heavy chains attached to its rotting lower legs. Cathy had looked continually at the gruesome sight of the severed spinal cord and trachea.

She couldn't help but see that the red greyish flesh around the spine was just like beef that had begun to rot. She felt physically sick but yet still completely captivated, analysing what was in front of her eyes. From out of the blue, the young WPC's emotions flipped, one minute trying to work out what it all meant, then she hated herself for wanting to look deeper, further, stronger at the sight which was in front of her.

Tears of sadness flooded out, as the realisation that this was a real person hit her hard. Visions of friends, relatives, lovers and all that accompanied being human. The Thames washed away at the skin, removing the silt and revealing dozens of tattoos. The rain was pouring heavily, but she didn't even register being wet, she was so numb.

'O'Conner! O'Conner! What the fuck you doing down

here? I told you to stay top side!' shouted the sergeant, running, or trying to run across the mud towards her. Even though she was a police officer, he wanted to protect her as she was different, plus he had orders to do so, orders from high up that no one else needed to know about, but she wasn't aware of this or the cash he received on a monthly basis from her father. He placed his arm around Cathy's shoulders and forcibly guided the young officer back up the bank. Meanwhile, the river police started to pull away in their boats as the corpse was zipped up in a bag before being carried to the road and placed on a waiting trolley.

1915 hours, later that evening

Her bed sheets were drenched through with sweat, her naked body glistening after subconsciously reliving that day's events. Over and over, it played. Cathy panicked as she awoke from a couple of hour's restless sleep. It was a few more seconds before she came-to fully, as the young officer realised, she was safe, she was in her new apartment; it was only a dream, but it hadn't been a few hours earlier. The troubled female drank plenty of water, continually glugging it from the bottle. At first, she didn't know how to deal with these horrendous events that had brought her prematurely from her nap. Since joining the police, she had witnessed the aftermath of at least a dozen stabbings, a couple of gang shootings, plus some suicides and several drug overdoses. Not nice, but she knew it was part of the job, and she could rationalise the violence and death, there was a reason for it. But this, this was different, a headless creature couldn't be put in order. She, for some reason still had not totally come around to the idea, that the thing was even human! Or had been. Feeling lonely and with a thousand questions flying around inside of her head, she grabbed for her mobile phone, but she stopped herself halfway through dialling. She looked on the screen and read the name "Helen". More water was needed but she sipped from the bottle on this occasion. *What should I do?* She posed the question out loud to herself. The phone remained in her hand as she paced around the kitchen like Alice in Wonderland she was sucked into the rabbit hole.

A decade ago.

    Two weeks prior to the kidnaping taking place, a female detective had investigated the murder of a well-known local businessman, who also happened to be a very important bank manager. He was found tied up, with his penis and balls severed and stuffed into his mouth; his office had been ransacked, the safe was empty. No killer, or more likely killers, had ever been arrested but it was believed to be a retribution murder, as the man had repossessed several businesses, including properties in the area on behalf of his bank, or that's how the paperwork made it to appear. The children of these business owners all had some link to child protective services, where files were available on them, yet the facts inside were incorrect, altered. This bank manager sat on the tribunal panel and didn't play fair. Discovered at the scene were dozens of documents; these named several paedophiles living in the town and surrounding area. Helen was assigned to the case of the missing girl and it was her first where she was second in command. Seven of the names discovered in the documents were previously known to the police, three of them were not, but one of these three names. Helen knew very well, and it was a struggle for her to comprehend that he was a child molester! Could the information be a hoax? But the missing girl in her mind was paramount and nothing would come between her finding the child.

Helen stood from the chair.

'I'll be an hour, Ted. Going over to question Mr Doodle. We need to rule him out. Can't see a problem,' said Helen, her arm through the jacket sleeve.

'Give me a minute, Hel, I'll come with you, you'll know what the guv'll say?' Ted swivelled in the chair.

'No, you stay and get the details ready for this afternoon. I'll be fine, can't see any problems with this one, a tick off the list job, certain of it.'

'Roger! Will you be back for the search? It's at three, remember, it should be a good turn out,'

Helen pulled her sleeve back: her watch hands said 13:20. 'I'll meet you on the common. It's on the way back in.' Helen then left the office.

Ted had made a note of her location in the shared dairy.

Forty minutes later.

She closed the car door, crunched the gravel under foot, her finger pressed the brass button. Helen thought of the Avon lady as the chimes sang, and it was only few more minutes later she was sitting opposite her ex-school teacher having a strong percolated coffee. In the air was that sense of, well she couldn't name it, a lack of life, energy and musty smell, some would say it needed a woman's touch, but she didn't want to be sexist. The place was in order, clean but only the places in regular use. He was passing over his version of why he had ended up on the sex offenders list 17 years ago, he declined to look at her because of the embarrassment.

'I know how it sounds, Helen, I do, but it wasn't like that, believe me. She was seventeen. Christ! Another month and she'd have been bloody eighteen. And it was her parents who objected, not Zoe herself. We were in love with each other.' He tried to rationalise his shortcomings. Both of his small hands wrapped around the big coffee mug, he leaned forward as he spoke, both his heels of the floor; his legs twitched at speed, still little eye contact. Helen listened but wasn't buying it. She knew the girl in question, and yes, he told the truth, she was nearly eighteen, two years younger than Helen, but Zoe looked twelve, and that was also her reading age. But again, she told herself this doesn't make a kidnapper.

Twenty minutes later, on her second fill of coffee, Helen received a phone call. 'I have to take this call, Mr Doodle, sir, it's my station,' She stood and turned, 'Cathy speaking?'

'Listen carefully, ...' spoke Ted.

'Yes, yes, no, ... it's on my desk, in a white folder. If it's not there, it must be at my house?' She turned further away, trying to disguise her shock. 'No, of course it's not a problem. I'll collect it on my way back, I'm just about finished up here, anyway. I'll leave now, shouldn't be long before I'm back to the station. You need the file for court. It will need to be signed by me anyway.' Helen had literally just repeated what was said to her as a "get out" of the house and now. After she had left the station, a second cop had come across an email about some footage of a possible van that was on their watch list in regard to the missing girl, and another girl, ten days earlier. Unable to read the number plate, it was sent off to a department in Whitehall. The number was retrieved by the specialist there and entered into the database. The results stated that it belonged to the ex-teacher, Mr Doodle. It was also discovered that previous to having been added to the sex offenders list, he had applied for a number of gun licences and subsequently purchased these weapons.

Helen turned about after the phone call ended and was again facing her teacher. 'I wi ...'

'You shouldn't have come here today, Helen. You shouldn't have meddled in my business. Now you leave me no choice.'

Facing her was the barrel of a very high-powered rifle. 'Let's just talk about this, sir. Why are you pointing that at me? I have no reason to continue questioning you. I'm finished here.' Calm and collected, she spoke knowing she had to personalise with him and quickly bring him back to the time when they were in the classroom.

'I'm sure we can work through this, you know, sir. Like you would say in class when we were struggling with a subject. You'd tell us, "let's take a minute and then come back to this little problem". Do you remember, sir?' Her lips squeezed her mouth corners curled.

'This is hardly a little problem, is it now, Helen?' The barrel of the weapon, pointed to the chair three times, Helen's breathing wanted to explode, instead she confidently sat as directed. The long rifle raised the butt sinking into his shoulder the barrel was aimed without any doubt at her. She could see how shiny the metal was inside and even the curly line they called rifling.

'Finish your coffee, Helen. ... Please.' He sounded so normal yet still his pupils didn't rest on hers.

'Sir, I really don't know why this is happening.' The barrel pointed twice to the cup.

'Drink. Before it gets cold, it's much nicer when it's hot? And its expensive.'

A silence replaced Helen's efforts to resolve the inevitable. She saw that his finger was not on the trigger, it lay against the brass. If it went there, she would toss the cup of coffee at him. She was going to die anyway, so one last chance.

'Behind the bookcase. And I am sorry, Helen, really I am truly sorry for everything. I tried not to do it, but it was too hard, I didn't have the willpower to stop who I call my bad man. Tell them I never wanted to kill the first one, but she was so, so noisy.

I would have never hurt her otherwise, honest. I would have looked after her forever, I must have crushed too many tablets. She never woke up? I tried to fight the urges again but she was so sweet and she liked it when I complemented her at the park. Remember to tell them, the other one died because she wouldn't listen to me, I'm no murderer, no monster like some of these ... child touching sick fucks. But Cathy is different. I've been watching her for a year. She is such a flirt, always cartwheeling showing of her pants to me,' The barrel moved, spun around, and entered his own mouth. His neck stretched, head right back, his thumb on the trigger, Helen's eyes closed tight. The resulting noise was deafening; the decibels bellowed, reaching over 150, bouncing around the room. Helen could feel his warm blood landing in a minimum of twenty places all over her face, the coffee cup hit the floor. Her eyes remained shut, her ears still ringing loudly as a sickly feeling came from her stomach to her throat.

Helen informed her inspector of the events that followed in her debrief, later that day; however, she still couldn't put a time on how long her eyes had remained closed. To her, the minute she re-opened them, what had just happened would then be a permanent reality. She continued describing the events to her inspector.

'He came out with it all, sir, including that he had taken and had killed the first girl.'

The shake in her hands prompted her boss to ask, 'Are you coping, Helen? Take your time?' he reassured, reading the upset as her mind recalled the day's events.

'I'm fine, sir, just the adrenaline subsiding.' She continued. 'Behind the bookcase was a small doorway, five feet tall by two feet wide, a bend down and twist job to get through the makeshift opening. After the bookcase came a tunnel, ten, possibly fifteen feet in length and on a slope downwards. Then the steel door, like the ones found on a submarine with a well over-sized wheel in the

middle. After that came some more tunnel, still sloping downwards but much steeper. My phone was switched on for the light. The next door I was at was made from some soft material, similar to that found inside a padded cell, sir. Again, no key just a thick piece of timber securing it. Next, instead of more tunnel, there were seven steps going further down. I was now in a small room. It was so warm and hard to breath, hardly any air, a change of clothes hung on wooden pegs. On the left wall, next to these, was a set of keys, long and old-fashioned. These fit perfectly into the last door's three locks, old, big and gothic and constructed of solid oak, as were the beams above my head. This room was clearly an entrance hall, and uncannily the warmth was accompanied by a sweet smell. I prayed that it wasn't "that" smell, sir, the one you never wanna taste again.'

The inspector nodded as he swallowed.

Helen continued with the debrief, her recollection as accurate as on the day. 'Keys in my hand, I stopped and was forced to take a step back, I knew I wasn't alone anymore. The scent I smelt was suddenly recognisable: it was decaying meat, and human! I rushed to the door, keys fumbling in the locks, my hand rapidly turned them. I felt a terrific heat and the smell became horrendous. I stopped myself from entering at this point, sir, I needed to take a moment, in fear of what I may discover, and the smell had become overpowering, enough to force short, sharp, breathes.' Helen went quiet.

'In your own time Helen, I know this is difficult,' reassured her inspector.

'The words that came next were welcomed and I'll never forget them 'til I pass, "Please, don't hurt me, please! I just want to go and see my mummy. She will be sad," Helen heard the soft words faintly as she spoke them but as well in her head in that tiny place we all have. "Cathy? Cathy O'Conner. Is that you? My name is Helen, and I am a police officer. Nobody is going to hurt you anymore." This, sir, is when I reverted to being a police officer, I am aware these predators would often set booby-traps. Everything in the room wasn't visible, as I was still only guided by my phone's torchlight. Coming to the corner, I turned, seeing little Cathy sitting on a sheet-less stained mattress. She was holding another girl, clearly the source of the potent smell, sir.'

The inspector watched Helen's face change as she recalled the sight of the dead girl.

'I asked Cathy who her friend was, to which she replied she didn't know as the friend didn't speak, poor Cathy thought she was asleep.

Helen's face changed again, 'At that moment, s... sir... the arm fell off the quiet girl. There was no blood, only thousands of maggots feeding on the dead flesh, they were spewing out the girl's carcass. I wanted to vomit, but instead, I asked Cathy to let her friend lay down because she looked tired, to let her rest there and for her to come to me. I told her we would send someone back for her friend, and not to worry. We then made our way out, sir. Outside dozens of vehicles had arrived, the shouting of orders began and only stopped when I walked out carrying Cathy, the applause started and grew, as we walked to the ambulance. A paramedic tried to take Cathy, she screamed so he gave up. I whispered to the sergeant regards the location and condition of the other little girl.'

Cathy hugged Helen and never let go, not even on the drive to the hospital, and the small 12-year-old, from that day onwards, vowed to be a policewoman like Helen who had saved her life.

Back in the kitchen ten years on.

Cathy recalled her last conversation with Helen during her final year at University.

Her phone was once more being tapped, but the name

"Helen" was no longer on the screen and wouldn't be from now on. Because of her family connections, Cathy had been put on a very, very fast track to becoming a high-ranking police officer. At first, Cathy was fuming about this, as she wanted to be a real police officer not an advertisement for equality and always knowing she was where she was, only because of her family name. She had gone to visit Helen and was expecting her to back her up, but instead. Helen's advice was to go for it, take the opportunity, but on your way up get involved, ask for a good mentor and work hard with them.

'I would like you to be my mentor. Who could be better?'

'Thanks for the complement, Cathy, but no, listen to me. I may have been the reason you chose this bloody career, but you want to get someone who you can trust and you respect, and most importantly is doing a real job, in London. If you're determined to go through with this, then make it count, do it well and don't stay around here. You'll never be taken seriously with your family name. You'll be thought of as a posh patsy,' replied Helen, proudly looking at Cathy, who in fact had been mentored by her for the last five or six years. Like a daughter she was, still is, and Helen was like a proud mother.

'How would I do that?'

'Read this article.' Helen had walked off to a table, came back and passed over the magazine. 'It's written by a female police sergeant and titled "The real female officer and her role in today's world". It's good, well-written and insightful, and she's no idiot. Then if you feel like you understand the piece, write to her and ask if she would be willing to advise you. Use my name as a reference, don't mention your family, she'll no doubt check you out, but flaunting wealth and prestige won't sit well. Tell her about all the volunteering you have done here, and at university. They like that sort of shit.'

'Do you know this sergeant? Helen.'

'Not really know her as such, but I've had dealings with her on a couple of occasions. And shall we say the way I met her was, well ...'

'How did you meet her?' Cathy's voice raised, eyes widened.

'I went to London for a couple of days with a close friend. She had booked us places and tickets for a ...'

'Emma, was it with Emma De Pen Court? My mother says Emma was one for the bright lights.'

Helen nodded. 'We arrived but Emma didn't feel well and opted for an early night, so I booked a taxi and thought I'd see some of our capital. The driver of the cab was talking away, pleasant, nice guy, quite funny if I remember properly. Then, from nowhere, a female came running out of the back door of a shop and straight in front of our cab. Her hands rested on the bonnet; the driver only just managed to stop in time. She started to shout at him telling him to get out his cab, informing him she was a police officer and wanted his car. He kept saying no, so she pulled open the door and yanked him out the driver's seat. She was in, set off and then noticed me. I remember her saying, "It may be best if you vacate the vehicle, ma'am. I am a police officer and in pursuit of a criminal."

Me too, I'd replied and fumbled about in my bag and produced my ID. Carry on, I'd said.

She told me to buckle up and I did. The night turned out to be a good night, she made her arrest, then we spent a couple of hours back at her headquarters where had a drink, much better than if I'd gone to the opera with Emma, bless her,' laughed Helen.

'Sounds really exciting,' added Cathy.

'Her name is Tanya Howlett, pretty little thing, yah wouldn't think butter would melt, but by Christ don't cross her. And whilst she is a serving police sergeant, she's attached to a special unit within Whitehall, it's all a bit hush-hush. If you do get the chance, learn from her; you will be fine, and a bloody good officer, but one thing Cathy, she doesn't do fools?' Helen passed over an email address. Cathy hugged her. Helen's arms also began to hug, but affection was alien in her life. The email was sent six weeks later towards the end of Cathy's final year of university. And the article she had read in the magazine was expanded into a massive, ten-thousand words and became Cathy's thesis. A copy was forwarded to the same email address.

Back in the present.

She pressed "call" on the phone. She thought of Helen, but she was ready to speak to ...

'Tanya Howlett?' the phone was answered.

'Are you free this evening for a catch up?' asked Cathy.

'I have a good workload to complete, I'm afraid. Archiving. Has to be done, but I could make it later in the week for lunch, say. It would be nice to see you. How are things in the Met? Have you settled in?' Tanya was speaking but still reading through reports.

'Oh... okay... sorry to be a bother. I should have known you would be busy,' Deflated by her friend's negative response, holding back some persistent tears, she became silent. Not wanting to pressure Tanya, and mad with herself for not being able to deal with this situation on her own.

'Is everything all right?' Tanya picked up on her sudden silence.

'Yes, I will be fine. Feeling a bit low, I shouldn't have called you at this hour, after five, with the work day being over. Sorry again to be a bother.' She was about to switch off.

'Don't be silly, you can call me at any time, that's what I'm here for, and five is more like my lunch break.' Tanya smiled. 'You don't need to apologise.' Tanya rose up from her laptop and walked through her living room towards the remote, to turn the volume down. She may have a lot to get through, but ten minutes on the phone wasn't a trouble. On the TV, the morning's events were all over the evening's news. She caught a glimpse of Cathy standing near the rear of one of the ambulances. 'Do you know what, forget the work. I could do with a break. I'll be at yours in around thirty minutes with a bottle of wine. Red or white?' she asked.

'Any Tanya. It's your company I wish for.' Her morale lifting. Phone down, Cathy went to shower after throwing the bed sheets into the washer, comforted by the thought of some good company at the end of a long and dark day. And if the questions in her head were to be resolved by anyone, it would be Tanya Howlett who supplied them.

5

TATTOO

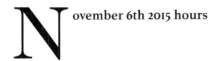November 6th 2015 hours

Savoy Theatre, West End, London

The fourth and final act was already well underway.

'You made it, my darling! I'm so glad you did.'

'Of course. I told you I wouldn't let you down for the world, my dear.' The minister smiled, leaned in towards his wife; her lips softly touched his cheek. He made himself comfortable next to her and his daughter, the theatre was warm with a mixture of very expensive perfumes floating in the air.

'Let me adjust your tie, love. It's crooked.' Her heavily jewelled hands twisted the shiny bow tie. Her eyes looked into his as she noticed specks of a red substance on the silk.

'I cut myself while I was shaving at the office. Don't worry, darling, I'm fine.' She finished. They faced the stage, while she became engrossed in the play, he calculated the profit he would be receiving after the first shipment to the USA had arrived. For Shoebridge, there definitely was going to be a special relationship with America.

Three rows back, another trio sat together. One of them looked at his watch then showed the others. Two of these formidable figures stood and began apologising as they shuffled their way to the centre aisle, two of them exited the building, one remained. The curtains descended, closing off the stage and it was only a few seconds before the applause began. The encore was over in a flash, but like all thespians the cast came back for more and more, eager for the approval of others. The minister and his family rose.

'This way, sir, ma'am,' directed the escort waiting in the aisle.

'Are we going to join the Grayken's for drinks, darling? We have been invited, and some of the cast are making an appearance, including sir Ian?' asked his wife.

'Of course, dear, I understand, but I will have to leave no later than nine-forty. I am unfortunately required to attend a meeting, which I cannot be excused from.' He placed his arm around his daughter as they reached the isle.

'You work so hard for this country and you care so much for your people,' replied his loving wife, her hand also firmly on their daughter's shoulder.

'Your car is ready and waiting outside, sir, when you require it,' advised the bodyguard, diplomatically encouraging them to move and now, aware that the security detail was blocking the aisle, not letting anyone pass. All three VIPs shuffled along. 'This way.' He pointed to the exit where a second protection officer had taken post and waiting for them, a female with braided hair, the sharpest blue eyes and wearing a men's suit followed the VIP's through the door. Outside the minister spoke through a smile.

'Knightsbridge please, Plumber, and drive very carefully, we have precious cargo on board,' said Shoebridge, who looked at his daughter the smile grew. One guard got in the front of their car, and the other two followed in a separate vehicle the woman squeezed on a helmet and followed at a distance on a motorbike.

~

Surveillance team - M1

'Shoebridge is in his car and he's leaving the theatre now, sir.'

'Keep back, Garthwaite. They aren't amateurs and we can't afford to be spotted,' warned the brigadier.

'Yes, sir. I have done this before,' replied Gary.

'No need for the clever attitude, lad. I was carrying out surveillance when you wore nappies. They're indicating, look - concentrate, lad,' instructed the brigadier.

'Good spot, sir! Well done!' replied Gary, attempting to hold back the sarcastic tone. He slowed, allowing the gap between the two cars to widen. Another vehicle turned down the same street, as Gary slowed down the other vehicle overtook them and cut in.

Surveillance team - M2

'We have a visual on the target vehicle, you can relax, M1,' said the occupants of the Honda.

'Remain three cars behind. Keep visual for another mile, M2,' ordered the brigadier.

'Roger that, ... sir. M2, out,' came from the second vehicle.

'Did you know the brigadier's out in M1 tonight?'

'No way. I thought Gary was alone on this one. Bet he wishes he was,' laughed Sam.

'The brigadier is alright, he's a good guy,' said Tiny.

'Yeah, he's a great boss, but would you want him riding shotgun in a surveillance car with you driving?'

'Good point. Hope Gary's on the ball.'

Surveillance team - M1

'Sir, is that your phone?' prompted Gary.

'Brigadier Howlett speaking,' he answered, without seeing the number.

'Sir, are you able to speak?'

'Yes, go ahead.'

'The Met have picked up a body on the banks of the Thames, a decapitated body with both hands removed as well, sir.'

'Someone didn't want an identification happening in a hurry,'

'Didn't want it at all, sir. The body had been chained and weighted down with an anchor, before being dropped in the middle of the river for fish food. A good guess is that whoever carried this out wasn't aware that the archaeological drag basket would be working in that area the same week, causing the body to break loose. Then some poor children discovered the remains on Wednesday morning, whilst out metal-detecting,' Tanya read, whilst walking.

'Sad affair, lass, sad affair. I saw all the commotion on the evening news. Tell me, why does this involve us? I am aware it's an unusual event, but clearly it's one for the top floor boys, is it not?' Charles remarked.

'Yes, you are correct, sir, and the murder squad are on ...'

'Pull back, Garthwaite, sorry Tanya. I seem to be on a bloody training run here.' The brigadier shook his head. Gary glared at his boss via the rear-view mirror, biting his tongue.

'I just feel we may have to take this one on, sir. Call it intuition. I have a friend in the Met. She calls me with a heads up when anything unusual appears on the radar.' Tanya collected up a few sheets of paper, tapping them neatly together on her desk, she rose whilst talking through the hands-free. She placed the sheets into the photocopier pressed a button then continued. 'The Met were going to sign the case off as just another addict, too far in debt to his dealer so they made an example of him. It would then be subsequently filed away as part of an ongoing investigation, into the drug wars, the bottom of the drawer, as we know it, sir. Especially since the start of operation Roadkill. However, a sharp-eyed mortuary attendant during the autopsy spotted a tattoo. Which to him appeared out of synch with what the police were looking into and their current thinking ...' Tanya paused, hearing Gary in the background. She placed the copied sheets and photos in an envelope, picked up her bag, shouldered it and left the office.

'Good night, miss,' said the uniform as he touched the peak of his hat. Tanya smiled and nodded then headed for the carpark.

'They're turning and stopping, sir,' Gary interrupted sharply.

'I'll call you back later, Tanya.' The brigadier cut the call. 'Slow! Slow! Slow! Pull in! Here, stop!'

Gary did what the brigadier ordered, but only because he was doing it anyway.

'Switch the ear on, let's see if we can get some audible.'

'Perfect, sir. I can hear everything - clear as day.'

'Good job, lad. You remain here I'll make my own way back. Call me immediately, if you come across any intel regarding flights or landing destinations, specifically any terminology relating to our distant cousins from across the pond.' The brigadier stipulated this as he got out of the car.

'Yes, boss, roger that. Will you be ok, sir?' Gary asked then pushed a gel plug into his ear.

'And less of the bloody "boss", we're not American! Yet.' The brigadier slammed the door, turned up his collar and set off. He walked past two others sat in a stationary Honda, three cars behind Gary. He kept walking and they gave the slightest of nods. Charles smiled to himself. He was the boss and a serving brigadier, but he loved being out with the lads on live jobs. He imagined, however, that they didn't feel the same way, yet all that worked for him would jump in front of a bullet headed his way, as he held respect that many commanders would have loved to have.

The top of Back Street split into two roads. Left was Ferry Road, and the right turned and led into Cannon Road, locally known as the underground river. This was his choice tonight, and it led him into or somewhere close to one of the side alleys that fed Oxford Street. Or so Charles thought? It had been a good while since he had been around these parts of the city, especially on foot. Twenty minutes passed and he was still walking, and the clouds were still spitting. A blessing in disguise really, as it was a myth that the famous London smog no longer existed. He crossed over the road after he read a text, he noticed an internal light illuminate the etched window. The words "smoke room and lounge", caught his eye.

One quick shot wouldn't hurt. Warm the cockles, he encouraged himself, pushing the un-cleaned brass plate fixed to the heavy wood and glass door. One screw was missing from the right bottom corner of the plate. His two fingers that had touched the metal were covertly wiped on his coat. The place was virtually empty of customers, just dozens of chairs originating from the late forties when the place was most likely fitted out. Each chair was over polished mahogany, matching the oblong tables, two of which had been levelled with a multi-use beer mat.

'A whisky, landlord, if I may trouble you,' requested Charles. His phone vibrated again in his hand, "in place" it read, it went back into his pocket.

'Coming right up, sir. Would you like ice with that?' the bartender asked, with added grace.

'Water, I'm not new age,' replied the brigadier as he looked around: he was in the lounge of a forgotten boozer. Clearly once very well used, the signs were there on the upholstery, now two-tone from all the shuffling on and off. The carpet in the standing area around the bar was virtually threadbare, with cigarette burns and years of ground in slops, on a warm day shoes would stick. Two other males were present. Both sat looking into half empty glasses, wearing frowns like chastised boys. Some shouting was coming through from the smoke room at the rear of the building.

The landlord slid over the whisky and a glass with a small amount of chilled water.

'Four pounds, when you're ready please, sir,' he asked as he entered £3.00 on the till's keys.

'Keep the change.' Charles passed him a deep-sea diver.

'Getting loud through there.' He nodded in the direction of the smoke room, glass raised, the contents about to be drunk.

'We getting any fucking service in here, you, prick?' came from the smoke room.

'I'll be there in a moment. I've only got one pair of hands,' the barman's head shook his face muscles gave away the tension.

'Get here now if you wanna keep your job, you useless fucking wanker!'

The landlord was gone long enough for Charles to finish his drink. The other two customers clearly weren't comfortable with the language. They supped up and vacated the place, one of them leaving half a pint and an unopened blue packet of Walkers crisps.

The landlord returned, trying to disguise a cut mouth with the bar towel. A rear door opened and out came three men. The one leading leaned over the counter and opened his hand, 'Money, cunt! Now?'

'I only have the float. You know we've been slack tonight, the till's bare.' The landlord's face red, palm open and pointed in the till's direction.

'Money! Now!' The fingers of the outstretched hand curled and re-opened then curled again.

'That's an interesting job you have, son. Your mother proud, is she?' stated Charles.

'Who the fuck is you, grandpa? Keep your nose out, unless you want it broke!' A laugh came.

'Charles! My name is, Charles Howlet, and I haven't been blessed with grandchildren as of yet, so your assumption is incorrect, and I like my nose the shape it is, and a lot better than you have tried to displace it?' answered the brigadier, finger and thumb either side of his nose.

'Hey, lads, we have a real live hero here. Thank you for your service - granddad,' the thug smirked as his ego inflated.

'Keep out of it, sir,' warned the landlord, in an attempt to smooth over the situation.

'Listen to him, gramps, or you'll get fucking hurt, I promise.'

The landlord gave over the money to the thug.

'Bye, gramps. Have a good night,' the thug mocked, waving the few twenties and a fiver at Charles.

'A pound of that belongs to me,' Charles spoke in a calm but strong tone.

'You're asking for a slap, that's what you're owed, gramps, I won't warn you again,' replied the thug, the other two gathering near to him.

'I'm asking you for my pound back and I said please.' Charles held out his hand.

'Just leave, Billy. You have what you came for,' pleaded the landlord.

'He's not leaving here, with my pound. I gave it to you, not him. If you don't want it, I'll take it back.' Charles pushed his hand a bit closer to the thug.

Billy looked at the other two standing behind for more encouragement.

'Slap him. Cut the fucker up,' they encouraged Billy.

'You should have kept quiet, pops, like I told you.' Billy clumsily produced a flick-knife he stood there like an imitation native American waiting for a fight.

'Another whisky, landlord, if you will.' Charles, with his two centre fingers, pushed the empty glass across the bar. He appeared to have turned away from Billy, but an eye was still engaged via the bar's landscape mirror. He looked to the landlord and without a care and spoke, 'It's times like these I wonder if Darwinism is still at play?' The landlord's eyebrows screwed up. The knife cowardly came from the rear. Charles knocked Billy's arm outwards on the turn, then easily landed a left on his jaw. The big lad crumbled and fell to the floor. The two others watching did nothing, both appearing stunned by the sudden action. The landlord instructed them to pick Billy up and carry him back into the smoke room.

'Well, he may think twice before he steals again,' Charles lifted the refilled glass.

'He wasn't stealing, sir. He owns the place. I just manage it for him,' announced the landlord.

'And you allow him to treat you like this. What's wrong with you, man, have you no pride?'

'I don't have a lot of choice. Pride comes at a cost? I went bankrupt last year with my own boozer. Lost everything: home and finances, all gone, then the missis did a Paul Daniels on me. Tell me, who's gonna employ a 45-year-old has-been, with a bankruptcy order hanging around his neck?' remarked the landlord. His tone contained anger and weariness. Angry with life and the cards dealt him.

'Write your name, number, date of birth and current address on a piece of paper.'

'Why? What for, sir? I don't understand.' He poured himself a drink.

'I may be able to help. Do you hold, a driving licence?' Charles lifted his glass finishing his drink.

'Yes, I do, sir, was a cabbie before the pub game. Fifteen years in whole. Completed the knowledge and everything. Good times.' The landlord split a beer mat in two and wrote his details on the inside then passed it over.

'Not promising anything, but I will have a word.' Charles gave him another fiver, beer mat in his pocket and he was at the door. Outside in the night air, his collar was instantly flicked back up. He had only walked 100 yards before he stopped, looked around: he was alone. He stepped backwards into the darkness of the shop's deep doorway. Thirty meters down the road a pair of eyes watched the brigadier as he appeared to vanish. Then the man leaned over, his hand dropped the glove compartment, his fingers curled around the grip. It took him ten seconds to tape over the internal light. And he was out the vehicle, a quick pace he kept, heading for the darkness.

The smoke room of the Coach and Blacksmith public house

'Here's your money, lads,' said Ned the landlord, passing fifty pounds to each of the three thugs.

'You didn't say I would get hit. My jaw is really hurting me. We're actors not bad boys,' moaned Billy, rubbing his hand on his face.

'Not very good ones. You were pathetic, and why did you try to stab him? And if you don't stop whining, yah bollocks'll be fucking hurting, you prick. You're lucky I'm still paying yah.' The landlord passed another twenty to Billy, then continued his de-brief.

'Remember what I said would happen if you speak to anyone about what you did tonight.' The landlord asked Billy for his flick-knife back. He took hold of the handle, spinning it at speed, then pointing the blade individually at each of the thespians, inches only from their heads. They were scared and mesmerised as he skilfully retracted the blade. He left the room saying, 'Get out now before I do something I'll have to fucking clean up!'

Back in the bar, he watched the last of the actors leave

the pub. Following them, he bolted the door, switched off the lights poured another tipple, then dialled a number.

'Sir, it's done. He took it hook line and sinker. No more than a couple of days I reckon, and I'll be in,' he boasted. The knife was back out and played with as he spoke.

'A £5000 bonus if they come back to you and the runner's job is offered. Are you sure he didn't suspect anything; you didn't go over the top?' asked the pompous voice.

'No, sir, not a thing. I'm sure, it was like conning a baby of its food,' said the landlord, confidently.

'Contact me if you hear from them, and don't be so forthcoming, the brigadier is nobody's fool, and you would do well to remember that.' Phone call over.

The landlord looked at the phone's screen. 'Bye then,' he muttered as he walked to the bar. Placing the glass back under the gin bottle, he pushed up the optic twice. What he'd told the brigadier about being bankrupt and an ex-cabbie was all true. What he'd neglected to pass over, however, was that he was on the payroll of Sir Shoebridge, as a back-room lobbyist. The Coach and Blacksmith pub had been re-opened only a week or so earlier and would be closed again in a week, if he were to be successful in becoming a runner for Charles and his Whitehall department.

Outside the public house, as the landlord talked on the phone

'You're light on your feet for a big lad,' pointed out the brigadier.

'Crepe soles and sponge linings.' The big man's hand slid into his open jacket. 'The photos and information on yah man in there.' He handed over an envelope as he nodded his head. He spoke again, 'Do you want me to hang aro...'

'No, and thanks for this. I will be okay. You call it a night,' said the brigadier.

'I'll leave my phone on, sir. It looks like the puppets are here.' And the man turned and left.

Charles returned into the darkness, listening, as the footsteps were approaching. One - two - three, he was out again.

'Hello lads, out for a walk, are we?' was said as he stepped out the shadows of the doorway.

None of them replied, only hunched over as a group. Billy's hand subconsciously went back up to his jaw.

'Are you going to hit me again?' He crouched in further.

'Now that depends on you, Billy?' The brigadier's head went sideways as his eyebrow raised.

'My name is not Billy, sir. It is Rupert, Rupert Kingston.' The thespian's posture altered. 'And I am a student at London University,' he told him with pride.

The brigadier had already worked out they weren't gangsters. Their performance in the pub had been farcical, bordering on the *Three Stooges*.

'Don't tell me that you're actually taking a course in acting?' Sort of laughed the brigadier. The three of them looked at each other and said in unison, 'Yes, we are, majoring in the dramatic arts.' Their expressions were the only thing about them that was dramatic.

'So, tell me, why were you performing in the pub tonight?'

'It was our first paid gig,' replied the one on the left.

'Talk to me. Was the whole event set up for me?'

'We were paid to act like hard men, to make you save

him,' said the one on the right, who then asked if they could leave now.

'Tell me how he got in touch with you and what his real name is, then you're free to go. That is if I believe you!'

'We don't know his name,' said two of them together.

'I was given a mobile telephone number and asked if I was interested in doing a bit of acting to earn some money. Honest, sir, that's all we know. I didn't think you would hit me.' Rupert had begun to panic; his breaths became shallow, racing. The guy on the left fished in his pocket and passed him his inhaler.

'Use it, you'll be fine,' encouraged Charles, his head pointed to the inhaler, he gave the man a couple of seconds, 'Do you still have the number he gave you?'

Rupert sucked in the gas released by the inhaler then entered his password into his phone and went onto the call log.

'Here it is, sir, he told me to delete it, but I didn't,' and he showed the phone to the brigadier. He took a photo of the number on the screen. 'Off you go, and we never had this talk! Did we, lads?'

Heads shook as they crossed the road and quickened their pace, Rupert requiring more gas. Charles set off and it wasn't long before he turned into another road. A smile warmed his face as he read the old black and white sign fixed on the wall. Dead Man's Lane, underneath this, in a smaller font, leading to Oxford Street.

Across the road, the man sitting in the car watched as Charles pulled out his phone. The watching driver pushed the key into the ignition waited a few more seconds before driving off.

'Tanya,' Charles said, answering his phone.

'Sir, shall I continue from earlier?'

'One moment, do we still require a runner?' Switching to a different subject, out the blue.

'Yes, we do, sir. I've started interviewing for the position, but with no success as of today. Why do you ask, sir?' Her enquiry was out of surprise, aware he would normally never have given this position a second thought.

'I may have a contender.' Charles fished in his Mac pocket, pulling out the beer mat. 'Check this person out. Ned Pearson, 18th April '72, residing at the Coach and Blacksmith, Lockington Road, contact number 07777435677. But not for much longer.' Charles laughed, then asked, 'Check out this number also 07999141323. You may find it interesting!'

'I will get on to it first thing tomorrow, sir. Could I continue with my earlier brief? It's imp ...'

'I would appreciate it if you could trace the number this evening. I will explain later.'

'Consider it done, si...'

'Are you still at the office?'

'No, sir. I'm back at my apartment. I've just walked in. Why?' replied Tanya, removing her outer garments.

'I'm just about to enter Oxford Street.'

'You sound as if you're outside, sir?' She heard the passing traffic and people shouting.

'I am, I'm walking. Why?'

'You're walking, sir? Outside?' She picked up the phone, switching it off loud speaker.

'Yes, and what's wrong with that, girl?'

'No... nothing is wrong with that, sir. Just slightly surprising.' She was glad and happy as he hadn't walked any real distance since the night of the ambush.

'I'll flag a cab down and come over to your place. You can give me this "important" brief when I arrive,' informed

Charles, heading towards the road with his arm up. 'Taxi!' Tanya heard him shout, then another voice. 'Where to, governor?' Then the sound of the heavy metal door closing.

'Kensington Place,' directed Charles.

'Right you are, sir.' The cab shot off, displaying the orange light.

'I'll be with you in twenty minutes or so,' spoke Charles, back on the mobile.

'Have you eaten anything this evening?' she enquired, but she guessed the answer.

'No, I haven't, but don't you be going to any trouble, lass. I'll get a club sandwich later. I have a meeting with the PM's aide.' The brigadier switched off his phone. Sitting himself back on the large seat, he thought about Shoebridge and the need to apprehend, or remove him. Not that anything would ever have gone to court. Just like the cocaine washing, it was stopped and was then forgotten about. The powers that be, would not allow such a scandal to emerge. But what was he meddling in now? Africa, America and what was he doing with this charity?

Tanya tossed into the hot wok a couple of handfuls of chopped onion, a crushed garlic, and finally a small touch of ginger and a pinch of black pepper. As these ingredients crackled in the hot oil, several thin pieces of soya chicken followed. Lifting the wok slightly from the heat, each time tossing the contents, which spit and spat as they re-landed. She sipped some wine then continued chopping peppers and leafy greens for the bulk, determined to get some decent food into the brigadier. The club sandwich to which Charles had referred was nicknamed the "Scooby". Its content was nothing but several red meats and lashings of oil-based garnish. The secret recipe was more than a couple of centuries old but had more calories and salt than a Friday night doner kebab.

Downstairs, a black cab pulled up in front of Kensington Place. 'We're here, sir.'

'Thank you.' Charles passed him some money. The cab pulled away after receiving payment. The light switched back to "In service".

'Good evening, sir. Are you well?' asked the doorman tipping his large top hat.

'Evening, Elroy. I'm good thanks. How are you keeping?' replied Charles, as the door was pulled and held open allowing him to enter the posh building.

'I'm good, sir. As well as can be expected, but missing the old days in the regiment, but we all have to get old.' His hand still gripped the long brass handle.

'You're nothing but a spring chicken, Elroy. But yes, I too miss the action and comradery, the injections of adrenalin when we got a shout. We were blessed to have had it at all, some don't.' Charles for a moment recalled Hereford in his younger days.

'I agree with that, but old I am, sir, seventy next month in fact.'

'You don't look a day past fifty.'

Elroy smiled as he looked down at the four shiny medals pinned on his chest. The brigadier patted the side of Elroy's shoulder then made for the elevator. With Elroy informing him he was coming up to seventy, he also felt old as his memory played back a good number of years to Elroy's leaving reception. He was there as a major and a young one at that.

The elevator doors slid apart, Charles entered and

pressed for the destination. He looked to Elroy who had gone back outside. A few seconds passed.

Fourth floor - please exit when the doors are fully open and secure, said the computerised voice. Only a couple of steps outside the lift, Charles was forced to lean on the wall for a second or two. His hand was up to his forehead, pressing inwards, forced to close his eyes to stop the spinning. A minute passed, as did the dizziness and slight blur in his left eye. He continued on to Tanya's apartment.

'That was quick, sir.'

'No traffic. What can I smell?' asked Charles, removing his overcoat.

'Just having something to eat. Would you like some?'

'If there's some going spare. I just spoke with Elroy downstairs. Were you

aware he is going to be seventy next month?' He placed his coat on the hook.

'Of course, there's some spare. Seventy! No! I thought he was in his fifties. He runs every morning. I see him in the park sometimes, a pretty good pace he keeps up as well, he always drops at the end of the run does sit ups and press ups.'

'Could we arrange something for him?' By "we" Charles was referring to the royal "we".

'I will look into it. His granddaughter often visits him. I've bumped into her a couple of times as she's leaving his apartment. I will bring it up with her, see if she has any plans.'

'Could we involve the regiment, if possible? Seems appropriate somehow. Don't you agree?'

'Yes, good idea. He always talks to me about Hereford.'

'Use my name and speak with Rupert. He'll want to be in on this.'

'Why?' she asked while stirring.

'Elroy was his sergeant for a few years, his right-hand man. Now, down to business. What is this report you believe to be so suspicious?' asked Charles, pulling out a chair at the table. Sitting down, he kept his left leg straight.

'Just one moment, this is really hot.' She was shaking and draining the pasta over the sink, her head pulled back as the steam dispersed. Next, it was placed on the square plates close to the chicken stir-fry.

'Tuck in, sir. Enjoy!' she said, drizzling some flavoured oil on the green leaves. She joined him sitting and began eating with one hand whilst flicking through a file with the other.

'Here, sir. This is the tattoo that has sparked all the interest.' She slipped a photo across the table, turning it around as it travelled.

The brigadier stared at the image of a man's lower back. The tattoo in question was in the format of heraldry. Presented on a shield with a red and yellow lion in the centre, it had hooves not claws for its feet, and an eagle's head. This was displayed on a black and silver background, an old helmet with a sword and axe laying crossed, at the feet of the mythical creature. Some words were ornately dressed on the outside; these were difficult to make out as the old font flowed and twisted, intertwining along a vine surrounding the creature.

'It's clearly a coat of arms that belongs to an old family, looking at the style of the helmet and axe. I'd have to hazard a guess at or around the 13th century. Maybe much earlier. But a lot of these crests were altered back then as the ruling families merged through marriage, alliances formed ensuring peace. Plus, territories expanded and were maintained through blood ties.' He picked up the photo, holding it out at semi-arm's length, attempting to read the words without the aid of his glasses.

Tanya handed over a couple more shots, close-ups of the words, anticipating her boss's non-compliance of wearing his specs.

'Two of them, sir, are written in Latin and the other two are old English,' confirmed Tanya.

'Servientes Custos; I don't remember Latin.'

'Serving Guardian, sir, ' Tanya translated.

'Efficacy Gelang.' Read Charles, managing a pretty fair pronunciation, then gave a translation. 'From what I remember, I'm sure that means "Success and Belonging".' He looked up at Tanya as he continued. 'Right, I can now see why this has captured your imagination. But can you explain to me why this is of relevance to our department?' enquired Charles, finishing his pasta.

'Close, it's actually "Success in Belonging", sir, and do you remember Lady De Pen Court?' asked Tanya, pushing her plate to the left.

'You leaving your pasta?' asked Charles, both verbally and with his eyes.

'Yes, but there is more in the drainer and there should be some pieces of chicken left too.' She had cooked way too much, hoping he would like it, which he always did, but if she suggested to him that she would make it, he'd tell her, "not that muck".

'Don't put yourself out.' He swiped her pasta. 'And I do remember an Emma De Pen Court. Wasn't she a friend of my brother, from Scotland, and if memory serves, she is part of a very prominent family?' His fork going to work on the pasta.

'Yes, she stayed at your country estate with us for a week, maybe longer. She invited herself after Jonathon's funeral.

She was besotted with you.' Tanya reached for the pan and placed it over his plate. 'Here, sir, there are a couple of pieces of chicken leftover.' Pan tipped, the pieces spooned onto his plate, she placed the pan in the sink and turned the tap on.

'She was WHAT? Besotted with me! Are you out of your mind, girl?' Then Charles thanked Tanya for the chicken, complementing her on the flavour.

'She was, I remember. She would continually question me about you during her stay with us. You were dashing back then. Emma wasn't your only admirer I was often asked if you were in a relationship when we went places.' She chuckled, knowing he wasn't that sort of man. His face frowned inwards, lips squeezing together. 'She was pretty, I'll give you that,' recalled Charles.

'I remember I walked by your study one night and the light was on, so I shouted and knocked, but you didn't come out and give me a clue written on a bit of paper as you always did. I walked off upset you hadn't replied to me and I didn't know why. At the end of the corridor, I hid between the small Chinese table and the big clock, and there I waited. However, it wasn't you who came out of the office, it was Emma! I remember the moment as clear as day, she was holding something in her hand, looking at it as she pulled the door too, her hand wrapped around whatever it was? She looked my way as if to ensure she was alone, then pocketed the object? She checked that the door closed properly before leaving, virtually left on her tiptoes. Then I saw Marlee. She told me you had left for London just after tea and would be back in the morning. You had been summoned, an emergency, a Cobra meeting had been arranged.'

Charles's eyebrows raised. 'Ha, yes ...' Then he went silent as a nostalgic expression came across his face.

'What's wrong?' she broke the silence.

'Nothing, lass, nothing.'

'Talk to me!'

'It's silly.' He used a word strange to his vocabulary. Tanya began her stare.

'Okay, I remembered when you said "Cobra". You would be scared every time I returned from London, in case I had a snake with me,' he laughed, but he was in pain: that's what the strange look had been, and it had hidden the happy nostalgic smile. Tanya topped up her wine and kissed him on his cheek. The melancholy had passed, as had the pain.

'I had Chang discreetly inform Emma that we were going on holiday to get rid of her. Do you remember, we said it had been planned for months?'

'Yes father, and of course I remember! I was very excited about going on a holiday. I'd never been away before, and we only left for six hours.' Tanya gave him a look.

'We went to the cinema and picked up pizza.' He managed the lip curl without pain, and continued. 'Thinking about it, it was around that time the unsigned ring went missing from my office. Chang and I spent two days going through the place, took the office apart, but to no avail. Today the ring is still missing. It has never surfaced anywhere?' The lines on his forehead rose.

'I don't remember the rings from back then, but take a look at the shield again?' Tanya said before continuing.

'It's virtually the same as on the rings?' his bottom jaw dropped.

'And yes, you are correct, Emma is part of one of the oldest families in the country and they own billions of pounds worth of property plus a land bank worth a similar amount, including a very nice collection in both London and New York. Add to this the two large castles in Ireland.

It's said their family's portfolio is above sixteen billion pounds. Each of the Irish estates are at least 10,000 acres, plus the one they reside at in Scotland. This must be of a similar size, they are very wealthy indeed, sir, and elusive with their affairs. Alison informs me that their team have invested over 3000 personnel hours, investigating the De Pen Court family, including assessing their assets. There's a belief that they have strong links to the American Irish society, including NORAID itself. Supplying financial aid for them too. I'm preaching to you, but you know how it works better than I do, sir,' added Tanya. Charles thought how ironic that he actually didn't anymore, yet he was pleased she was superseding him, especially given his circumstances.

'All very interesting, girl, and it sounds grasping, I agree, but, and I don't mean any disrespect, because I can see you have this "bit" between your teeth. If Alison's lot are looking into it currently, that would make it come under Alex's domain, would it not?' Charles rubbed his leg while he poured himself some water, green bottle down. 'So, I'm still not seeing the connection to our department here, apart from my brother being a friend of the family. And that must have been... well, well over 20 years ago.' Charles made his way over to the stove. 'This is really tasty. Do you have a takeaway tub?'

'Emma's son Henry is an only child. He would be my age now, sir. He went missing ten years ago, after a major row with his father. Henry actually tried to knock his father down with a Bentley! The car was his 18th birthday present. Three years ago, Emma lost all contact with him. At first, he was thought to be behind some animal rights demonstrations, of which two were particularly nasty events - resulting in fatalities. A couple of clinics were taken over and it all ended in a doctor and a security officer being killed. A few more members of staff were also pretty badly hurt, hospitalisation being required. This is when Henry disappeared off the radar completely. A week or so after these events, I received somewhat of a panicky phone call from Emma, begging me to look into Henry's whereabouts as she feared he was dead.' Tanya took hold of her wine glass, her fingers turning it round in her hand, reaching into the cupboard with the other hand for a takeout tub.

'That explains you turning up at the office a lot then as you were still in University.' His eyes opened wide. 'Did you find anything out regarding the lad?' enquired Charles, fork in pasta again.

'I asked Sandra to put Gary on it when he was still Delta, she did give him two days when he was recovering from the showdown. He did well and discovered that Henry was in fact living on the streets, of no fixed abode. I know it's hard to believe when you take into account his mum is most likely in the top ten of the richest people in the world.' She sipped the wine. 'He gave me an address of a squat down by the canal, an old Victorian pumping station on Stoneferry Road. I took over from Gary at this point and arranged to meet up with Henry, but he made a condition that I remain silent and to tell no one of his location. Not even which city he was in. After listening to his explanation of the incidents that killed those unfortunate people, I assured him that I would keep any information he gave and his locations to myself, but I persuaded him to allow me to at least, inform his mother he was safe and th...'

'Was he involved with the killings?' demanded Charles.

'No, sir, not at all. He had stumbled into the activist scene after leaving home, via a girl he had met. The group must have done their homework on him, as a lot did back then, being frightened of infiltration by undercover police or MI5. My guess is they found out he was a rich kid and let him tag along. A fund source, sir, more of a mascot and possibly a potential I think, rather than a serious player. He just doesn't have the stomach for killing. He actually burnt all the skin on his left palm trying to open a door and let the doctor and guard out on the last incident. His father found out Emma was putting cash into a bank account for him to access; he stopped all his money and the gang subsequently dumped him. But not before laying the blame of the bombing and two murders at his feet. He had the living daylights kicked out of him and was left there to die, with all the incriminating evidence placing him in the two clinics that had been blown up.' Tanya refilled her glass and offered the bottle to her father.

'So, why all this concern now? We don't do family squabbles. Nothing good ever comes from interfering in old family affairs, girl, you know that!' He shook his hand, declining the wine. His hand squeezed the small plastic bottle in his pocket.

'It was the tattoo. When I last met with Henry, he had just had a tattoo inked on himself. He was complaining of the pain and finding it awkward to sit back in the chair as we talked. I enquired if he had hurt himself; he didn't reply. Instead, he showed me the image he had taken with his phone the day previous in the tattoo artist's studio.' She sipped some more of the wine.

'And it was...' The brigadier tapped on the image of the photo with his finger.

Tanya nodded, confirming his assumption; he continued, 'So, you're saying you would like me to inform Emma, Lady De Pen Court, for old time's sake that her son has been found dead. Not a job that I relish doing.

However, you're right, it is the decent thing to do, at the end of the day. And will this finally satisfy your curiosity? I need you focused on our cases, not some CSI job, we're not A...'

'Not American, sir?' she smiled; he gave a look. She spoke. 'You are aware that your men go around saying to each other they aren't "American yet"?' She sipped some wine, a twinkle in her eye.

Charles paused then nodded, then continued, ignoring the comment. 'You're not making much sense, and add to this the fact we are extremely busy, needing to find out who the American connections are, not to mention our staffing issues, or lack of,' Charles continued spooning out more of the pasta. 'What is on this?' he digressed.

Tanya remained focused. 'That's just it, sir. I said the last time I met Henry he showed me the tattoo on his phone, but the last time I saw Henry was on one of our mobile surveillance films. He was taking a booklet from Shoebridge's Mercedes. And that was only a couple of days ago. And the pasta has a parsley and mint sauce mixed in with it.'

The brigadier turned sharply to look at his daughter: his interest had sparked when she mentioned the minister's car. 'I was there when that shot was taken. Garthwaite was taking the photos, I believe, but we couldn't receive any audible.'

'That's correct, sir, Gary signed the authenticity of both the pictures, dates and locations, stating you were also present and could confirm with eyes-on if required.

'Yes, it was a strange night, Garthwaite believed their car had been fitted with a deflector or screen, worrying as this gives concern to Shoebridge being aware he has a tail.'

'I don't know, sir, he is a very cautious man, and more so

after you blew open the drugs supply, he had going.' Tanya sat back down. 'How is the leg, sir?'

'Healing, but slow, yes you're correct he would obviously be more cautious.' He pushed the plate away 'You have done well with all this, lass.' He smiled at Tanya, who had started to put all the sheets and photos away.

'Thank you, but it was down to the attendant and then Cathy for bringing it to my attention.' She started cleaning up, tipping the excess food into the container.

'I must head to the club, I've a meeting?' His hand reached for his coat, he stopped, 'Wait a minute, you've just eaten chicken? Have you given up the plant eating?'

'No, father you have just enjoyed soya chicken pieces,' she gave a great grin and held up an empty packet.

'Let me know about Leroy.' his eyes gave her a touché. She came over took hold of either side of his coat's collar and straightened it. 'I'll drive you to the club.'

'Nonsense, girl, I'll call a taxi, plus I may take Leroy for a drink first, yes I will,' I'll see you tomorrow,' He was out the door.

6

INFORMED

November 15th 1643hours
Hereford
'Sean, thank you for coming at short notice. Please, take a seat, we have things to discuss.' The speaker was half out of his seat but sat back down as if not sure what was best to do.

'I'm okay to stand, if you don't mind, sir.' Sean didn't like the fact he'd been called by his first name, especially by his commanding officer during work hours; this in the forces wasn't good.

'Have it your way, Doyle.' The officer looked away from him for a second, gazing towards the door.

'Hold all my calls for the next thirty minutes, Bailey.'

'Yes, sir, of course, sir.' The full screw left the room, pulling the door too behind him.

'Are you sure you wouldn't like to sit down, Sean?' The officer held onto several sheets of paper.

'I'm fine, sir. Like I said, I prefer to stand.' Sean's manner was one of self-protection. As he was well aware of the back-room discussions that had been taking place about him and his latest injury. To him, standing was a demonstration of his fitness and maybe his defiance.

The officer placed the collection of papers, face down on the organised desk as he released them, he stood up behind it, the legs of the heavy chair scraping the wooden floor. A few steps and he was over at the grey filing cabinet. The top drawer was pulled open, he gripped several files together; these drawn forward, he returned to his guest.

'Sit down, Sergeant Doyle,' ordered the officer, as he did the same.

Doyle's knees didn't bend. The officer stared at him; his mouth curled. The knees bent.

'Thank you, now Join me, Sean, will you! Oblige me, humour me, disguise it however you want, but don't make me order you to drink, that just wouldn't be British, now would it?' He released the two shot glasses from his fingertips. They rocked then stopped. He tipped the half full bottle of *Teachers*.

Sean did oblige but sat as rigid as he'd stood.

'How long have I known you, sergeant?' asked the officer, as the bottle was placed on the desk.

'Seven years, four months and ...'

'Okay, Doyle, okay, that's precise enough.' The officer sipped the whisky then lit a fag, drawing in deep as he leant back in the chair, the clean light entered through the window highlighting the pile of papers.

'Thank you, sir.' Sean threw back the full contents of the glass, replacing it, back on the same spot.

'Sip this one, sergeant.' He leant forward and the Teachers bottle tipped again, clinking as it did so, bottle to glass caused by the shake in the officer's hand. Sean noticed the ash on the end of the cigarette bending, about to fall.

'Is there a reason you wanted me here, sir? Or was it

because you just didn't want to drink alone?' Sarcasm didn't come natural to Doyle, but he could be good at it when he wanted.

'I have received some news about your Grandma Mary, and it's not, ... good news I'm afraid to say.' His tone lowered naturally, as he spoke he watched Doyle, whose expression remained the same as when he had walked into his office, just a few moments earlier. Without looking at the cig he placed it in the ashtray, perfect timing the fag cracked in two.

'I will read the report as I received it.' The sheets of paper were tapped square on the desk, as he cleared his voice like a presenter on *News at Ten*.

'Mrs Mary Ward was discovered by one of her employees on Tuesday 25th November.' The officer swallowed before been able to continue. 'Her body was found at 1116 hours. She had been placed inside a coffin in the parlour's chapel of rest. She had been laid out, pre...' he looked up at Doyle.

'Can I ask, how did she die, sir?' interrupted Sean. On the outside, his demeanour never changed, not an alteration of any muscle in his face. On the inside, it all poured out about the dream lady: she used to take him out, he felt special, then she gave him a gold ring, then disappeared, came back and collected him from the hospital, many, many years earlier. Removing him from a life of cruelty and neglect at the home, to one where he would be loved, wanted and impressed upon.

'Sorry, Doyle... Sean, ... it says here ... th ...' he looked at Doyle, 'That she was shot in the back and chest three times - at close range.' The officer closed the folder and topped up Sean's glass, this time the clink of the bottle somehow resonating the time with Doyle, ensuring it was marked in his memory forever, as the date of 15th of November was, why didn't he go to see her?

'Can I leave now, sir? My troop are about to embark on a mission overseas.'

'You're partially correct, your troop is, son, but without you. Sergeant Elise from red troop has already been briefed and is taking your position. You are in no fit state to be on active duties. Surely, you must agree with me on that, Sean?' The officer poured himself a second glass, a large one as he reclaimed the cigarette from the ashtray a small inhale and it was finished. Pushing it back down he twisted the end, a couple of stubbs, the grey smoke gave a last swirl.

Sean's open hand morphed into a tight fist, yet he remained silent. Truth be known, he wasn't sure how to deal with this news, or the emotions that came along with it.

'Like you so accurately pointed out a few moments ago, Sean, I have known you for a very long time, and may I add, proud to have. I refreshed my memory with a quick glimpse over your record. The youngest recruit to ever pass selection, heavy weight boxing champion three years running, and then retired - unbeaten. Marksman, weapons expert, trained in all forms of combat... and the list goes on. The best bit for me, however, isn't any of the macho stuff. All of us here, are good at that shit, it is why we're all here after all. It was during your last tour in Ireland, when you were seconded to intelligence. I remembered having a number of conversations with Rupert Oliver about you. He was full of nothing but praise for the investigative work you carried out, according to him you prevented a second mortar attack on Downing Street. And the splendid retrieval in Syria...' The officer's words to Sean faded into "blah - blah - blah". He thought of nothing but the gold ring. Then Mary's face entered his mind; above this came Tony. Doyle's images faded and the officer's words again made sense, not that he wanted to hear them. He wanted to hear the two people he'd just remembered, and say sorry to one of them.

'Rupert's team still talk about your retrieval in Syria at dinner parties, even today. As you know, son, there is a lot of speculation at the moment regarding your fitness, whether it be true or not. Off the record, I personally have no issues with you, or your fitness. You are still probably one of the best operatives we have. But unfortunately, times are sadly changing Doyle, even for the likes of us, the ones who are called when there's no one else to turn to. We now have to account for ourselves, and in return we have to be seen to be an employer of good standing.' The officer picked up the lighter and fags, his eyebrows lifted, he swallowed struggling to part with the following words. 'I'm therefore giving you six months personal leave, Sergeant, commencing today.' He pulled out a separate folder opened it and began writing on letter-headed paper, he spoke more, but his eyes remained on the paper.

'I feel you need a break and also some time to sort out your personal affairs, back home in London. With all that has happened to you and your family recently, I feel a six-month break is warranted. And it will of course help your physical recovery, that must be a bonus?' He stopped writing, flamboyantly signed the bottom of the sheet, rubber stamped it and handed it to Sean. It was his pass-out of camp, with two dates stamped on it; these would be in place until it was all made official.

'We'll be in touch with you, sergeant, sometime in the first three-month period and take it from there. You will also have to attend a couple of meetings with a unit at Whitehall, boxes to be ticked, hoops to jump through, nothing radical. You understand, I'm sure. With this being a prolonged personal leave situation, we must be transparent.' The officer lit another cigarette. 'Have you any questions for me, Sean?' He closed the second folder and sat back enjoying the nicotine influx.

'No questions, but if you force this leave on me, sir, I'll apply for discharge immediately.' Again, his tone remained the same.

'You wouldn't, by any chance be trying to blackmail me, would you, Sergeant Doyle? Because if you are, let me remind you that I still have a medical report to submit on your behalf, regarding your leg injury. And of course, there are the psych reports to review. However, Rose was very professional in her comments, but she too recommended a long break followed by a final couple of sessions with her. She feels you are tired, Sean. But either of these could see you discharged much faster than a self-request. Do I make myself clear! Sergeant?' The officer spoke sternly, with full eye contact.

'You do what you feel you have to, sir. I feel my days may be numbered here anyway, so whichever route appears first, I'm ok with it.' Sean replaced his beret, stood up and saluted perfectly, bringing his heels together with a snap. He walked to the door, his hand placed on the brass handle about to turn.

'Doyle, no one is an island, son, everyone needs somebody, sometime. Remember that. And take the time off, it's a plus. I assure you,' The officer's tone increased with empathy for the young man who had just been informed of the murder of a loved one, but he also was well aware you didn't show too much emotion to their kind.

'Why sir, and who said we all need someone?' Sean left the CO's office, pulling the door to, not slamming it, but not softly closing it either. The corporal, from behind his desk, stared at Sean, but no words were exchanged between them.

The officer's finger pressed a button on the digital intercom, simultaneously, with the other hand, topping up his glass, the cig gave off more mini smoke signals in the ash tray.

'Corporal Bailey, I require contact with Brigadier Howlett in Whitehall? Do it as a matter of urgency, I need his counsel as soon as,' instructed the officer, uncannily speaking with a shadow to his words.

'Yes, sir, right away, sir.' Corporal Bailey, wondered what had gone on with the CO and Sean, especially as Doyle said nothing on departure.

Doyle spent the next couple of hours working out in the camp's gym, to the point of exhaustion. His troop had left for some backwater village in Nigeria two hours ago: Operation "Witch Doctor". The orders came from a government minister with instructions to retrieve some paperwork, and to do so at any cost. Fourteen minutes past midnight Sean threw his kit bags into the boot of his Audi and left Hereford, heading for old London town.

As Doyle drove out the camp gates, he clocked the CO's office light remained on, he saw the figure of Bailey at the desk. He waved to the guard as the barrier raised.

In the CO's office. 'Thank you for returning my call, brigadier.' Bailey then pressed the hold button and dialled the CO's home telephone. 'Sir, I'm sorry to contact you at this late hour, but I have Brigadier Howlett on the phone, as you requested. He's returning your call from earlier today. He apologises for the late hour himself, but he has been engaged in meetings all day.'

'Thank you, Bailey. The hour is of no concern. Put him through will you.'

'Connecting you now, sir, goodnight,' Bailey pressed both illuminated buttons together, replaced the receiver and made his way to the top draw of the filing cabinet.

'Charles, my good friend, thank you for getting back to me, and I do hope I haven't pulled you away from urgent matters.'

'No, not a problem, David. And urgent matters seem to elude me somewhat these days. What is so important that the regiment needs my counsel?' asked the brigadier, opening his fridge door.

'It is I, who require your counsel, Charles, not so much the regiment, but we will always value your guidance.'

'There is a lot of flattery coming my way. What are you after?' Charles laughed.

'Do you remember our conversation some months ago, a few days post Operation Vault, in Thailand?'

'Yes, of course I do. Not a good time for the regiment. We lost a few good men and a couple of bad injuries were sustained. You also needed to take some time out, reflect and see where this left you personally, if I remember.' Charles spoke quietly, recalling the incident and the state his friend was in at the time.

'Nothing wrong with your memory, its correct, and one of the injured soldiers in particular was a Sergeant Dol...'

'Doyle, of course, young, headstrong, but very committed, like a wild dog. I remember reading his personnel file at the time, as I was a part of the fitness for work panel, his leg took a lot of trauma. And wasn't he put forward for a medal, but he declined? Instead, he named a fallen comrade as a substitute, calling him the real hero. Corporal Long was then awarded with the medal posthumously, all the result of Doyle's statement. Very impressive, and not many would do that, and didn't it mean

Long's widow would receive a higher pension?' recalled the brigadier.

'Correct, Charles, twenty percent higher, and she will also receive benefit for housing for a period of no less than five years. And good, it sounds like you are up to speed then, as it looks like the time has arrived for Sergeant Doyle to leave the regiment. And I wondered if you would maybe keep an eye on him. He is a good lad and an excellent soldier, with the ability to carry out investigative work. A lot like yourself in many ways, "a wild dog did you say"? David went quiet.

'Not any more, I'm grey around the mouth,' Charles took the complement as it was intended.

'But I can assure you Charles, he's a bloody good all-rounder. But he doesn't possess your cricketing skills.'

'No need to keep flattering me, David. Seriously, I will be happy to put Tanya on it, as it happens, we are in need of more staff for the department at the moment. And your man did a good turn for me when I needed a fresh face a couple of weeks back.' Charles knew what sort of a man this Doyle was, and he would be an asset, in fact, he had his eye on him, before this contact, the minute he'd read his file. A one percenter with morals is rare.

'I will send the paperwork over to her office, first thing. Thank you again, my friend, and have a good evening.' David was ready to place the receiver down.

'And you. We must get together soon. It's been too long, and we're not getting any younger.'

'I agree, the next time I'm in the capital we will meet up.'

'Do you remember Davy Elroy? The bull,' asked Charles.

'How could I ever forget "him",' replied David, laughing hard.

'WE are arranging a special party to be held at the

regiment hopefully. He's seventy at the end of this month. I'll make sure you receive an invite.'

'Look forward to it. I owe him a drink at least. I wouldn't be here today if it wasn't for that man.'

'While I think on, I'm looking for a candidate for a special operation that I have running at present. It involves investigation, and the targets being observed, are, well, shall we say of a high calibre. Most people are frightened of their status and don't follow through, but to be fair, one has also disappeared and two have refused to continue after being hospitalised and their families threatened. But they won't say why?'

'I guess the word has been spread,' interjected David.

'Would you forward a copy of Doyle's contact details over to me? On the PQ. I wouldn't mind an off the record chat with this chap, before this goes mainstream.' Charles became interested as the penny dropped, realising Sergeant Doyle's profile would be a perfect fit for a difficult position he was struggling to fill.

'Of course, Charles, your luck may be in. Goodnight my friend.'

The call was finally over, the brigadier sent a text to Tanya "Add David to the birthday list".

7

REAL LADY

Scotland, far, far north

The doctor remained blindfolded and bound when the helicopter landed. A stocky man facing him in the Lynx leant over to remove the hood.

'NO! Leave it on him 'til he's inside the house. The governor doesn't want an outlander to see anything, especially the external areas of the place. It may make it possible to identify where we are from a map,' warned the pilot.

'Got yah, right.' The man pulled the hood back down, re-drawing the cord tighter than before, squeezing the plastic toggle into the doctor's Adam's apple, feeling nothing for the man's discomfort.

A sucking sound came from under the hood as the medical man gulped in air.

'Be quiet! Or I'll tighten it further?' ordered the thug.

'Loosen it! We'll need him to be able to talk, not pass out,' instructed the pilot, in a much more sympathetic tone.

The doctor quickly picked up on this, giving him some hope for his life to be spared.

'Where am I? Please, please tell me, where am I? What do you want with me?' His voice muffled from under the re-fitted dark cloth. Barely audible but loud enough to be picked up.

'Shut up!' the man said again, before slapping the doctor across the head, hard enough to knock him over, the doctor landed on his left ear, the side of his head flat against the seat. The blades above them slowed, coming to a total stop. The door was slid open; the doctor was pulled quickly and dragged forward.

Hooded and still bound he sat terrified listening to at least three people speak at once. He hadn't a clue of his whereabouts or what the intentions of these kidnappers were towards him. Only a few hours ago he was sitting in his office after carrying out a clinic in the hostel, he was halfway through filling out a death certificate for a homeless man, when it happened.

Just outside the door one man joined the other two, 'How was the guest?'

'Been no trouble at all. He passed out, shiting himself when me and Harry kicked his office door down. He's still sat in wet trousers now,' mocked the stocky man.

All three of them laughed; this stopped when the pilot appeared.

'Come on, let's have him up. I don't want to be late for the governor, do any of you?' The pilot didn't have to say anything else after mentioning the governor, the governor word, as good as a whip carried by an overseer. Two of them entered the helicopter.

The doc felt many hands grab him at once, all the large fingers sinking into the soft tissue of both his upper arms. Remaining still, petrified, he was suddenly yanked clear of the seat - he didn't need to use any of his own effort.

'Mind your head,' a voice advised. 'Shit, too late,' the same voice said as the doc cracked his forehead on the steel frame. His head hurt, a sharp stinging pain. A thin long cut opened, and then came the sensation of the blood running down his face. He fell a couple of feet onto the spongy grass, his weak legs nearly giving way on impact with the turf. Not that it would have mattered: the two men pulling him wouldn't have noticed the extra weight. He began to cry uncontrollably, unable to stop himself welling up. The blood had soaked through the bandages and his forehead had begun to sting. He knew he wasn't a brave man; this had been proved over and over right throughout his life. And what was the point in pretending, he was, after all, about to be killed, and at any moment, or so his imagination informed him, but why? The only reason he thought, was the gold teeth he'd kept for himself, a secrete pension pot. Sobbing, he felt the ground underfoot change from soft slippery grass to hard uneven slabs, his toes and heels catching each of the cracks as the pace of him being dragged virtually became a run. It wasn't long before they stopped dead. He tried to talk once more but was ignored, if he was even heard. He wanted to scream but stopped himself for fear of punishment.

'Side door, take him straight into the scullery, lads,' directed the pilot.

'Please, what's going to happen to me? Please, I can get you money. I have money, I do, and gold. Just tell me how much you want. I have a lot of cash,' begged the doc as the hands pressed firm on his shoulders, forcing him down on a hard-round chair without a back. 'Pleas...' he tried to ask again.

'Shut - the - fuck - up, cunt,' was growled in his ear, an inch from the cloth, by the same person who had secured the toggle in the helicopter. Then his hand slapped the back of the doctor's head. He couldn't ever remember being hit harder in his life. The slap really hurt, feeding his imagination about being killed. Beckoning his demise, the blood began to run again.

'Alice, any tea in the pot?' grunted the head slapper.

'Yes, of course. I've just this minute made a fresh brew, but I'll have an apology first,' replied the middle-aged plump cook, while peeling away the thick slices of bacon, laying each of them down individually in the large heavy frying pan; this was spitting at her as the meat dripping warmed.

The man who owned the voice realised he'd sworn in her kitchen. 'Sorry,' he apologised, his hand retrieving a fiver from his wallet. This was squeezed through the slot on the jar lid with a picture of a young boy and girl on the front, voice not so gruff, as he replied to the cook. 'You know how I dislike bad language.'

She looked at Alex, he knew she was asking regards the bacon, 'Not for me, Alice,' the pilot said quietly as he left the kitchen. He started climbing the steep and narrow steps, his broad shoulders forced on an angle, as this stairwell was built for people of the 16th century not the 21st.

He appeared through a panel at the top of the stairs, the pilot was now in the house; no longer was he in the rabbit runs meant for the latter-day servants. He was in a large hallway, one of sheer splendour - ten foot high ceilings and doors over eight feet tall and four feet wide. Antique artwork adorned the ancient wooden panelling. Alex the pilot, walked along the corridor, and as usual he avoided eye contact with the portrait of the seventh laird, perfectly positioned at the far end, dressed in a dark jacket, the clan's tartan flowing up from the kilt and around his left shoulder, a good-sized leather sporran and a large beret with a peacock feather. Alex lifted his head as he came to a stop adjacent an entrance.

'You're expected,' croaked a skinny man, standing nearly the same height as the door, looking at his watch without the need to pull up his sleeve. The giant's wrist flicked, his bony knuckles sharply tapped on the door, his Adam's apple dancing as he cleared his throat. 'The pilot has arrived, ma'am,' he announced, then proceeded to open the door. He didn't cross the threshold or say anything further. It was closed after the pilot walked through. He left to carry out his duties.

'Alex, thank you for joining me. Did you have a good flight? I saw that the weather was to be dreadful?'

'Yes, governor, bit of side wind, but nothing to worry about. We flew above the worst of it.'

'And how was our guest? Was he co-operative, and did he travel here of his own free will?' asked the female, dropping small fish into a large glass tank.

'Hard to say, ma'am. He passed out when Harry and Barry entered his office, and at some point, following this he wet and messed himself,' replied the pilot, watching and praying for the little fish trying to swim for their lives as a large scaly creature chased, caught, and ate them.

She laughed, turning to the pilot. 'So, we are dealing with a real fighter, are we, Alex?' She continued to laugh. It was actually a feminine laugh, and pleasant, but somehow Alex was freaked by it.

'It seems that way, ma'am,' he replied, falsely mirroring her laughter.

She walked over to the ebony and ivory drink's cabinet; a one-off piece of furniture finished with long lengths of gold leaf. Chinese figures were etched into the glass doors. 'Will you join me?'

'I'm flying back to London in an hour, ma'am. I think it best if I don't. If that's okay with you?' he spoke with hope.

'Surely one would not affect your abilities, would it, Alex?' Her piercing diamond blue eyes captured his glare; he couldn't look directly at her.

'A small one, ma'am. I don't want my judgment impaired.' He knew better than to refuse her ladyship twice. He wasn't stupid.

She made her way to some chairs that were nesting in a deep fur rug near to a crackling fire. She lifted the glass in the pilot's direction. The crystal glistened as it sent an array of colours onto the walls. Alex joined her and accepted the very large whisky.

'Well, we can get straight down to business with this doctor. It looks like he will listen very carefully to my proposal, and given the fact he has had thousands from me to date, I don't foresee any resistance?' she chuckled, before continuing. 'Did you manage to pick up the documents?' She sat forward in the golden silk chair.

'I did, ma'am. I have them here. And the man said to tell you he had taken some photos and you would know what this meant?' Alex unzipped his flying suit and removed a flat brown envelope.

'Thank you, Alex. You didn't let me down.' She took hold of the package.

'You appear warm and you're perspiring. Feel free to remove your outer garments, I understand flying suits are warm.' Her voice practically nurturing.

Alex was captured again by her icy eyes. As if hypnotised, he unzipped the suit fully revealing only shorts and a white PT shirt.

Most men would have wished to undress in the company of this stunning female, her eyes artificially full of love and lust, inviting you to seduce her, but Alex already had the scars to show from previous encounters. She walked to the mantel and opened the lid of an antique wooden box, oak with Celtic symbols. Alex swallowed the full amount of whisky. The glass remained in his fingers tight, he shivered, knowing what lived in that wooden box. Lady De Pen Court was only concerned about getting what she wanted, and she always did.

Below in the kitchen

'Can I give him a cup of tea and a sandwich?' asked the cook.

'Sure, don't see why not. It can't do any harm. I guess, everyone's entitled to a last meal.' The man laughed as he pulled off the hood and began removing the tightly bound bandages from the doc's head. The release of the pressure caused the cut to bleed once more. A long sigh was heard as the medical man breathed in deep. Slowly he opened his eyes to see the kind rounded face of the cook. He was about to break down, panicking after hearing the comments about the last meal.

'Don't you be cruel to him, Harry. You know the governor only wants to have a chat with him. He's to be our guest for a couple of days, not our prisoner, behave yourself,' admonished the cook, noticing the doctor's fearful expression, then she caught a whiff, someone could do with a freshen-up, a shower maybe? She looked to him like a teacher to an infant on their first day at school after their parents had left, and their mind hadn't yet settled. Her stubby hand placed a soft towel on the cut.

'You look really tired. We'll have to get you freshened up, and dress that cut properly, it looks like it could turn nasty.

And we don't want that do we?' She mothered him, full of niceness and hope, the soft touch of her fingers helped calm him. He looked away from her to the direction of the man the cook addressed as "Harry". Not seeing the same traits in him, the doctor quickly glanced back, frightened his stare would be returned. The kitchen was full of natural light, it entered through the large window. He felt better as he watched the cook preparing vegetables, chopping them into large square-ish lumps, before they were dropped into the biggest pan the doc had ever seen. The radio was on, some local talk show, with a host speaking. Harry was talking to the other man-mountain who was blocking the light from entering the doorway. He shivered as his eyes recognised him as the one who had kicked his office door down, the event which had started this, "Tales of the Unexpected" episode. An on-going twisted nightmare of which he had no understanding, thus far. The doctor took hold of the pint mug gingerly with both hands. Slowly pulling it across the cloth covered table, the soft plastic material rippling then falling away, so on and so forth.

He was trying hard not to draw attention to himself. His peripheral vision was on guard. Up to his lips, he began to slurp at the strong but milky sweet tea, his eyes focusing on the stained chips on the mug's rim. Normally, this would have set off his germ phobia, but he didn't care right now: it was warm, wet and comforting. His confidence grew; he stretched out his arm for the bacon door-step. This slid easily: not enough weight to cause a ripple.

'Right, ten minutes and the governor, wants to see him,' spoke Alex, coming down the stairs. Re-entering the kitchen his hair was a mess, eyes red and a cloth held tight to the centre of his left arm, where the elbow hinged. His complexion was pale in colour.

'Is there still a chance of a sandwich and a pot of tea, Alice?' he asked the cook, semi-angry, but not towards her, it was towards himself for allowing that to happen yet again. Hated it, he did. Some could let her do it to them, like water off a duck's back, but not Alex. Every time it happened it would be days before he felt normal again. His only reassurance was that others benefitted from his pain, or at least he had been told that.

'Yes, yes of course, my dear, sit yourself down,' she replied, wiping her hands on her floral pinny, before making her way over to the larder, unable to make eye contact with the pilot.

The kitchen became a quiet zone, even the host on the radio strangely played soft music. Everyone, bar the doctor was aware of what had happened to Alex upstairs, but no one would dare say anything. It had happened to them all at some time, and still did on the odd occasion. However, Alex was special, which made him a regular for her ladyship. Every time he visited the big house, she did it to him. The doctor nibbled away at the large sandwich, the bread hand cut, and not frugally. Overflowing with bacon and thick rind, the real butter melted, dripping onto the cloth. He watched the two heavies quietly acknowledge the pilot then leave to go outside. Smelling the cigarette smoke soon after they'd left, explained their destination. He raised his head slightly in the door's direction trying to get the smoke into his lungs, as it had been a good few hours since he had been snatched, and he had a habit of fifty a day. So, any amount of floating nicotine coming his way was truly a blessing.

'Would you like a smoke?' asked the pilot, watching the futile attempt at sniffing the air. Not able to reply straightaway, the doc looked around to make sure it was him who was being addressed. The packet of Marlboro was pushed closer. His eyebrows raised whilst his finger pointed to his own chest. 'Me?' he dared to ask.

'You look like you could do with one!' Alex tossed the fags on the table, the lighter held in his hand. 'Thank you - really, thank you.' The lighter was alight, the doctor drew in, the hot red glow digested the paper.

'Outside, take that dirty thing outside, NOW!' shouted Alice, waving the tea towel at him.

'Come on.' Said Alex, wearing a schoolboy smile, encouraged the doctor out the door.

'*Boo!*' went Harry in the doctor's face.

'Give it a rest,' suggested Alex.

'What's up with you? It's just a bit of fun, init?' replied Harry.

'Not for him, you *prick*,' His voice emphasised the word "prick". Alex was a pilot and until recently a professional soldier. He wasn't well-suited to working with these off the street, wannabe bodyguards.

'Who you calling a prick?' Harry asked aggressively. Alex moved like lightning and was up in his face. 'You, ya prick!' Half his size, but Harry looked into his eyes and dropped in stature. Alex didn't move.

'No hard feelings, mate, and sorry about the door this morning. It was an accident.' Harry offered his hand out towards the doc, watched by Alex.

The doc was about to shake when... 'How do you kick a door down by accident?' Still no grip in place.

'Well?' Then came a silence. The doc's hands opened, waiting for an answer, backed up by his newfound courage.

'I was messing about. Just joking around, really. We were to meet with you and ask if you would like to meet with Lady De Pen Court, I put my foot up, like I say just having a laugh, yah know as if I was gunna kick the door and I sneezed. I was trying to explain what happened when you dived under the desk and started screaming. The next thing we knew is some security guys arrived and the shit hit the fan; I grabbed you - threw you over my shoulder, Barry sorted the security and the rest is history. The two hands met and shook, followed by Harry giving a quick glance at Alex. Harry and his overzealous partner may have looked the part, and they were good at being hired hands, plus, to the majority with their stature and looks, they scared people. But they knew Alex was the "part", an ex-marine who had joined the air core for a couple of years. He was only working for Lady De Pen Court whilst he accumulated enough flying hours, then he was off to Alaska to start his dream life. Harry was an ex-pub bouncer and Barry was a former Welsh Guard, who left the army under a cloud. He still thought he was in his 20s even though he was 39, living like a lot, on past achievements. He strangely enjoyed the fame that came locally from people been scared of him, and if they weren't, he made sure they were. He'd been a bully all of his life and just like his dad, he would die a bully.

8

RECOVERY

To his left, he could see the reflections as if they floated on the river. Although it was dark, the number of vessels travelling on the wide body of water were many. Mesmerised by one in particular, he stared through the glass.

It was a fire boat he presumed, which had been converted into a floating display. Watching as it sprayed high pressure water uniformly into the night air, it was a colourful display, made more spectacular by the rain droplets acting as mini prisms as they ran down the window. After a couple of minutes viewing, he sat back against the seat. In the air was a vague scent of vomit mixed with disinfectant. He imagined that the seat was damp, but he convinced himself that it wasn't. The pouches stitched on the back of the two front seats were stuffed full with leaflets for food, entertainment and places for a weary traveller to rest their head. The inside of the cab was clean, very clean: the driver definitely took pride in what he did.

'Busy night, driver?' he asked, more out of politeness than real curiosity.

'Yes, yes, sir, very busy.'

Looking through into the front, he saw dangling from the mirror was a beaded necklace and something made from birds' feathers. These were attached to a ring covered with coloured cotton. The dashboard had been turned into a shrine, built around a large gold statue of Ganesh. The taxi slowed down. The passenger was in an unfamiliar part of the city. He became uneasy. The worry of the damp seat was now insignificant.

The taxi slowed further. The man told himself to calm down and relax. The car came to a halt.

'What we stopped for, driver?' was asked from the rear seats of the plated Toyota.

'The policey, sir, have set up plenty, many check point, on all out road of city, sir,' the Asian cabbie explained.

'Why? What's happened? Any idea?'

'They have seal everything off, an child is gone. Some take her, sir, on radio early-a. We have been here for good time, lots of car in front.' The cab driver turned around and looked over his shoulder, a sad look displayed through his kind eyes, and that was all that was visible, as his turban and unclipped beard covered the rest of his face.

'I'll walk from here, mate. Thanks.' A twenty was passed over the seats.

'Tank you, sir. Ya - wait. I give change.' The blue nylon bum pouch was unzipped.

'Keep it, mate. You're gonna lose an hour at least, looking at that line of traffic.' The man's head nodded forward.

The car door slammed, and he was out. One leg in front of the other, he took the first fifteen steps. He felt plenty of pain, which made him wonder whether walking was the right decision, it was only just over a week ago he had been struggling to get ten feet, with support bars on either side of him, plus there was a physio at the end encouraging him to keep walking. But he had a schedule to keep to, and his mind told him to keep going, never give in and all will be well. He had thought this way for years, many many years and on the whole, it worked, although it didn't seem to prevent him finding trouble. But for now, he was going to have to keep thinking that, because one leg wasn't working the same as the other. The embarrassment of a limp helped make him try harder, but it couldn't fix the hip. He strolled while his trained brain took everything in. Laughing to himself after noticing everyone was wearing gloves. And rightly so, it was getting to the end of November in Old Blighty, wet and very cold.

But he couldn't wear them, they made his hands tingle. During his basic training in Kent, the staff would sneak up and check if any of the recruits had them on during an exercise. If yes, the offender's hands were dipped in a bucket of freezing water. It was supposed to make you a man! But all he remembered was it made his hands fucking cold, and the irony - the hands doing the dipping were always gloved. Sean thought it was true, the saying that is: "Those that can't do, teach". He managed another smile as he remembered being 16 years old, his first posting at Infantry Junior Leaders Battalion, based in Folkestone. Halfway through his training, a chubby faced corporal by the name of Blant fell outside the lads' room whilst out running, clearly hurt. A few of them had run out to help. They removed the corporal's rucksack and discovered that it was in fact stuffed with two pillows, weighing nothing. Sean and the other two lads pissed themselves laughing. They received seven days restriction of privileges, what for, was never really said. But the sad muppet called Corporal Blant lost that much respect he had to leave the training camp.

At the top of the road, he came to a junction. Stopping for a second, he looked both ways then set off and turned left in the direction of the bridge. The pain had eased somewhat; the dodgy joint felt free. He slowed slightly, trying to remember a route he had only travelled once, and a good while ago, as a passenger on a motorbike. All around him was constant noise from the static traffic, engines ticking over, plus the aeroplanes flying above. Several sirens sounded from many directions as emergency vehicles tried to get around the congested roads of London. People walked past him as if he were a ghost. They didn't see anything or anyone, all too busy chatting, texting and reading on their mobile phones. He heard fragments of every conversation from, "I miss you", to "I'll finish it in the morning, just leave it on my desk" and "It's your turn to grab a takeaway. I'm on my way now". His pace was leisurely as he tried to enjoy the scenery along the Thames. Yet his brain still focused on one source of information and he couldn't shake it. It grew, as it had been doing for weeks.

Eventually across the bridge, his pace changed from slow to lightning. In a split second he was down behind a car. Two young girls in their teens wearing hardly any clothes, their large coat's open, showing off their mid-sections - in November! The pair walked by, arm in arm, sniggering at him. A car exhaust had backfired; Sean instinctively took cover. Getting back up was again at a different speed. It seemed to take forever. And this time it was his powerful arms that pushed up his bodyweight. The bolts in his hip locked like inter-connecting Meccano. Sliding up the side of the car, his leg stretched out. Sean took a breath: he only had a few hundred yards remaining as a cold sweat broke. He knew that starting back as a club bouncer tonight was premature, but he had little choice as all the other work had dried up. No one from "work" had visited him in hospital. His only visitors had been Tank and Bear from the C and P, which is where he was heading to now. His savings had shrunk down to the point of embarrassment, and yesterday he pawned the only piece of jewellery he owned. A solid gold ring that was an old family heirloom. He told himself that he should have just sold it. After all, he had no one to pass it on to. Three weeks out of work for anyone was a long time for the wallet. Twenty yards from the boozer, his phone rang. 'Sean Doyle,' he answered.

'Hello, Sean, it's Tanya, Tanya Howlett. How are you bearing up?' she enquired, her voice soft, holding the slightest amount of guilt.

'Good, I'm good. Surprised to hear from you, if I'm honest with yah, very surprised.' His voice wasn't soft, but yet there was also a small amount of guilt.

'I don't blame you, but you know what our world can be like, Sean, a cruel mistress at times.' She knew he had every right to be pissed off, and if he ended the conversation there and then, she wouldn't blame him, but she had to try to help. Her conscience demanded she did that much, at least.

'I can't really talk. Just going into work.'

'WORK! You're kidding me, Sean. You can't be well enough yet.' And she knew he wasn't. Tanya had visited him, and many more times than both Tank and Bear, he just didn't know this; in fact, after checking with the hospital only a day previous to his discharge, they informed her he had self-discharged a week early, and against the surgeon's advice.

'No choice, Tany. Landlord wants his rent and bread snappers to feed. You know the drill, it's the cost of being part of the rat race.' His head nodded slightly as he saw a rat near the bins.

'You don't have any children and you own that tin can you live in. And what about the funeral parlour? That's doing well, isn't it? I saw it on the local news. All the building work that's going on. Looks like you're expanding,' she pointed out, perplexed by his comment.

'Well people are dying to get to us?' he chuckled.

'Very funny,' she told him.

'Good job, eh, Tany.' He went silent; so, did she - the line remained open.

He broke the silence first. 'Right, if that's all? I'm about to go into the Cock and Pussy.'

'Wait! That's that biker's hangout, is it not?'

'Your point being?' He waited a few seconds. 'At least they visited me in hospital.'

What he said, the sharp words cut her deep. She was desperate to blurt out, but she was way too professional to allow herself that pleasure.

'Sean, listen to me. The reason for my call is to inform you that payroll has emailed me. It appears there has being an oversight on our part, and apparently, we owe you £1800. I will transfer the full amount into your bank account tonight. So, you don't need to go into that place, do you?' Tanya had her laptop open and transferred the promised amount from her personal account. There was no payroll email.

'It's done, Sean. That will keep you going for a couple of months, surely.'

'I guess a thank you is in order, but I need to go in now. Don't want to be late on the first day back, do I?' He knew he was being dramatic, but he had a good reason to keep her in the dark. He wasn't okay with the deceit, but she mentioned the cruel mistress first! Plus, he wasn't privy to the reasons why.

'One more thing before you go in there. Would you like to do some surveillance work for us?' She hoped this offer would lead to breaking bread.

'You're fucking kidding me, Tanya - right?' Sean turned off the phone and completed the last 20 yards. He was skint, but Tanya had been right, he had no rent to pay for the container and no little rug rats depending on him. But the funeral home made no money, well, no profit. It only just managed to pay back the overly inflated overdraft and cover its own payroll, and his sixty percent wage from the army soon disappeared on the building's maintenance, which had been overlooked for a good few years. And what was left over his generous personality dispersed. He had made some changes and upgraded the computer systems. And there was the old saddler's workshop. It was literally collapsing, in fact the sewer beneath had, thus bringing down the walls of the workshop. That was the building work Tanya had referred to. The council had footed eighty percent of the cost; Sean had to find the remaining twelve grand. She, however, wasn't privy to the fact they had successfully won a lottery grant for the conversion of the workshop, but these works went over budget, which he paid the extra from his savings. To him, that was a separate entity in his life: to be able to help others without the glory, was just him.

Sean loved the parlour, and in memory of Tony he'd never sell it, or see it go under, not on his watch. But equally he somehow couldn't see himself working in the grave trade for the rest of his life. It was only known to him, but the business hadn't been in profit for well over ten years. He had been sending money home to Mary because she had stopped taking a wage, trying to reduce the overdraft. The banks kept on moving the goalposts as they were keen to get their corporate hands on the old historic buildings and the good bit of water-side-land that came with it. Mary had, had to borrow heavily just after Tony unexpectedly passed away. He had forgotten to alter his will and twenty percent of the property belonged to a cousin living in New Zealand. A distant cousin and the last in the line, with the name of Barchards. He decided he would like a lump sum, instead of the regular monthly payment he had been receiving from Tony, who was also the last male of the Ward family.

Less than two metres, and Sean was at the door of the Cock and Pussy.

'Sean,' loudly acknowledged the bald-headed man with an un-groomed Z Z Top beard. He shook Sean's hand, and with continuous movement went in closer, threw his left arm around Sean's back, bumping shoulders at the same time. A couple of slaps on the back and they separated.

'You sure you're okay to be here tonight?' asked the big man.

'I'm good. What's the crowd like?' They walked further into the club.

'It's not rammed, bro, but we've some guys in from another club doing a deal, so we may have a bit of refereeing to do later,' Bear replied, as another big man walked up.

'Here, wet your lips, and nice to have you with us. But you sure you're up for it? No shame, mate, if you just fancy hanging around, and don't worry about wages, we'll sort yah out, you know that, your Tony was a founder member of this place.' Sean was passed a bottle of beer.

'Thanks, Tank, but I'm good and looking forward to working, need a distraction. Leg's a bit stiff, that's all.' Sean grabbed the bottle, taking a large swallow, a subconscious show of strength. The door opened.

'Easy there, big boy! There's plenty more where that came from,' said the young waitress entering the club. The slim, barely legal redhead removed her coat, holding it out at arm's length like a film star. Tank, needed no encouragement, he eagerly relieved her of the garment, remaining speechless. She mimed and blew him a kiss then walked off towards the bar, her perfectly formed peach only just covered by the shortest denim skirt.

Sean watched the haplessly in love Tank drool like a greedy child, then he pressed his hip hard against the wooden bar, this somehow relieved him of the dull ache. The oversized gutful of beer he had just digested worked like an injection of pain killer. He remained with his hip in location for the count of ten and two more injections before he set off.

'I'll show my face.' He left the bar side, and the further Sean entered, the darker the room became. The side walls were only thirty five feet apart due to the bar having been built in the arch of an old railway bridge. The place must have been eighty feet in length. The front was like a guarded Second World War pillbox. You didn't get in if you weren't invited. Once inside, the first fixed item of furniture was the wooden bar, constructed from railway sleepers, built to last, with its half dozen well-stained York stone slabs forming its countertop. This ran along the left side wall for no more than twenty feet, give or take a foot. The thirty-year-old bar served the purpose perfectly for what it was made to do, and that was to be a bridge for money - and traffic was heavier one way - and that's all the leather clad bikers cared about.

Dimly lit, with mirrors fixed to the walls behind the bar allowing the punters to catch a glimpse of the scantily dressed girls. This ensured that the glass jars, sat next to the tills, were kept full, boosting the bitches' wages. Either side of this repurposed archway, were garages: one selling new and used bike parts, the other fixing bikes and the odd car. Everyone in the area knew the Cock and Pussy as a well-known bikers' club, and it had been for as long as anyone could remember. Including Sean, who would meet Tony here when he was a kid. But what most didn't know was it had no licence to sell alcohol, and it never had. After the bar, against the right wall came some stools and small tables; these occupied the next twenty feet. The punching balls hanging from recycled bike frames followed. Next in the interior design layout came even smaller tables. These were over four feet tall with two round pegs sticking out of the tops for arm wrestling. The last ten feet had been walled off with a steel door fitted. Above this, a camera eye panned the full club. The all-seeing eye lived in an armoured case covered with thick mesh. The steel door was never opened, but the office space behind was in regular use 24/7 and accessed via the mechanics shop next door, through a false panel in the toilet block. The office acted as a money counting unit, clearing the thousands of pounds the Fallen Angels brought in on a daily basis.

Tanya's apartment

'Sir, I am sorry to call again so late.'

'Never a problem, is all fine?' asked Charles, leaning his head downwards, the phone pressed hard to his ear.

'I have just offered Sergeant Doyle further work with our department.' She waited; her phone held away from her ear.

'One moment, I'm struggling to hear anything.' Charles rose from the worn leather Chesterfield. He began walking away from all the chatter.

'Try again, girl. I can hear you now. What was it, you said?' He had reached the door.

'I have offered Sergeant Doyle some surveillance work with our department, sir,' she repeated again, and waited for the onslaught.

'Please tell me that this is some form of a prank, and you've had too much wine, lass.' The brigadier began to walk further through the door, taking him out into the club's foyer.

Tanya was adamant about her decision. She knew Sean was a good guy and that her father was stubborn, very stubborn. Sean was so similar to her father, she thought the two of them would have been closer, but instead of working together they did the opposite.

'I thought we had had this conversation a while ago and put an end to it. You were to have no contact with Sergeant Doyle.' Charles turned away from the manservant as he spoke to Tanya.

'He saved your life, father, and I have lost enough people in my life, as you well know. He deserves another chance.'

'We don't know what he was doing there on that night, and he still refuses to say anything regarding the event. He has had plenty of opportunities to explain himself to me, and yet he remains aloof regarding all matters.' The manservant removed himself from the foyer, aware of the conversation warming up.

'He was carrying out surveillance, and because of this he refuses to tell you who the client was. Would you expect him to reveal to someone else if he was working for us, sir?' She waited again.

'You are just ...' His phone went dead.

'Thank you, daddy,' she said out loud, happy knowing that it was a yes, or at the very least, the beginning of a yes.

Now all she had to do was convince Doyle. She left her apartment heading for Cathy's, wearing a smile.

'Thanks for coming over.' Cathy threw her arms around her mentor. At first Tanya was taken aback. She was not one for full on emotional displays, but given the circumstances that had brought her over, she allowed the squeeze to continue for a couple of minutes. What Tanya hadn't prepared for and didn't allow to continue, were the tears, then the heightened sense of fear followed by lots of incomprehensible rapid ramblings.

'Cathy! Cathy!' said Tanya. 'CATHY!' she shouted, but to no avail. Tanya performed the slap. Straight across her face, not soft, but hard enough to leave a good print. The hysterics stopped instantly as Cathy stared at her assaulter with her mouth wide open. 'You hit me!' Innocently stating the obvious.

'Pull yourself together, or resign from the police and go back home, today!' Tanya's eyes didn't blink as she stood steadfast.

'What do you mean, go home?' Cathy was no longer sobbing or achieving high notes with her vocal cords.

'As simple as that, go back home. I know what you saw was horrific, but this is what you signed up for, is it not? To be that very thin blue line between the public and the ...'

'Evil that exists,' ended Cathy. 'Forgive me, Tanya. Now I am embarrassed.'

'Don't mention this again; however, I will ask you once more, whether or not you are going to resign and go back home or step up and strengthen the line,' asked her mentor.

'I'm not going back home. I would be bored in a week. I am going to step up.' Cathy appeared to have a weight lifted from her shoulders, her confusion resolved.

'Right, it may be time I increased my responsibilities?' Tanya filled the wine glass.

'It's fine, really. I understand how busy you are.' Cathy sat cross legged on the sofa, submissively expecting to be bypassed, humoured, not taken seriously. It was the same with her colleagues at the station. To them she was a rich little daddy's girl who had purchased a career in the police service, and partially, this was the truth.

'It isn't fine. I am busy, yes. That may even be an understatement; however, I believe that actually being your police officer mentor is not where my time will be best invested. You have acquired all the knowledge, passed all the relevant levels and exams. And from our conversations, it's clear you hold a good grasp of the law.' Tanya looked at Cathy, who was still sitting crossed legged, her chin resting on her hand, then elbow and so on. Her interest was there for real, but where was the sharpness, the streetwise intelligence, the toughness to be a police officer, a copper and a good one?

'Cathy, do you believe you have what it takes to be a police officer?' asked Tanya, as straight as she could, realising, of course, the awkwardness of the question.

'What do you mean by that? I have never wanted to be anything else.' Cathy had sat up, her back as straight as a steel rod. She unfolded her legs, meaning her feet rested flat on the ground, then she was up, standing tall. 'Why do you ask this, Tanya?' Her back still straight.

A small warm smile appeared on Tanya's face. 'That, right there.' She looked Cathy up and down. 'All the reports I have read tell me how perfect you are, how smart and a quick learner, part of the team, will achieve a high rank, bu...'

'Reports, what reports? Regarding myself?' interrupted Cathy, feeling somewhat like a child.

'I receive a monthly report on your progress. Nothing to worry about, merely part of the mentorship programme you're currently in. They are held in your personnel file. They are all perfect, but my concerns are that they are too perfect, because like it or not, with your family connections, you will reach the rank of superintendent, and I wager, just after you turn thirty.' Tanya re-filled her glass.

'So, you are letting me know that all I'll be is a show piece for equal rights.' Cathy passed her glass to Tanya to be refilled, face displaying the internal thoughts.

'Eighty thousand pound a year, by the time you hit thirty-five, and think of all the good you could achieve for the community.' She handed the full glass back.

'My sister receives that amount a year, plus pressies for doing nothing. I am going to be a real copper! It's not the money?' She held her glass out and waited for Tanya to do the honours. 'Cheers, and thank you for the home truths. NOW, help me!' Cathy threw back the wine as if making a statement. 'Please!' she added.

'When are you back at work?' The smile had returned to Tanya's face.

'Friday, the late shift. I have leave booked for the following two weeks, after that. I was returning home for a few days.' Cathy advised.

'Today is Tuesday. I will clear it with your duty sergeant, so you don't have to go in on Friday or the following three weeks.'

'I don't require all that down-time. I'll be fine for my duty on Friday.'

'You will be fine by ten in the morning. When was the last time you went for a run?'

'Two weeks ago, maybe three. Work has a tendency to be hectic, timewise.'

'Do you trust me?' asked Tanya.

'Of course, why wouldn't I? You are a police sergeant.'

'And so will you be, in eight weeks, or I shall drive you home myself?'

An expression of shock materialised on the 24-year-old's face. Tanya's eyebrows raised.

'Thank you for the offer. See you tomorrow, Tanya,' said Cathy, still standing tall.

'Sergeant Howlett to you for the following eight weeks. If, and seriously, it is a big if, you pass or even finish the programme I have in mind for you, you can then call me whatever you like, if you don't pass, our path hits a 'Y' junction do I make myself understood? Good night, PC McDonald.' Tanya left the apartment. Cathy, or Catharina as her family would address her by, didn't move initially. She remained standing with the glass in her hand. 'What a bitch!' she said loudly, before she poured the last of the wine into her glass. 'I want to be just like her.' She spoke into the mirror, with so much meaning and vigour. 'I can do this. I can do this. I can do this.' She continued with the affirmations; the day's events not given another thought.

'Dave,' said Tanya into the car speaker.

'Tanya, is Charles alright?' he asked quickly.

'Strange response, but yes, he's fine and at his club as ever. Just spoke with him matter of an hour or so ago.'

'Just woke up, and your name was flashing. What's up?'

'I require someone to go through the mill.'

'Not sure exactly, your point. Is this official, or is someone bothering you? If it's the latter, I'll come down myself. Now!' Dave's already masculine voice rose.

'No, nothing like that. I may have the wrong term? What

do you call it when you turn a young person from civi street into a soldier or they quit and go home?' she rephrased for clarity.

'Now I'm with ya. They go through basic training. Not a lot of sleep. They get fucked about, screamed at night and day. Physically and mentally pushed to their limits. After a few weeks of this you'd be left with a couple of thirds of the intake. Then real work starts. The few who pass start on the rebuild, and we will bring them back up with an increase in self-esteem, strength, both body and mind, mind set altered. Sorry, Tan. I say we, as if I'm still in.'

'No need to apologise to me, my father does the same ALL the time, the regiment this and the regiment that.' She slowed and stopped the car at the side of the road.

'Anyway, strange question. What's it all about?'

'I have six weeks, maybe two months, and I want to turn someone into, well, how can I put it? Tough. I would like a person toughening up. Is this something you could facilitate? Invoiced of course.' She waited in hope.

'To be honest, Tan, we used to run a CPO course a couple of years back, before the horse-riding accident, that was designed for people who had never been in the forces and wanted a qualification, giving them a way in to babysitting celebs. Sadly, in most cases, it was a reality check. We charged a grand a week for the basics with six people simultaneously taking part, and £800 a week after the fourth week. That's if the candidates continued on to the advanced part, which lasted a further eight weeks. They were also guaranteed two months' work with us, after satisfactory completion of the full twelve weeks. And if you had on your CV that you'd been contracted by us, you would get a start anywhere.' Dave bragged a little. 'But as you know, Tan, it was Sarah's department, all that training shit. Gary used to help a lot. They got on well. Gary Garthwaite: he's with you full-time now. Of course, you know that, he works for you?' Dave's voice slowed as did his thought train, after mentioning Sarah.

'I do apologise, I had forgotten that it would bring back unwanted memories for you.' Tanya was genuinely sorry. She was well aware that Dave Sissons was the hardest bastard she had ever known. Even the brigadier, her father, with all his time in the SAS commented on Dave's "abilities", as he would say. But when it came to Sarah Kennedy, Dave was a pussy cat.

'Don't, Tan, nothing for you to say sorry for. It's been long enough, just wish she hadn't left like that. Then to receive a letter telling me she didn't want to be a burden to me, now that she was permanently in a wheelchair.' His voice was still low.

'Me too, I really miss her do you remember when we first met with her? I had been undercover in the police station she was assigned to, and didn't you punch her and knock her out?' Tanya's tone rose jovially.

'I, yeh, I did.' He recalled the day Charles had contacted him explaining what was happening, that a female police officer's life was in mortal danger, and could he drop everything and travel to London - ASAP. With a team of at least four operatives.

WPC Sarah Kennedy is an American with dual citizenship with Britain. She has made allegations against a fellow sergeant involving child sexual abuse and murder. Unfortunately for her, she wasn't aware that this particular sergeant had connections to people very high up, so high up, it hit our radar. She would not last the day. Dave and Bash cornered her in a small alleyway as she left the police station. They were aware of the two police officers who had followed her, and not for her own safety. Sarah head-butted Bash and ran shouting for help. The pair of uniformed cops at the top watched as Dave caught her. He winked at them. She opened her mouth to shout. His left-hand hit, goodnight Sarah; he threw her over his shoulder and walked off. The cops waved to him. Back at the van, Bash opened the rear doors. Sitting there were two men tied up with rope, next to them, a holdall containing eight grand, a pistol, handcuffs and enough Ketamine to put ten horses to sleep. Sarah was kept under very close protection for the following 24 hours.

Twenty seconds before Dave hit her, he was in love, and never had he felt like this before, if anything he was emotionally barren. The feelings grew and grew, changing him, and still today, he had never stopped.

'Dave, I will call you back if I still need the "basic training" course.'

'Yeah, not a problem. Call any time, Tan.' He pulled the drawer open and took hold of a photo.

'Goodnight, Dave,' replied Tanya, instantly re-dialling another number.

'Hi, boss,' spoke the new voice.

'You knew Sarah Kennedy well, didn't you?'

'I did, boss, but she was your friend, wasn't she, and why, what's brought Sarah up? Last I saw of her was getting on two years.'

'Cut the shit, Gary, you and her were like siblings, she told me so herself. You were struggling with your fitness, she helped you a lot. You're still in touch with her, aren't you?' She wasn't messing around, but she had no idea if he was in touch with Sarah or he wasn't. She prayed.

'How did you know I'm still in touch?'

'That does not concern you. I need to speak with her, Gary.'

'I don't know, boss. Really she sh...'

'Gary, we know each other well, and have done for a long time, have we not?'

'Yes bo...'

'Tanya, call me Tanya. Do you think I would ever endanger Sarah in any way?' She was speaking genuinely from the heart.

'Of course not. And I never wanted to keep it from you, that I was still in touch? But ... wit...'

'With what? Spit it out?'

'Dave, ... she thought you would try and persuade her to go back to him?'

'I see that, and she is likely correct, but no, this doesn't involve Dave. I have a proposition for her. I need an individual training. Good money, but I need the best to do the training. And if Dave recommends her, she's the best' Tanya spoke the truth, well the main part of it anyway.

'I'm meeting with her tomorrow at ten. Come with me, but stay in the car and wait for me to come for you, if Sarah agrees to meet. Promise me, Boss?'

'I promise, and thank you. Goodnight, and thank you, Gary.'

'Night, boss, and I'll be outside your apartment in morning.'

The service flat on the ground floor of Tanya's apartment block

She stood there for a moment; her knock was fast but quiet.

'Mr Elroy! I apologise for knocking so late.'

'Don't you worry about the hour, miss. Don't sleep a lot these days. How can I help? Would you like to come in?' replied the doorman.

'No, I don't wish to intrude, I know it's your day off tomorrow. I was wondering if you would be going out for a run in the morning.'

'I will. Miss, why?' he was puzzled.

'I have a trainee coming over at 1000 hours, you may have seen her, she is next door to me but a floor higher, pretty, tall blonde she will be in a police uniform, or partly.

Leroy's head nodded as he recalled. 'I have, she's always smiling, and very polite, it's a bit of a puzzle her father visits in a £200,000 Bentley.'

'That sounds like her, she is titled but doesn't wish for that to be known.' Tan's eye brows raised slightly; Leroy gave a nod in acknowledgement. Tanya continued, 'Unfortunately, I have been called away on an urgent matter. I wond... no, I was hoping you could possibly take her with you and report back to me on the level of her fitness, please. I am aware you finished your military career as an instructer.' She held in her hand a piece of paper.

'No problem, miss, I usually go around seven, but I'll wait. Look forward to it. What's her name?'

'All her details are on here.' She handed over the piece of paper, then turned on her phone. Her thumb started scrolling, then stopped. Turned the screen to him.

'Yes, that's her, and she's smiling there too.' He smiled, before continuing, 'Is she in some trouble?'

Tanya was caught of guard, 'Trouble, not what I am aware of, why do you ask?'

'Like I say her father visits in a very expensive car, he also offered me a £1000 a month to, well as he put it, "Be a little more vigilant around her apartment".'

'From what I have gathered, her father is very over protective. Thank you again, Mr Elroy.' She held out her hand; he shook it softly.

'My pleasure. Looking forward to it, miss, and give my best to the brigadier.' Tanya returned to her apartment and almost immediately began rummaging in a drawer in the spare bedroom.

The following morning: 07:52 hours

'Gary?' Tanya spoke in her morning tone.

'You ready, boss? I'm downstairs.'

'I thought you said ten o'clock?'

'We're meeting her at ten, boss. And it's a good distance. I've got you a coffee and bagel. Come on!' Gary was really enjoying the moment as it was usually Tanya chasing him.

'Two minutes.' She pressed "end".

'Sit back and relax. Here!' He passed her a paper bag and a Costa Coffee.

She took his advice and relaxed. The coffee was enjoyed; the bagel wasn't touched. Not a lot of conversation happened between them, which was unusual. Tanya tried to establish the whereabouts of her friend's new home, but Gary was not singing to her tune. Seventy miles had been added to the vehicle's clock.

'Ready for a re-fill, boss?' asked Gary, as he flicked on the indicator.

'No, I'm good, thank you.' She looked out the side window.

The Audi pulled up level with the fuel pump. Gary was out the car for nine minutes. He got back in opened the packet of chewing gum, filled his mouth, offered to Tanya, she declined. He set off to re-join the motorway. With just a hundred meters to go he pulled over again; this time the engine remained running. 'Sorry, boss,' said Gary as his hand went inside his jacket pocket.

Tanya's head turned. 'You're kidding me, Gary. Why?' She couldn't believe what was in his hand. A man she had known and worked with for years and who she thought she knew well and believed he knew her well.' Dozens of cars, lorries and vans shot by the parked black Audi as Tanya stared at the blindfold.

'I spoke with Sarah and she insisted that you were to wear it for the last stretch.' He spoke to her as his shoulders raised a little and his hands opened. He waited with a dumb expression on his face. Tanya wanted to discuss it, but he had already done a lot for her, and also Sarah, her friend had the right to stay incognito, and a part of this was the location. He was well aware of how good his boss was, as was Sarah, and given any inkling she would be able to re-find the location.

She nodded and took hold of the stretchy thick black band. She sorted her hair and placed the blindfold on, then let the chair go backwards. 'Ready when you are, and if you tell anyone and I mean anyone about this, me and you will have a problem!' Her head turned his way even though she couldn't see.

'No, course not, boss,' answered Gary, as he pressed to take a photo of her with his phone, it was all he could do not to laugh; the pic was shared with a couple of colleagues. Forty-five more minutes and the Audi came again to a stop.

'We're here, boss.'

Tanya sat up and removed the blindfold, eyes squinting a few times. 'Where are we?' she stared at the cows in the fields, a bridge and water. Wherever they had ended up, it was a beautiful location, and the fact that the car was on some grass answered Tanya's question, of why the last half a mile or so had felt so rough. The far distance held several buildings, more than likely farms, she thought.

'Stay in the car, boss. I shouldn't be long.' And Gary was out and walking. Tanya watched him for at least thirty metres before he disappeared around the bend. She was desperate to follow and got out the car, but her honesty turned her back after ten feet. She sat on the bonnet and waited as promised, eager to get some help for Cathy and excited to see a good friend.

9

REGENERATION

'You're late, Plumber. Explain yourself!' Shoebridge pointed out climbing into the back of the Mercedes.

'I had a tail on me, sir. Been shaking it off for ten minutes.'

'Are we clear now?' asked Shoebridge, ceremonially glancing over his shoulder.

'Yes, sir, but I'm going to swing by the pit and quickly take the car for a wash, if that's ok with you, sir?'

'Yes of course, we must do what we have to. We cannot afford to be followed, and definitely not tonight, of all nights.' Shoebridge sat back and started to take stock of how far the American deal had come, especially since the initial talks had begun only a few months earlier. In one year's time, if this charity connection blossomed as well as expected, personally he stood to make millions of pounds. Unlike the exporting to Africa, which netted £20,000 a month, and this came with high risks that he didn't care for. Plus, the people over there and their mumbo jumbo superstitions, not to mention them dancing around in grass skirts, blowing smoke and praying to gods, with names that he couldn't even pronounce. The sooner this African deal ended, the better, at least for him. But it had filled a gap since the drugs trade had abruptly ended.

A quick left turn and the Merc drove into the all-night car wash. The front wheels locked into the pull along grid. Plumber pressed "send" on his mobile. The minister's eyes were drawn to the windscreen as the massive wool roll came off the bonnet ready to wash the glass. Plumber flicked on the windscreen wipers, at the same time turning around. 'Be ready, sir. We won't have long to switch.' The roll continued revolving, but no longer was it moving upwards. Standing in front of the car wearing goggles was a tall gentleman with his thumb up. Plumber was out and went straight to the back door.

'Quickly, sir, quickly.'

The tall man approached and threw a heavy-duty rain mac over Shoebridge then gave a set of keys to Plumber. 'For the blue BMW! Its sorted,' he shouted, then got into the driver's seat of the Merc. Plumber was being soaked as the water began to reappear from the overhead pipes. 'This way, sir.' Blinded by the soap, he rapidly ushered the hunched over minister to a side door.

The Merc finished being cleaned and left the drive-through. The exchange had only added on twenty seconds if that, so any eyes watching wouldn't have realised the occupants had swapped. The minister and Plumber hurried down a poorly lit man-made warren, several times turning side ways to squeeze through, ending up in a back-street garage. Plumber aimed and pressed the small silver key fob. *Bleep, bleep,* the blue BMW's indicator lights flicked on and off twice. 'Get in, sir,' he instructed, opening the rear door. He ran to the wall and started to pull down on the long chains. The rollover shutter crimped into itself as it rose. At five feet high, Plumber told himself that would do.

Into the BMW, he drove under the partially risen door, stopped, quickly jumped out, then ran back. Arm around the pillar, he pulled free a large steel pin and retrieved his arm at speed, moments before it was severed by the heavy door unrolling under its own weight, then clattering to the ground.

'Fifteen minutes, Plumber! Will we make it?' asked the minister.

Plumber didn't respond. He was off down a couple of alleyways, then a quiet road, making the noise of the bins flying even louder. After this was the main dual carriageway. He flicked a switch set into the dashboard. Blue beacons inserted into the front radiator grill and wing mirrors started to flash in unison with the now blue indicators.

'Ten minutes, Plumber. If you blow this deal, I will blow you away! Do you understand?' Shoebridge tapped his driver's shoulder with the Browning's barrel.

The customised BMW spun like a formula one car into the tight bend. Coming out the corner, Plumber's foot went to work. 'We're here, sir,' he shouted, as the car shot forwards, smashing through the steel and mesh gates, doing over a hundred miles per hour.

'Slow down, man, you'll kill us both. Slow down! You fool.' shouted the minister as he checked his watch. Browning still in hand. 'Stop! Will you?'

Plumber obeyed the last order. Full of adrenalin, he braked, his passenger nearly kissed the back of his head.

The area in front was a vast wasteland of concrete. To the far left sat derelict warehouses. Their 100-year journey had ended when the docks declined one decade ago. Panning to the right, the buildings were tin clad with steel fabricated legs. These were still in use, but as storage only and open at the fronts and sides, displaying vast amounts of timber. At the end was one more warehouse. This was frugally illuminated, or maybe it was a deliberate act so as not to draw attention to its valuable wares held within. Hybrid brick and block with a steel fabricated frame wrapped with a heavy-duty steel overcoat, was also visible, its front elevation covered in the same shiny steel. Above the door was a simple sign: Bonded Warehouse No. 6. That was all it read and all it needed.

'The door's opening,' said the minister. 'That's the signal. Off you go, Plumber,' ordered the minister, loading a magazine into the bottom of the pistol.

Every foot that the door raised in height, the BMW travelled ten meters. The gap now seven feet, the car drove over the raised threshold and stopped dead.

'Fucking hell, sir!' spat out Plumber, shocked at the sight of eight new Range Rovers, all parked perfectly in a horseshoe, the vehicles black bodywork reflecting in the highly polished floor. Lined up in front of these expensive cars were over thirty armed men, all of them wearing uniforms that didn't clash with the vehicles, balaclavas providing each of them with anonymity.

The door was back down to four feet, three, two, one, and it kissed the raised rubber seal. The wind stopped blowing. 'Go on, what you waiting for? Get out and announce me,' directed Shoebridge, leaning forward and slipping the Browning into the rear of his pants.

The BMW's door opened. Plumber climbed out. Silent and still shocked, he remained stood next to the bonnet. He wasn't a weak fellow by any means, but in this scenario, he was not sure if anyone would have been strong. All the men wearing black, raised M16 rifles. The Range Rover in the centre immediately facing the BMW - became his focal point. The passenger door opened. A male, somewhere in his 50s, wearing a big cowboy hat and bootlace tie was facing him. His face round, mellow, chubby in the cheeks and under the chin, not scary, not hard, but his eyes, his eyes, were darker than a sharks, this showed a different world.

'Where is Shoebridge?' he demanded to know.

'In ... in th ... the ... v-vehicle still. I'm his driver.' Plumber became unsteady as all the rifles raised together a touch more, and still the barrels were aimed at him.

'FIRE!' ordered the Texan in a calm manner.

'I ... I do ...' Plumber's words were stopped instantly as all thirty-six M16s let rip. His body unable to fall due to the hail of rounds passing through it, he, or what was left of him, finally fell five feet behind the BMW. The Texan remained with his hands over his ears. The echo bouncing around the unit was deafening.

The weapons were lowered, except for the rear two that switched position, their sites now on the minister. He gulped as the red dots came through the BMW's windscreen and danced on his chest.

'DON'T SHOOT! PLEASE! DON'T SHOOT ME!' screamed Shoebridge at the top of his voice. He sat on the back seat with his hands on his head. The smart 50-year-old Texan lowered his hands and shouted.

'Come out of the vehicle, slowly.'

The two M16s remained aimed at his chest as he moved. Shoebridge quickly pulled out the Browning. Dropping the pistol onto the rear seat, he shuffled to the door, slowly pulling the handle. His leg gave way as it slipped on Plumber's blood. He fell to the shiny floor. *Crack!* One of the

M16s fired: the lead chipped the paint only a foot from his head.

'Get up and walk this way, slowly. Hands up, no sudden movements, unless of course you wish to join your driver,' laughed the Texan, looking at his armed posse.

'Yes, yes, slowly,' confirmed Shoebridge, his hands up. He was walking like a military man behind a coffin. Tense, scared, aware of all the eyes focused upon him, only just lifting his feet off the floor. He slid each one forward with the anticipation of a tightrope walker.

Ten feet from the yank.

'Get down! Get down! Don't move! Spread your legs! Arms behind your back!'

All these words took on powerful meanings as they were dictated at Shoebridge in very high decibels. Four of the armed men passed over their rifles and ran to him. Two plastic ties pulled tight around his wrists; a couple of the men slipped their hands into his armpits. Shoebridge was picked-up, carried just like a mechanic's dirty rag.

'Do you know who I am? You can't treat me like this!' he shouted at the Texan.

Nothing was said; the stillness of the room made Shoebridge sweat.

'Do you know who I am? Do you understand what I can do to you?' he shouted again, used to getting his own way. The Texan smiled and walked the last couple of feet towards Shoebridge, who silenced as he looked into the American's eyes.

'A fool. That's who you are. A fool, sir,' said the cowboy.

Shoebridge was dumbstruck by the American's unexpected answer. He watched as the cowboy opened a large wallet. His hand went inside, but his shark eyes remained on Shoebridge. At the same time, he nodded to one of the guards. A knife was produced. The guard approached the minister; Shoebridge panicked, 'Whoops, a little accident. Sir?' the Texan was making reference to the damp patch appearing near the minister's groin. The sharp blade cut the plastic. His hands were released. They came to the front, his fingers and thumbs massaging his wrists.

'What the fuck did you do that for? Why kill him?' Shoebridge asked, with some courage returning on the release of his arms.

'How long has "that" been in your service?' The cowboy's head pointed to Plumber's remains. And remains is what they were, like road kill.

'Ten years at least. A good fellow. I have never had cause to chastise him and he had my trust,' replied the minister, still angry at the death of his loyal employee.

'A fool, sir, like I said, a fool. Here!' The American pushed several photos hard into his guest's chest. The minister's mouth dropped open, then he raised his stare from the glossy pictures towards the Texan.

'How? When? Where? These are not real, they ar...' he rambled, obviously shocked with the content.

'First one, a week ago, second, just two days later, and the location is of no importance. One of my informants took them. You see, sir, we never proceed until I sign off on it and its all clear, and I always look under the bed, as you never know what monsters lurk there.' A satisfying raise of the eyebrows came on the narcissists face.

'How do you know he was working for him? He may have been chatting, that's all, he ... kno ... knows the brigadier ... he has done ... so for a good few year, and it has ... well, worked to my advantage.'

'You are correct about that: he knows the brigadier "very" well. He's been paid by his department for nine years. Are you aware that his correct name isn't Steve Plumber, its Mick Lavender, an Irish thug? The brigadier got him an early "get out of jail" card, from the Maize, as he was in solitary due to being a snitch. And in return... well, I'm sure a clever man such as yourself could work the rest out.' The satisfying expression remained as a second wallet was given to Shoebridge, pressed even harder against his soft fleshy chest. The Texan nodded to the man behind Shoebridge, as he continued to talk, 'Take that one home! It will make good bedtime reading.'

Shoebridge remained on the spot; the lights in the unit dimmed to the level of dusk. 'Get down onto your knees! Don't move until the lights come back on. Do you understand me?' asked the deep voice, as the M16s nozzle was felt on his head. The lights dimmed further; he could no longer see anything.

'Yes ... I do ... I understand. Don't move till the light is back?' A towel was thrown over Shoebridge's head. It was clean, he smelt the fabric softener. Then a glare from the grey polished floor informed him the lights were back on. Waiting a further minute or so before he pulled off the towel. Right there in front of him was a small box that was branded with the image of an apple. The only things left in the unit were ten yellow cleaning cones, sitting where his BMW had stopped. It was 15 minutes before he had the iPhone assembled and working.

10

KIN

I t took Tanya three or four days and lots of phone calls just to get to speak with Sean again. But she was not going to give up, that wasn't in her make-up.

The brigadier was not happy because, yes Sean had saved his and a couple of his men's lives, but what was he doing there on that particular night, and more importantly, at that specific time of night? Doyle point blank refused to say who he was working for, even under official interrogation and with the threat of prison time. Tanya knew exactly who had commissioned him and why they had done so, because it was her who had employed Sean Doyle to follow as a backup on that fateful night.

She had received a tip-off on the same day of the operation. But the brigadier and Dave had dismissed it as unreliable, a folly if you will. Four hours later, the driver of the Range Rover was killed instantly, shot in the head by a sniper. This caused the vehicle to flip over and over before sliding off the old timber dock into the dark murky waters of the Thames. Sean broke cover and dived in after the Range Rover pulling the door open, getting some of them out. After saving three of the guys, he got help for the unconscious survivors. As he walked away, a car came from nowhere, knocking him over and leaving him for dead. The operation was a very well-kept secret and had taken part in an out of the way location, due to the fact they were there to collect an Iranian defector, arriving on a US submarine. So, Sean's reluctance to say why he was there at that time cloaked him in suspicion, even after his heroics. And given the fact he hadn't officially been attached to the unit; it didn't go down well. Tanya wanted to tell her father it was her who had organised it, but Sean demanded she remain silent.

'If I can't be trusted on my word, then fuck the lot of yah. You hear me?' She had never seen him upset before, but made a promise to do as he asked, and the silence hadn't yet broken.

She tried once more to make contact.

'Tanya, stop calling me,' he urged. 'There's no hard feelings, I'm out of that life, and glad to be. I want nothing to do with it anymore, too much politics for me.' He sounded genuine.

She listened to his words, but at the other end of the phone her heart was becoming heavy with guilt. She knew he meant what he said, and if truth be known, she didn't blame him at all. He had been treated badly and she felt responsible.

'Okay, Sean, I won't call anymore, but I felt that I had to try, you understand. Take care and be lucky. And remember, if you ever need anything, I'm here and I genuinely mean that, anything, anytime.' She was sad. A good guy had saved her father and two men she knew well. He'd nearly been killed himself. Instead of a medal and some recognition, he got shunned and a titanium hip.

Two days after she had promised to stop calling him, Lady De Pen Court had been contacted by the brigadier, to inform her of Henry's death. She took it surprisingly well, thought Charles. But the well-to-do class, with their stiff upper lips and reluctance to wash their laundry in public. Meant they seldom showed what we all call emotion, not in public anyway. The day after hearing about Henry, Tanya was contacted by Emma at her office. She was seeking advice and a possible recommendation with regard to someone looking into the circumstances of her son's death. After passing on her condolences, the conversation continued 'His name is Sean Doyle, a sergeant in the SAS.' She added where he could be found. 'Oh and don't say I recommended him to you, please.'

'Why ever not? You're singing his praises,' asked Emma, curious as she had just given him a glowing reference. Emma scribbled the name on a sheet of paper: Sean Adrian Doyle.

'Let's just say things didn't end well when we parted company. Emma,'

'You two were in a relationship, I presume?'

'No, God no, friends and colleagues. His work is top notch, and he is very professional, yet I must add, in an unorthodox way. He's no conformist, but you will have no concerns and he gets results. He is a handy lad, but with brains and a heart.' Tanya's tone changed slightly as she mentioned Doyle in that context.

'This Sean character sounds a very rare commodity. Thank you again, my sweet, Tanya. I will speak with this Doyle fellow at some point over the next few days. You have put my mind at rest, and for that I thank you. Please give my best to your father, as I was slightly shaken when he called regards Henry.' She was about to hang up when Tanya felt the need for more of an explanation.

'As the name "Cock and Pussy" suggests, it's not maybe a place you would be used to frequenting, Emma,' warned Tanya, awkwardly.

'I am sure I will be fine. I'm a grown woman, but thank you for your concern,' replied Emma with a slight silent chuckle, again about to replace the receiver.

'Also, if he is not at the club, you should be able to locate him at Barchards and Ward. It's a funeral home off little high street. I know he is spending some time looking into his family tree, so he may be out and about a good deal.

The receiver was finally down.

Sean counted out the £400 in cash in different notes, creating separate piles on the glass counter of the pawnshop. 'Shit, sorry, looks like I'm a tenner short, mate. Can I owe you it until tomorrow?'

The attendant passed over the heavy gold ring. 'Don't worry about the ten pounds, sir. However, if you ever want to sell the ring, please will you give me first refusal. I'll put a couple of noughts on the end of what you pawned it for.' The attendant nervously adjusted his bifocals. Sean held the ring up to the height of his eyes.

'Forty thousand! .... You're having a giraffe! It can't be worth that?' The ring remained at the height it was at.

'Actually, sir, I would be offering £35,000, as you're paying interest on the loan of fifty pounds. But I would be very happy to negotiate, and I could arrange for the payment to be in cash, if that would be more favourable to sir's circumstances.' He smiled and once more adjusted the heavy bifocals. Sean lowered the ring as he noticed the red mark on the bridge of the man's nose.

'I'll think about it. That is a lot of money. You really believe it's worth that amount?' Doyle's brow furrowed, astonished at his ring's value and thought of how many times he'd come close to losing it.

'It could be worth a lot more, sir. We could do some form of bonus commission as well. Perhaps if I said I would receive, Thirty percent of what I make for you over 40,000?' The red mark spread but never faded as the man's eyebrows separated.

Sean nodded as he went to leave the shop. The Victorian brass bell clanged.

'Sir?' the attendant asked in a curious tone.

'Yeh,' Sean turned.

'May I enquire as to where you first came across the ring? Sir' He waited his mouth held open by anticipation.

'To be honest with yeh, I don't really remember when, but I also can't remember never having it with me, from being a very small child. Why is that of interest?' The reply that returned was not to the question posed.

'I hope you find no objection, but I took the liberty of giving your ring a polish, sir. And whilst removing the years, and I do mean years of pitted in dirt, I discovered some very unusual words engraved inside. Latin, I do believe, is the language. Well, a very old academic version of the forgotten language. These scribblings had been very cleverly hidden with the use of a separate thin band, a very fine inlay of gold this alone would have required a skilled crafts man, the inlay is hundreds of years old itself, however, not as old as your actual ring. Very intriguing I found it, sir, very. I have an interest in hidden words that have a meaning or more than one meaning, you see,' emphasised the unusual shopkeeper.

'So, what do these *scribblings* tell you?' asked Doyle, interest piqued, feeling like he was in the twilight zone.

'I would have to take an impression, and that may affect the value of the ring, or we could have it sent off for translation and they will require the actual ring itself, sir. Oxford University ... I do believe they have a professor in residence there.'

'How is it that no one else has seen these words?'

'Look at the ring now, sir.' Fagan nodded towards the gold band still held in Sean's hand. 'Can you see any sign of a separation line?'

He did, as directed and looked, close at first, then held it up and out at arm's length. 'I can't see it, nup, nothing,' he said, slightly annoyed with himself. He stared harder,

'Well, if you put back all the grime that I've removed, I'd say the last time those words were read was at least a couple of hundred years ago, maybe more, and the lack of any real dirt under the inner band itself, tells you it's not been off, or not often. And most definitely not for long.'

Fagan was going to continue; Sean nodded, ending the ring's autopsy.

'Thanks, I may bring it back, see what it says. Gets you thinking.' He nodded; the Victorian bell charmed softly again. The ill-fitting door didn't quite close, due to the swelling from the damp weather. Sean gave it a sharp pull to bring it home. The bell rang again.

The conversation did make Sean use his old grey matter: the thinking started.

Not so much about selling the item, although it was a lot of money that had been offered, and for sure he could do with the extra cash right now, it would sort a few things on the to-do list and make a big dent in the overdraft. He thought more about the ring itself, not just the intrigue Fagan had created for him.

A family heirloom it was, but he hadn't really had a family, well at least not in the conventional terms of a family. His earliest memories were of him in an orphanage, one which was run by some Catholic nuns. He'd be about three or four years of age. A horrible, dark and very dingy place, filled with violence and negative teaching. The only happy times he remembered started about a year after when he'd be five. These ones consisted of a female with nice round friendly eyes visiting him. This kind lady would come to the home and take him out for the day. They would have fun and laugh, belly-ache laughter, even if all that they did was to walk and play around in the park.

He would run and shout for the lady to come find him, she would cover her eyes and count to ten, "Coming ready or not", She'd tell him. They would enjoy ice-cream together and sometimes go to the cinema. Back at the home, in front of the stone steps, she would always slip six sweets into his pocket. One for each day, she told him. Sean would cry when she had to leave, but his smile would emerge again when he ate the last jelly baby, knowing the nice lady would be returning the next day. Then the times she visited became less and less. From once a week on a Sunday to once a month, if that. Then they just stopped altogether, and no notice, no explanation was fed to him. Giving it some thought, this is when Sean recalled seeing the ring for the first time. He smiled to himself as he remembered the nice lady. She had held his shoulders tight, but not to hurt, to hold his concentration, and she told him, 'You're never to show this present to anyone, promise me?' his head went up and down nodding at speed, 'It's yours and yours alone, do you understand me? Sean,' She placed the large ring in the centre of the child's small warm hand, curling his fingers around the precious metal, looking him straight in the eyes.

'One day, you will know why you have it. And it ..., no, that's enough, sweet thing, you won't understand the rest. But one day I promise you I will tell you all about it and you will be free of this dreadful place. I promise you this. I am so sorry for ...,' She kissed his forehead and wiped her eyes. 'Come, come let's take you on the merry-go-round, one last time.' She took hold of his small hand and they made their way back to the ride.

At five years old, all Sean cared about was that he had something, something that was his and only his, a big thing in an orphanage.

Twenty years previous

Sean was now eight, going on nine and had put the memories of the nice lady down to dreams. Two years had passed and not one visit had taken place. None of the nuns ever mentioned her. He had grown tall and toughened up, but still his frame held little meat. He had become strong, and he had needed to as he was bullied and constantly pushed around. One day, after lessons and dogmatic chores followed by strict prayers. Sean remembered watching one of the teenagers whipping his own back with a cat o' nine tails, crying from the pain it caused as he carried out self-flagellation. The prayers were for the boys, they were forced to ask God for a hard life, a punishment for them being undesirables, and that it was their own wickedness that prevented them from being adopted by decent folk.

Later that day at around eight, the two dormitory lights had just been switched off for the night. Three of the older lads were up and out of their beds, they ran over to a new boy's bunk. They started beating on him. Sean, like the rest of the lads, lay in his own bunk, sweating, thinking of when this had happened to them. A real fear as these poor youngsters had no one to turn to, and no one to protect them.

'Leave him alone, Michael, Daman, Oscar, get away from him!' Sean shouted loud and clear across the room naming all of them.

'Shut up, Doyle, or you'll be fucking next,' shouted Daman. The other two laughed at Doyle.

'Get off him, now!' Sean shouted again.

The bullies ran to Doyle's bed, but he was out of it in a flash, arms up and ready to fight, Michael knocked him straight down. The kicking started with Daman putting the boot in. The room became so quiet then the kicking stopped. They left him and went back to the new boy's bed to resume the handed down initiation. Sean lay on the cold uncovered floor, quietly sobbing, his fingers turning white as he squeezed hard on the ring. From out of nowhere a form of energy took over him. A feeling of power came with a need to protect this younger lad. He was up and grabbed hold of a chair, smashing it straight over the head of the big lad, Oscar. He hit Michael next, once across the face, hard, he went off and cried. The third boy, Daman stayed and laughed, he pulled out a pen-knife. Sean went ballistic on him, he had wanted to for a long time, he had seen Daman really hurt some of the kids and in a sick way. His hands flying like mini missiles, he knocked the crap out of the bully, the last punch came as young Doyle launched up, coming down he hammered his fist on the sick bully. The rest of the dorm, who from time to time had all suffered at the hands of these three, were up and bouncing on their beds, every one of them shouting the name "Doyle", over and over again.

'What's going on in here?' they heard as the door flew open. The nasty looking nun demanded to know what the cause of the disruption was. No one replied and the shouting continued. The 12-year-old Oscar lay still on the floor, unconscious, his nose bleeding. Michael sat against the wall, still crying with his hands over his eyes. Daman was battered but still conscious. 'I "will" kill you for doing this, you hear me, Doyle? You're dead.' Daman stared at Sean. Sean created this fantastic grin, and with this his eyes lit up, he knew now, nothing could keep him down.

The nun grabbed hold of Sean's wrist; pillows were thrown at her as the shouting of "Doyle" continued. Shackled at the wrist, she dragged him at speed down the hallway, the vicious female's long dirty nails stabbing through his young skin. Sean was ordered to remain quiet and sit on the cold quarry tiles making up the old floor.

'WAIT THERE! And don't you move an inch, I'll fetch Mother Superior!' shouted the nun. A voice that he could never seem to escape.

He sat there crossed legged, head drooped, looking at his wrist. He watched in the dim light as his skin replenished from the nipping marks she had caused. His fist held tight, but bulging, as it contained his one true possession. Across the hall in the office, he heard some raised voices. As he concentrated, one of the voices made him look away from the red indents as he listened carefully all other sounds ceased to exist. It sounded familiar: the kind lady who used to come and take him out. The office door flew open, clattering against the wall. He saw her, it was her, he was certain of it. She was there, large as life and shouting loudly at the Mother Superior. Had the nice woman from his dreams come for him?

She continued to shout at the fat Mother Superior. 'I'll get him back, he's mine. I promise you; I'll be back for him. I love him. You have no right to keep him from me?'

She turned to see Sean. She was full of tears, but now of both kinds. Sean smiled opened his hand and showed her the ring, but then the lady of his dreams was surrounded quickly by at least a dozen nuns; to him, she'd vanished again just as she had some three years previous. The overweight male caretaker wobbled down the corridor, coughing, trying to clear his lungs. He arrived on the scene, his fat fingers fastening the buckle on his wide belt.

The caretaker was ordered by the Mother Superior to force the woman to leave. She kept on shouting whilst being physically evicted. Sean heard the caretaker shout, 'She's fucking bit my nose. Its bleeding?' The shouting continued as the group moved as one and evicted the dream lady. The last words he heard were,

'I'll get him back, you'll see, he's mine, give him to me now.' The gathering subsided; the shouting was distant. The confused small child squeezed his hand tighter as if the pain this caused let him know he was still awake and not dreaming about the kind lady from the past.

Sean was later told by his so-called caregivers that the woman was a local mad lady, a "witch", and she didn't know what she was saying. He was then punished for beating up the bullies. Sentenced to five days under the stairs in what the lads called the lockup. The young Doyle sang every minute of the day and night whilst doing a Bobby Sands. On the third day the singing suddenly stopped. Sean had to be rushed to hospital with severe dehydration.

'When was the last time this child drank? And dare I ask, ate anything?' enquired the doctor.

'He's refused to eat for three days, stupid, stupid child,' was her pleasant reply.

'We will keep him here for four days at least, Sister. I'll send a message to your place when you can collect him,' advised the doctor, with no eye contact and a reluctance to even talk to her. He knew how these children were treated at that home. But it seemed no one cared, as all his previous complaints had fallen on deaf ears.

'Good! It will give us a rest. He is the devil's child, that one, spawn of a demon.' With that, the sister left the ward, crossing her chest and muttering words in Latin. Three nurses she pushed by, without a courteous word spoken, one of them falling sideways onto a bed.

'What is that you have in your hand?' asked the doctor.

'It's ... mine..., mine,' replied Sean, with a severely croaked voice. He covered his left hand with his right.

'I don't want to take it off you, just have a look at it, make sure it won't make you poorly. Would you open your hand for me?' encouraged the young doctor. Sean rolled over onto his belly with his hands tucked under him.

'We really need to see the object. We won't take it, I promise you that,' added the quietly spoken nurse. Sean looked at them both several times, trying to work out if he could trust them, he wasn't sure, but they seemed nice, not like the nuns or bad men that came to the home.

'Please don't take it, it's mine, and I didn't steal it, promise. I was given it by the dream lady,' alibied Sean.

'That's nice, is it from your father?' enquired the nurse, as it was clearly a male ring.

'No. I told you, the dream lady, she gave it to me, she's nice.'

The doctor moved closer to the bed, looking at the ornate piece of jewellery. He wiped the ring with an antiseptic cloth then gave the ring back.

'I believe you didn't steal it. Would you like some ice-cream, son?' asked the doctor, with a smile. He wasn't just being kind; he'd noticed how red and sore the little lad's throat was. The nurse asked Sean if she could look at the ring, a few seconds, 'It's a nice piece of jewellery,' she too wiped the gold before it was returned. And left the ward to use the telephone.

Sean ate some food followed by a small amount of ice-cream and then fell fast asleep, relaxed and snuggled into the clean warm sheets. An hour later a different nurse attended to the weak boy, speaking to him with soft kindness. The whisper was only for her and him to share. Sean was fast asleep. Her last words floated into his ear, picked up by his subconscious mind.

'You will be safe, that I do promise. I will change your life, as you are here for a purpose, from a line I cannot speak of,' She left for the office to make a call.

'Oh..., doctor, you're still here. I thought you had left a good while back.'

The doctor couldn't reply verbally. He nodded, raised his hand, his finger pointing outwards.

'Yes, that should be okay, as long as the results are best for the young boy. If it's higher than four, by even a fraction, I want to know personally, you understand. You have my mobile number.' A number was read back to him, 'Thank you.' He placed the receiver down. 'Sorry, I was on with the path lab. You have a good shift.' His head swung around. 'Are you new? I don't recall seeing you here before.'

'I am new, doctor, my first shift tonight in fact, hope to see you again?'

'You have stunning eyes. Really beautiful?' added the medical man.

She smiled in response to his complement, as if she hadn't heard it before. The doctor left the office. The nurse re-lifted the receiver and dialled a number. When she finished the call, she returned to the children.

The time was coming up to 9.00 PM and the paediatrics ward was being prepped for the night's rest of its precious patients. A second nurse had arrived for the night shift. Two nurses walked up and down, checking each bed.

'Is this your first time with us?' asked the tall nurse who'd just arrived.

'Yes, I'm bank staff but usually work on the men's main ward, up on the fourth floor, so I'll follow your lead on here, if that's ok?'

'Of course, well it's time for a break right now. Do you want to follow me for a coffee?' asked the tall nurse with a giggle.

'I would love one, and I've made a cake.' In the office she fished in her bag and pulled out a round tin decorated on the outside with roses.

'That looks really lovely. Would you like sugar?' asked the tall nurse, holding up the spoon.

'No ... no ... thanks,' replied the new nurse, cutting the cake. She took her time, a perfectionist, measuring the slice twice before she made the cut.

'It's chocolate sponge with vanilla butter, seasoned with a sprinkle of cinnamon, and all fresh today.' She passed her new friend a slice of the cake.

'It's delicious, you made it, for real? You'v...' The tall nurse stopped talking as the second bite was swallowed. The new nurse rushed to her aid, at the same speed as a baseball player on the last spot, catching her head as she fell sidewards. 'Don't worry, you will be awake in an hour. Bit of a sore head, that's all. I promise.' She flicked a blanket into the air, guiding it over the tall nurse as it landed and then she vacated the office, heading straight for Sean's bed. She pulled back the sheet and looked at the little lad's face, then quickly at a photo cupped in the palm of her hand, flicking between the two for a moment. She already knew he was her "mark". She'd scanned the picture at least a dozen times whilst stood in the phone box before entering the hospital. It was from the phone box she had made the call to Carol, the nurse who should have been on duty tonight.

An hour previous.

'Hi, Carol, Sue from personnel. We have overbooked for tonight on your ward, and as you helped us out over the Christmas period, you can have the night off.'

'Wow! Thanks, Sue. Are you sure though?' Carol queried, aware of the lack of staff.

'It's all been cleared with your matron, Liz. Enjoy the evening, and it's on pay, so don't be worrying.'

The photo cupped in her hand was a clear recent picture, taken two weeks earlier, through a long zoom lens and it was a perfect match. Speedily back to the nurse's station, phone in hand, she dialled a number and heard.

'Hello, Bar...'

She cut the person short. 'Are you, Sean Adrian Doyle's mother?'

'I am ... y ... yes, of course I am. Who are you? Is ... he ok?'

'He is in hospital.'

Mary looked at Tony in shock. He rose and went to his wife to comfort her.

'My Sean is in hospital,' she told him. With the receiver pressed hard into her pinny, she brought it back up to her lobe and listened.

'Are you willing to take him home?' asked the female voice.

'Yes, I am. When? Now? But isn't he unwell?' Mary looked again at Tony, joy now in her eyes, fed by the words "take him home", still resonating, but still the worry of him being in hospital remained.

'Come to the Royal now. You have no more than minutes. Do not bring anyone with you and do not talk to anyone about this call, including the police. Is that clear, Mrs Ward?' stated the female caller.

'Clear, yes I understand, talk to no one. I'm on my way.' She replaced the ivory coloured receiver.

'My Sean, he's in hospital. The Royal. I have to go. Can you call me a cab? I'll quickly swill my face.' Tony didn't question his wife, he carried out her request.

'Hi Stan, can you send me a car around to Barchards please, right away, or yesterday would be better?' Tony laughed, trying to disguise his urgent demand.

'Not a problem, Darren's leaving now, five minutes.' The line was cleared.

The taxi met Mary at the front, outside the parlour's reception. Thanks to the traffic and the god of green lights being kind, she was at the city hospital in under ten minutes. A further three, out of breath, she walked through the self-opening triple doors. Looking left and right a couple of times, she spotted the nurse slightly raising her hand.

'Tell me he's alright!' she asked the nurse, breathless, dazzled slightly by her diamond eyes. 'Come this way. I'll take you straight to your son, and please, don't worry, he is run down that's all, nothing serious I promise, so don't be getting all upset,' the nurse affirmed. All the usual formalities bypassed, she waved at the security officer; the love-struck puppy waved back at her, not even questioning she was not a regular member of staff.

'Read this, please.' The nurse gave an envelope to Mary as they entered the elevator. It read "Do not talk whilst you read this. Do not question the nurse, she is only a messenger. Do not panic. Your son has been brought to this hospital after being treated unfairly at the convent home. We have arranged for all his hospital admission papers and his files at the Magdalene home, to disappear. Are you willing to become his mother again? If yes, do not say anything, just nod when you finish reading and give this letter back to the nurse.'

Mary nodded without hesitation and gave back the note as instructed. The doors opened and the nurse pointed out the entrance to a ward, above it read "Sparkle Ward - Ward Eight".

The nurse led Mary to Sean's bed. The twenty minutes were up as she knelt next to her son. 'Do you want to come and live with me, my sweet Sean?' Mary whispered several times into his ear as he slept. She couldn't have been happier.

Opening his eyes, he was still exhausted but smiled when he saw the dream lady. She had come for him just like she had promised to. He managed a small nod. His arms lifted up to see if she was real, but they jerked as the fluid drips were still in place.

'Come on, Mrs Ward you must hurry before anyone sees you. We have two minutes, that's all, two minutes,' ushered the nurse, looking to her watch.

'Thank you so much for this, whoever you are. I'll never forget what you have done for us, and we will remain in your debt till I die,' thanked a tearful Mary.

'Don't leave this behind. He will need it one day.' It was

balanced in her hand, then she passed over Sean's ring. 'Not wishing to cross any boundaries, but when and where did you get this from?' she asked, eyes engaged.

'My father handed it to me and my grandfather to him. Why do you ask?' Mary felt a lump in her throat mentioning her pa and grandpa. She took a moment for herself before continuing. 'He gave it to me on his death bed. I know nothing more of it, apart from it was to go to my son if it felt right to do so. He held my hand tight and made me promise as he took a last breath.' She made the action with her hand then looked at the nurse.

'Can you confirm both your father's and his father's names?'

'Shamus and Jack, Doyle of course,' said Mary. The nurse nodded.

'Thank you, really, thank you for what you've done for me and Sean.' Mary hugged the uniformed angel then left, pushing a wheelchair. The nurse walked to the nurses station and injected the sleeping tall nurse in her upper arm. She placed a ward transfer file with Sean's name on the front on the main desk, checked every child, quickly, made Sean's bed and then remained at the ward door until the nurse was up, swaying slightly but up and about. She left and within ten minutes a call was received by the tall nurse, 'Are you ok to remain on your own as the bank nurse has escorted the child to St Cuthbert's?' The tall nurse replied yes.

The return journey for Mary didn't take more than fifteen minutes, and the taxi pulled up outside the century's old coach house, which was now an undertaker's parlour. The car's engine was switched off; its internal lights came on, following in sequence, one, two, and three, and the parlour was also illuminated. The light shone through the glass and wooden, door which led into the parlour. The door opened and a man came out, shoulders touching both sides of the door's frame. He joined the woman as she was about to lean into the back of the cab. 'Here, let me get him, Mary,' he said. Bending over into the car, he scooped the nine-year-old up in his arms from the back seat.

'What do I owe you, Sidney, darling?' Mary asked the driver, her purse in hand, fingers ready to retrieve whatever sum was requested.

'Nothing, not a penny, Big M, on the house this one. You and Tony gave a great send off for the mother-in law last month, and her indoors was very proud, plus, I was passing, going home anyway. So, don't you be giving it another thought.' Sid waved to Tony. Mary smiled as she closed the back door. Sidney tipped his cap and drove away. She entered the parlour of the undertakers. Closing the door behind her, her hand found and dropped the brass latch. She turned to face her husband and the many questions she anticipated. And they came, every one and more.

'I can't believe that you just took him, Mary, just like that, without ...' voiced the man holding Sean. He'd cut himself short not really knowing what to say. Or how to say it.

'I told you Tony, didn't I, before we married. I told you right at the beginning of our relationship that ... I, I would get him back, at all costs. I've always made that perfectly clear,' Mary stated, in an attempt to justify tonight's actions, even though it hadn't sunk in with herself yet. She now had Sean living with her. Was she now dreaming?

'I know that luv, I do ... but ... I thought ... you meant you'd do it legally. You know, through the courts luv. Not bloody carry out a covert SAS raid on the local hospital, for Christ's sake. What were you thinking? Do you know how much trouble we could get in for this?' Tony wasn't shouting but his naturally deep voice caused Sean to open his eyes.

'I tried it that way, they won, but you know why, damn church.'

'I know, Mary.'

'Look at him, Tony, go on.' Her head energetically bobbed in the lad's direction. 'Just look at him. He's well underweight, pale, and well, he's just not ...' She became silent.

'Not what, luv?' asked Tony, with Sean still tight in his arms.

'Not happy, he's just not happy. And he's my boy, my flesh and blood, he should be happy, he should be with me? I should be making him happy.' Mary began uncontrollably shaking, crying. Years of trying to get Sean back with her and out of that dreadful place. It had all caught up with the 40-year-old mother.

Tony was a big set man, with a face to match and hands like shovels. Mary always said he was her bear. But his heart was bigger than his hands. Sean could feel this man's arms securing him, he felt his heart beating strong and the muscles of his chest. And strangely, he felt safe and secure, as he moved about in the giant's arms amid the smell of a mixture of sweat and wood polish, and something else, but Sean didn't know the third ingredient. He felt safe that was enough, even though most of the adults in his life, up to now, had in some way abused him or treated him like a commodity. Today was different.

Six weeks passed and Sean had put on at least a stone. The colour had returned to his cheeks, and he went everywhere Tony went, following him like a new puppy. Mary could not have been any happier: the two people she loved most in this world complemented each other perfectly. Tony wouldn't admit it, but he loved his new role. He made out it was a pain, but he felt younger and he spoilt young Doyle. Not with money or gifts but time and commitment, plus installation of invaluable self-belief in the little lad, a priceless gift and something that Sean had never had. Back with the Magdalen Sisters, instead of self-belief he'd have been taught self-flagellation at the age he was now.

Tony was the 14th generation in Barchards and Ward undertakers, which was an extension to a very old family carpentry trade, centuries old. In 1642, during the civil war, Anthony Ward was given by Oliver Cromwell an acre of land to make coffins. In 1810, the Ward family sold off nearly a third of the land back to the Crown, as the Regents Canal was dug. The Barchards building company built the buildings that stand on the land today which are the funeral home, saddler's workshop and blacksmiths forge. Tony was looking forward to Sean being the next custodian, and he hoped he would carry on the family firm.

Four years soon flew by. It was a normal Monday, late afternoon. Sean had returned from school, not a care in the world, his uniform grey trousers torn on both knees.

'Big M,' said Sean.

'Yes, love,' she replied, not having seen the torn knees.

'Can I ask you a question?' he asked hesitantly, slowly lifting the lid of the biscuit barrel.

'Of course you can sweetie, you can ask me anything, you know that.' She opened the oven door, turning away from the heat wave, smelling of fresh pastry.

'But if you're asking for a pasty, then NO, they're for a buffet tomorrow. Mrs River, has passed,' she advised in a slightly firm tone.

He replaced the lid softly, having taken a ginger biscuit,

thinking about the question he was about to pose. 'Why did you come and get me from that place?' he asked, biscuit intact.

There was a silence, not awkward, but it lasted a good few seconds before she could answer the young lad.

'I knew your mother, Sean, and I made a promise to her that I would look after you to the best of my ability. She was very special to me, you see.' Mary was now committed to this line of explanation, or at least until the young lad was a little older and more settled.

'Can you tell me more about her, my mother? What colour hair did she have? What colour eyes? Do I look like her? And where is my father? Did you know him? And the ring - why did you give me the ring?' He was energised for answers.

'Wow! Where has all this come from? All in good time, Sean, but I promise one day I will tell you everything. I want you to know where you come from, discover your family and with that will come the details about the ring, you'll see. Now come, let's wash up. Tony will be in for tea shortly, then you two are going to the cinema.' Mary hugged the lad, stood back and ruffled his hair. She was so proud of him, a sweet kind boy, full of life, eager to learn and wanted to help anyone, and all this even after his start in life, he was still smiling or grinning?

'Do you like living here, with Tony and me, Sean?'

'I love it, love it! And you and Tony,' responded Sean instantly, then he ran to the sink to wash up, *fairy liquid* squirted in abundance on his hands.

Tony never made it in for tea on that Monday afternoon, or ever again. He'd had a massive coronary in the middle of the yard. Died instantly on the spot, said the paramedics, his aorta blew apart.

'Thank you, Burt ... for giving hi ... him a loving send-off. Tony would have been so jealous.'

'Aye, that he would Mary dear, that he would, the big oaf. And he would have also done the same for me if fate had flipped our destinies. We look after our own, don't we?' He placed his arm around Mary and squeezed gently. Burt was another local undertaker; he had just completed the service for Tony. He gave her another hug and walked away, with his parting gift of, 'Anything I can help you with, Mary, you know where I am.' Genuine words, and Mary knew this.

She wanted so much to allow the amassing tears to roll, yet she knew her Tony would be watching and very proud of how she was holding up. 'Good show lass, good show.' He would say to her after a long day. She recalled his words as if he stood beside her. Bolstered by this, she set off to mingle and thank the hundred plus people, for turning up.

That night Sean went missing. Mary was beside herself. She was in pieces; as both worry and grief merged, her world had blown apart.

At 10:45 pm the phone rang, the loud rings made her jump. 'Hello,' she answered, way too tired to go through the parlour's full spiel, which was always delivered on the parlour's line whatever time it rang, but tonight the only soul she thought of was Sean's.

'Mary, its Sergeant Scales, and I have that young lad of yours at the station.'

'Is he alright, sergeant?' she asked, desperately waiting for an answer.

'He is, Mary. Don't be worrying yourself; however, ...' his voice raised a touch,

'Five shop windows on the High Street aren't alright, shall we say.'

'What ... what ... why ...?' she asked.

'I know what has just happened to Tony is terrible. I miss him myself. He was a great man and liked by everyone. But we can't just sweep this under the rug, Mary. For one, the financial implications regard the properties, which I guesstimate is at least 4000 pounds. The shops owners will want recompense,' warned the sergeant. What he had said took its time sinking in. She was just relieved Sean had been found.

'Could you come to the station and collect him? I'll sign him into your custody for now. However, he will be under house arrest for a couple of days, until I have chance to speak with the inspector, and he's away until Tuesday. He doesn't go out of your house! Mary, can I be assured?'

'Yes ... no ... yes, I mean, of course, I understand. I will set off right this minute, and I can pay for the windows. I'll make sure Sean takes every penny to each of the shops that have been damaged.' Mary grabbed her coat and car keys.

Sat in the car, the key about to be turned, the relief of finding him soon passed and the realisation dawned on her. If he has to go to court, the law will discover how she snatched him and he would be taken back there, to that hell on earth.

"Oh, Sean, what have you done, son?" She started the car and drove to the police station on Spitalfields Road. After signing for her son, the sergeant spoke some stern words to young Doyle.

'I hope he listened and it registered, we have enough little shits on this manor,' said the sergeant, watching them as they left.

'I believe you made him think. He'll be okay, he's a good

kid at heart,' added another officer, standing beside the sergeant.

'I hope you're right, Rhodes. I hope you're right.'

In a few minutes, the station was in a panic. The all-glass door closed after a young female officer came running up. 'A chemical spillage on the bypass, sergeant,' she advised, full of anxiety.

'Call the fire service. We'll get a cordon in place. Which way is the wind blowing?' The sergeant didn't hear the last comment.

The journey home was shared with silence. Sean tried to speak twice but was hushed by Mary, not for punishment, she just couldn't talk, as her thoughts were filling up with more thoughts of a court case, and all that would then encompass their world, she'd just lost her husband, how could she lose her son?

A few awkward days passed. There hadn't been a conversation between Mary and Sean. She didn't hate him, or blame him, in fact, the opposite, she felt nothing but sorrow for him. What had happened to Tony had shaken her world, but it was profound for Sean. His world, which had been at last happy and secure, was rocked to the core.

Late on Monday evening, gone ten, Sean walked past the lounge. He heard the sound of sobbing. The young lad stopped and reversed. Mary was quietly crying, holding a small glass of the hard stuff. It was about to spill. 'Let me take that,' offered Sean, rushing into the room, catching the malt at the right time.

Mary smiled up at him, her make-up a complete mess, eyes full of sadness: Something Sean hadn't seen a lot of since leaving THAT place. He sat down next to Mary and hugged her. 'I miss him. Why did he leave me?' Sean letting it all out,

'I miss him too, Seany, dear, I really do,' honestly said Mary, hugging the boy so hard.

The embrace was interrupted by heavy knocks on the front door. The knocks came again in quick succession - both mother and son broke apart. Marry panicked a bit as she looked at the suitcases, 'Sean, push them bags behind the sofa.'

'I'll see who that is at this LATE HOUR.' Mary was, attempting to straighten her long curls on the way to answer the door. The cases were being filled as Mary intended to flee.

'Sergeant Scales, what a surprise. Was I expecting you this evening?' Her response was high-pitched, she tried to hold it together, thinking of the cases, her hands back up, trying again to sort out her curls, not out of vanity but decency with a touch of the nerves.

'No, you're not and I apologise for just turning up at your door, especially at this hour, Mary, and unannounced. We were passing and I saw the lights still on. I have some news regarding Sean, and I wanted you to hear it as soon as. I know you have been very worried regarding the outcome of his detention.'

'Of course, yes ... yes, you did right. I have been worried. Alan. Come on in, please, come in, the sooner we know what's going to happen then we can move forward, deal with whatever faces us.' Mary moved aside, allowing their entry.

'This is Officer Rhodes, Mary,' introduced the sergeant. A much younger, tall, muscular man, forced to bow, followed the sergeant in. Removing his hat, he nodded to Mary. His face was square, hard, but honesty was held within his eyes, that she saw clear as day.

'Sean, Sean, the police are here to speak with us,' semi-shouted Mary, looking again to the cases, how would she explain them, 'Sean?' was shouted again, walking back into the lounge.

Young Doyle remained silent sat back on the chair. He looked down to the carpet, a sheepish smile on his face. He knew what he had done was wrong, very wrong. He had thrown bins and bricks through the windows of the butcher's double frontage, the newsagent's, carpet shop and fish shop. The repairs for the damage set Mary back three and a half grand. Sean had also, off his own back, volunteered to work at each of the stores for two weeks, free, to say sorry.

'Please, please, the pair of you sit yourselves down. You're making me dizzy.' She semi-laughed. Officer Rhodes smiled. Mary was relieved, Sean had hid the cases well.

'Can I get you a drink or something to eat maybe?' offered Mary. Sean rose and ran to his bedroom. Returning in seconds, he took his place back next to Mary, his left fist tightly shut, knuckles white.

'No, we're fine, relax, Mary. I understand that you're on edge, that's why we're here to talk. But please ... don't be putting yourself out ... just relax, you've been through hell of a lot recently.' The sergeant was sincere. Every word he spoke was truthful even though not every word was music to Mary's ears. Although she had an outcome that allowed her to keep the only thing she cared about. After the sergeant finished talking, the young officer became involved. His passion and his words were chosen carefully tailored for young Doyle's ears. Sean listened intensively at what was being said, picking up on the officer's honesty and big brother authority.

'So, Master Doyle, if both you and Mary agree and sign this contract, instead of this matter going any further legally, you will be required to attend my boxing club three nights a week, and half a day on a Saturday. If you have kept your nose clean for a year, the slate is wiped clean.' Officer Rhodes finished his chat and passed over a couple of booklets to Sean and some paperwork to Mary.

Sean looked at Mary. She stared back, and both acknowledged the relief the meeting had brought. The officers vacated.

There was no more silence in the flat from that moment onwards. Sean kept his word and worked after school at each of the shops for the given period. The butcher kept him on two hours after school on Tuesday and Thursdays, and on Saturday afternoons he did deliveries on his push bike. Half of his wages he gave straight to Mary to pay back the damage costs. If truth be known, it wasn't just the wages that kept Sean working at the butchers. He had become good friends with a girl who also worked there called Specks, then afterwards a boy named Kev who followed Specks everywhere. Mary, watching from afar, was pleased as Sean had not before then, made any friends. The three of them became inseparable, Sean had never missed a session at the boxing gym, Danny Rhodes had taken a shine to him and Doyle flourished with the knowledge he once again had a strong male figure in his life. Sean kept up with the boxing and it wasn't long before he was fighting for titles, and his friendship grew with Specks and Kev.

11

COCK AND PUSSY

The new Daimler pulled up in front of the Cock and Pussy MC. Both the front passenger and the left rear doors opened together. Two highly polished left shoes were placed on the ground simultaneously; two smartly turned-out men in grey suits exited the expensive vehicle. They did the alpha male walk up to the entrance of the club.

'Can we speak to a Sean Doyle?' asked the one with a Welsh accent.

'No! Fuck off!' instantly replied Tank, his face muscles reciprocating his polite words.

'I will repeat myself once more, I suggest you comply. Can we sp...'

The Welshman was on the floor, his hands covering his bloody nose. Tank had head butted him and had hold of the other man around the neck. Sean came running out to see what all the commotion was. Another shiny suit left the Daimler and ran at Tank to free his colleague. He started fighting with Sean. Tank was squeezing the life out of his captive. Lady De Pen Court had exited the car and watched as the grown men brawled like adolescent children. Two fingers in her mouth, she whistled louder than a *Manchester United* referee. It had its desired effect as the brawl stopped dead. Tank's prey was released and fell to the ground, gasping for air, sharp indents either side of his windpipe.

'Which one of you children is Mr Doyle?' asked Lady De Pen Court.

'Your lucky night, Sean,' said Tank, slapping him on the back.

'Who wants to know?' asked a playful, yet wary, Sean.

'So, you are Mr Doyle, are you?'

'I guess, as long as you're not the tax man.'

'I am the opposite. I have an offer of some work for you, Mr Doyle, if you are interested of course.' She stood tall not intimidated by the place or the fighting.

'And what sort of work would a fine lady such as yourself, have in mind for a man like me?' Sean laughed, but there was genuine interest in the question. Tank joined in. Giving him another slap on the back.

'Gigolo are we now, Sean,' bantered Tank.

'Don't flatter yourself, Mr Doyle, and I actually doubt it very much if you could handle a real lady.' She saw the challenge and rallied. She thought of sweet Tanya warning her of the place.

'I tip my hat to you ma'am, you have some balls, I'll admit that much, coming here to a place like this. Your only undoing was to turn up with these has-beens.'

'Shall we continue this conversation elsewhere? May I suggest somewhere a little quieter, maybe.' Her voice hadn't changed, she spoke with absolute confidence and an authority worthy of her status, most definitely upper class but in no way condescending.

'Well then, ma 'lady, let me think. Given the fact I have

no clue who da fuck you are, how you even know my name. Add to that, you turned up here in a very posh car with some out of shape hard men, who appear to be lacking in manners. I think maybe I'll decline your offer, if that's ok with you, ma'am.' Sean bowed slightly and turned away to return to the club.

'You can reach me at the Plaza Hotel. I will be in residence there until Thursday evening, and let's just say, Mr Doyle, it may be worth your while visiting, at least to listen to my proposal and give it some consideration.' She smiled.

'Sorry, I make it a rule not to chase money, and I definitely choose who I work for.' Doyle turned towards the club's door, no longer interested in the conversation.

'I wasn't talking about financial reward, Mr Doyle. Of course, there would be payment for the work if you decided you would like to come on board. I was giving reference to me helping you along with your family tree, which I am led to believe you are currently researching. Your ancestry may be a better way of stating the facts.' Her tone still remained the same, as did her presence.

He stopped dead in his tracks and spun around on his heels. 'What do yo...?' He watched as she bent over and entered the car, the men in after her. The Daimler then drove away.

'Who the fuck was that?' asked Tank.

'No idea, mate, not a clue, but she was classy,' replied Doyle, still watching the Daimler, the brake lights became bright, the left indictor came on, the car was gone. 'How did she know I was tracing my family?' he said out loud.

'Attractive, if you like the older, well-dressed sophisticated type.'

'You like all types,' replied Sean, shaking his head.

'I like the fairer sex to enjoy all of this. It wouldn't be fair not to share, would it?' Tank turned his hands inwards and pointed to himself.

Doyle smiled, shook his head some more and left for the bar. A lot would have found it difficult to understand how Sean was a part of the biker club scene. Truth be known, a lot of ex-squaddies are drawn to the comradeship and excitement that these clubs provide. Young men join the armed forces and become men, and like the rest of the world's population, they need guidance and leadership. This may not have been completely true in Doyle's case, but the club took his mind off a few things, and then there was Tony.

The Plaza Hotel was a small family-run concern, yet still one of the finest in the big city. It held a worldwide reputation for excellence, and if you weren't on their stay list, you wouldn't get in. If you were on the exclusive list, a night in residence here would set you back just shy of four grand, just for starters, or so the rumour mill said. No one had ever seen an invoice. All done via word of mouth from the hotel administration to the personal administrators of the exclusive clientele. The cost was really for privacy, room and lodgings, and maybe a few extras. Again, nothing ever appeared on paper.

Sean finished his shift at the Cock and Pussy around one in the morning. The rest of the night had turned out to be peaceful.

'You want a lift home?'

'Yeah, will do, if it's no bother,' Sean, straddled the Harley Davison. Ten minutes later, twelve miles covered, two red lights run, Sean climbed off the bike.

'You gonna meet with her then?' Tank waited.

'Not sure, bro, bit strange her just turning up like that, and how did she know I worked at the club? And like I said, how did she know I was tracing my family; nobody knew that. Thanks for the lift.' Sean gave back the black skid lid and ran his hand through his hair.

'Call me if you need someone to go with ya, hold ya hand.' Tank winked and rode off.

The rest of the night what followed was full of restless tossing and turning. When the insomnia eventually left and he fell asleep it was full of dreams of Mary and Tony. The following morning, he was up early, and although tired, made his way to the office and swallowed plenty of coffee.

The door opened. 'Seany,' greeted Ann, pleased to see him, somewhat of a surrogate for Mary.

'I'll be out most of the morning.' He drank more coffee. 'Is there owt you need before I leave?' he asked, with the cup back to his lips.

'Have you drunk that full coffee pot? I've only just turned it on.' Ann's eyes opened as she approached the table. 'You have, haven't you?' She shook the empty glass jug at him. 'You'll be wired lad, wired.' Her head shook as she re-filled the percolator.

'Sorry, Ann. Bad night's kip, trying to wake myself up. I'll be back around one.'

He yawned as he was going out the door. No taxi called on this occasion, Shanks's pony was to be the method of transport, powered by all the recently consumed caffeine, as our friends, the yanks, would say. Six blocks later and Sean was nearing his destination. His hip was still giving him jip, but he wasn't letting that stop him.

'Well, slap me some, that you, Chalky?' said a surprised Sean, approaching the arched canopy protecting the entrance door to the posh Plaza Hotel. Bright green and shiny, it matched the heavy camel coat Chalky fashioned. Even had the same words written on it.

'Sean! Sean fucking Doyle himself. All the lads said you had gone abroad, working private shit getting big money. How's the leg? Still owe you,' replied the smartly dressed doorman, nodding towards Sean's leg.

'Abroad? No that's not for me, back in the city for a while, see how that goes, and the leg was doing okay 'til I got myself knocked down a couple of months ago. Just before I got out the regiment, doing a "small" job. A favour.' Sean subconsciously rubbed the leg. 'You working here then, Pete? Good gig is it?' Sean looked to the Canopy.

'No, I'm stood here looking like a right prat for a laugh. What do you think?' It was clear that Pete hadn't found his ideal vocation, but unlike Doyle, he did have rug-rats to feed. Three beautiful daughters he adored.

'Still got a sense of humour, I see. Thought you'd have been over at the club with Tank. I'm doing a couple of shifts with him. I'll have a word, if you fancy it?' The two shook hands. They had served together for a few years in the regiment, as had Tank, but he was before their time.

'No, mate but thanks, if I work at the Cock and Pussy, the ex-misses 'ull stop me seeing me kids.'

'You split then, sorry to hear that, mate.'

'Yeh, she constantly pestered me to leave the regiment, then three months out and she's filing for a divorce. Met her fucking ex on Facebook, he's a wanker now, sorry... banker.'

'You ok?'

'Yeh, just live for my girls now. What you up to? Don't tell me you're staying here mate?'

'No, no, wanted to have a word with one of your guests, a

posh lady, bit tidy and very confident,' reeled off Sean, recalling last night's image of her.

'You mean Lady De Pen Court.'

'She's a real lady then? Well, doesn't surprise me, she has class, and some balls.'

'Careful, mate, that one has a lot of contacts and a lot of heavies with her. Rumours she's involved with the Mafia.'

'I've already met the heavies, nothing to worry about there. They could all do with a few weeks in the gym,' laughed Sean. 'I'm here under her invitation actually. Apparently, she would like me to work for her, but as to what I'm to do, it isn't clear yet.'

'Well! Fuck me, never thought I'd see the day when one of us was mixing with the likes of one of them, she's Rupert material.'

The pair shook hands again just as a second door man appeared.

'What have you been told about fraternising with the public, White?'

A growl appeared on Chalky's face. Sean could see what he wanted to do to the asshole stood behind him.

'Actually, he is being of great service to me. I'm here to meet with Lady De Pen Court,' interrupted Sean, his hands in the pockets of the grey hoodie.

'I don't think Lady De Pen Court would mix with the likes of you, in fact, I'm certain of it. Sling your hook, you're lowering the tone,' said the overzealous doorman. Sean was about to reply...

'And how would you know whom I would, and wouldn't mix with, may I ask?'

'Forgive me, I did not see you standing there, Lady De Pen Court. I ... I ... wa... errr, err ...' rambled the green penguin.

'You were assuming to think like me, were you not?' She made him shrink.

'I apologise, Lady De Pen Court. I ... I ... I apo...' grovelled the doorman, bowing cowardly. The perfect image of a jobsworth.

'Come on, get out of the way, White.' He tried to regain confidence in his position by passing on the belittlement he had received from Lady De Pen Court. Chalky never moved.

'So, you are a real lady,' said Sean, his eyes looked straight into hers.

'I have a title, yes, Mr Doyle, but call me Emma, please. I wish to keep this casual as I seek your advice on some fragile matters and have been told I can trust you. You are also somewhat of an expert in the field I wish to discuss.' Her tone had lowered.

'Prove it,' said Sean, his eyes still connected.

'Prove it, Mr Doyle. How so?'

Two of her guards, the pompous doorman, plus Chalky, watched him with intrigue, never having seen someone talk like this to Lady De Pen Court.

'Well, if you trust my advice so explicitly, like you say you do, I'll give you a bit for free.' His arms helped his words.

'Please, do so, Mr Doyle. I always appreciate a bit of good counsel.' She was also now intrigued and waited his answer.

'You could do with another minder, no disrespect, lads.' Sean looked at the Welshman and his mate who Tank had bitch slapped the night before. They didn't reply, yet the anger on the Welshman's face was clear and growing.

'Would you be enquiring if I have a position vacant, Mr Doyle? Is this to what you refer? I do like a person who can get straight to the point.' She continued their game, and noticeably, she made a small movement of her head to the left.

'I would be, yes, but not for myself, your ladyship, my friend here, Chalky. He could run rings around the men I've seen of yours so far.' Sean pointed to Pete.

'Chalky?' said Lady De Pen Court with an unexpected frown.

'My name's Peter White, ma'am, hence the ...' He spoke as if speaking to an officer back in the army.

A smile appeared on Emma's face. 'And are you as good as he says you are, Mr White?'

'Well, er, er, not su...' stuttered Pete.

'Humble and strong, I like that combination in a man, you're hired, Chalky. Is it acceptable for me to call you that?' She asked, then looked Sean straight in the eyes. 'Does that show you my intentions are honourable, Mr Doyle?' She never moved her stare.

'It does and I'm very grateful, plus, you have a good man there, please say when and where. I'll meet with you and listen to your proposal. But I'll only listen, I'm not guaranteeing anything. Just want to make that clear.'

'Right at this moment, shall we? Please join me for morning coffee, and to just listen is acceptable.' Emma about turned. Sean followed after Pete had sort of hugged him. 'Owe you another one, mate. Thanks.'

As Sean walked through the revolving doors, out of the corner of his eye he saw the pompous doorman collapse. 'You still got that left then Pete?' laughed Sean. Within four feet, after entering the Plaza, he had spotted at least five real 'A' list celebs, one of which impressed him, as he was somewhat a hero of Sean's.

Lady De Pen Court spoke into her phone. 'I've forwarded it on to you. Call me back if you do not receive it in the following ten minutes.' She placed the mobile back into her bag and turned to Doyle. 'Are you a little star struck, Mr Doyle?' she was still playing the game.

'No, yeah, well a bit.' A sheepish look overtook his mug.

As he sat down, Emma raised her hand a little. A waitress speedily arrived.

'Can I be of service, Lady De Pen Court?' asked the waitress, with a polite curtsey.

'I will take my usual, and Mr Doyle will take the same, thank you.' She looked at him in a shielding way, as if saying "you are in my world now, allow me to lead".

'I will return with your beverages shortly ma'am.' The young waitress disappeared. Emma looked to her left.

'Nice to have met you, Lady De Pen Court,' spoke a muscular man, in a German accent.

'And you, Arnold. I take it "you'll be back",' replied Emma, in humour.

The big man chuckled loudly. 'You English, you crease me.' He walked off, accompanied by Sean's stare.

'Shall we get straight down to business, Mr Doyle?' Emma returned to the point to be discussed. She pushed back a little on the sofa, but remained up-right and proper.

'However, you want to play it, and call me Sean, it's strange to keep hearing "Mr Doyle".' Sean was still gazing at the people.

The coffees arrived. 'Two Jamaican Golds with cream and caramel, Lady De Pen Court,' said the waitress, placing the large quiver-shaped cups on the table then backing away slightly.

'Thank you, Kelly, they look absolutely amazing, as does your hair today.'

Emma smiled at the waitress who was now walking on cloud nine, because she had remembered her name and complemented her. Kelly was young and came from a part of town she would never mention. But she had worked very hard to get this position, and Lady De Pen Court, to her, was the pinnacle of her own aims, not the title or wealth, just herself, her upstanding manner.

'I would prefer to continue addressing you as Mr Doyle. It's different, you see, in my world, with the gossip and rumour mills constantly on the churn and me without a husband. It is as if I'm fair game. I am sure you can see the point I try to make.' She leaned in to retrieve one of the coffees. 'Please, tell me, what you think to my choice of drinks, Mr Doyle?'

Sean picked up the remaining cup while Emma observed closely.

'You are an interesting man. However, I cannot make out if you are trouble, or not.' She leaned back, eloquently sipping the drink, without acquiring froth all over her top lip, unlike Sean.

'It's a knack, of which you'll eventually become acquainted, I'm sure.' It tickled her, she laughed genuinely, and it felt good.

'So, Lady De... Emma, how can I help? It seems to me that you have your shit together, and who put you in touch with me? I can't see we would run in the same back alleys.' Sean was being flippant, and he knew it. But although he was thankful for her employing Chalky, he wasn't a hundred percent convinced of her integrity. He saw no immediate red flags but the strangeness of the way this real lady had just appeared in his world from out the sky, it would seem.

'Let's say an interested party recommended I speak with you, and very highly too, may I add. However, I have a policy to never mention associates. I find it slows things down, don't you, Mr Doyle? As questions get asked then the whole thing becomes cloudy and the focus leaves the subject matter. Plus, real confidence and trust are a rare commodity today, and I feel I am lucky to have both of these in my life.' She smiled once more as Sean again covered his lip with froth.

'It's nice but difficult to drink, and I think I am getting an audience.' He reached for the table and picked up one of the printed cotton napkins.

'Don't let it concern you, it won't be for your skill at coffee drinking. They are mostly likely speculating as to whom you are. And to what OUR relationship is. The gossip and tittle tattle doesn't stop at the door, not even in such exclusive establishments as this one.' Emma chuckled tastefully, more for the observing eyes this time. Yet her smile was still one of genuine happiness. She had the ability to not care what others thought of her, which Sean saw as a plus.

'Your world,' replied Sean.

'Now you are getting it, Mr Doyle,' she complimented him. 'Right, down to business. The work I wish to offer you is to find out who killed my son and why?' She focused on her drink when saying the word "son". Eyes down, there was no witness to her expression, and rightly so.

Sean was stunned: he didn't see that statement coming. 'I'm sorry to hear of his death. Can I ask how long it has been?' His coffee was placed back on the table.

'About a week, I believe.' She masked any emotion to the point of not feeling.

'A week ... seven days?' replied Sean, his voice raised with the surprise of her answer and the shortness of the duration.

Emma nodded, her gaze still fixed firmly on the Jamaican Gold.

'Surely the boys in blue will be still looking into it I'd

have thought?' he asked with an empathetic tone. Then he stared at the onlookers. He wanted to tell them to fuck off, but he knew this wasn't his turf, that was for sure. With the stained cotton napkin in one hand, the posh coffee back in the other, he waited for her to answer.

'Sadly, and as hard as it may be to comprehend, Mr Doyle, Henry, my son, at the end of his life was a homeless person living on the streets of London. And his whereabouts for the last nine or ten years are a complete mystery to me. And of that fact I am not proud. I would give all of my wealth and my own life to bring Henry back.' She, at this point, gave off genuine emotion but still could not regain her eye contact with Sean. She proceeded. 'I feel a lot of shame for this outcome, but families aren't always what others believe they are observing. Do you not agree, Mr Doyle?' Now she was able to look right at him just as if the allotted time of being ashamed was over. Her composure was in place, yet he noticed her eyes had somewhat de-illuminated.

'Amen to that, and I'm no expert on families. However, I'm not convinced that I would be the right man for what you require, Lady De Pen Court. I wouldn't want to hinder the investigation in any way. It's clearly very important to you and surely a local PI would be suited better than I would. I haven't been in these parts for a good few year.' Sean felt, given the very sad moment, it wasn't right to call her Emma. That would have required some history between them. He noticed her underlying grief through the regained smile. She, in Doyle's eyes, was a one-of-a-kind individual.

'I will pay you whatever amount of money you require. Money to me is not an obstacle that I have to overcome, and I stand by what I said outside that nice club of yours. I am able to pass over a lot of quality information, that I am positive will help you regarding your beginnings in this life. Which I am led to believe you have an interest in pursuing. I could help you discover the identities of your parents. Let's call this information a bonus, of which I am confident you will earn.'

Two of her minders approached the table.

'Ma'am. We've received the information you're waiting on. You have an hour to be there before your plane leaves for Brazil.' The speaking man never once looked at Sean, or any other guest for that matter.

'Thank you for informing me, Lance. I will take the Range Rover if that suits your plans. Please have Derrick be ready will you. Would this then possibly leave you some free time? If it does, please be a dear and take Chalky to the tailors, have him kitted out. I feel ashamed of him dressed like that. And fill him in on what his duties are to be, will you.' Her hand touched his forearm and went limp while she spoke. Doyle noticed her kind, friendly, yet professional way with her men, and they appeared to have respect for her, and maybe some more.

'Yes of course, ma'am.' Lance nodded his head a touch, then left. Still no glance towards Sean, but he did acknowledge the head waiter. A friendly nod came back from his cousin.

'I will have all the paperwork that I have acquired to date with regard to my Henry's case sent over to your place, Mr Doyle. The package will also include a credit card for expenses. I won't put a limit on it, I am sure you are honest. As for your salary, shall we say £400 a day, and a week's advance of this amount will be deposited directly into your bank account. The cleared funds will be there before you are able to reach the cashpoint machine. Do you have any questions for me? I appreciate I have reeled off a lot of information.' She waited for Sean's response, her pretty face full of a confidence all of its own. Her hand took hold of the Jamaican Gold and raised it to her lips whilst she waited for his answer. She believed it was already in the bag, a done deal, as was the majority of deals she had, had input with. But she had already acknowledged that Doyle was not your typical man, so a small amount of anticipation was present; however, Lady De Pen Court had a sixth sense when it came to weighing up the measure of a person. And what was required to be their puppeteer.

'Only the one question: so why do you need me? With all the information you have gathered with regard to myself alone, surely it would be easy for you to ask about your son, with all the resources at your beck and call.' It was a straightforward question for Doyle. However, two answers lay behind it.

'With regard to your information, that was, as you mention relatively easy, Mr Doyle. The reason being, you are like most of us. A member of the rat race, you leave both a digital and paper trail of a size you wouldn't believe. My son had somehow managed to live behind the curtains, of this so-called wonderful society, making him a little more clandestine.' She placed the drink back onto the glass table and rose. Kelly materialised at her side to assist with her coat.

'Please do not feel as if you have to leave too, remain as my guest and finish your drink. If you would like anything else, don't hesitate to ask, just mention my name and it will be taken care of. Until we meet again, Mr Doyle.' He half stood. She turned and walked away with the grace of an old-fashioned movie star, one man picking up her shadow at the door. The answer she didn't feel Sean needed to be aware of, was that it was the embarrassment this "tittle tattle" regards

Henry being homeless, would cause her, with rippling consequences. Doyle was also expendable, to her he may be a good asset, and him not being linked to her was her bonus. Emma had learned to play chess from a very young age.

Sean attempted to stand but then sat again and remained seated for a further ten minutes. Truth be known, he was enjoying the surroundings, puzzled by not only the job offer, that had been presented his way, but the fact that this real lady knew everything about him. In his hands was a file as good as what the army had on him, if not better. It was without a doubt a facsimile that contained thirty pages. However, the index had forty two lines on it, the last twelve had been de-personalised. Everything, it appeared, regarding him was held here in the aged and shabby folder. *How the fuck...* he thought, especially his personal bank account details. He had only just opened that account, not even two full days ago.

Sean had always imagined that he was not really on the grid. Doing his best to pay cash for most stuff, even in the army, he wasn't, on the electoral roll. I guess, like Chalky said, she has a lot of contacts, even so the folder's contents were old - dated, this hadn't just been thrown together. The first entry was his first day at school, this took place 4 weeks after Mary had snatched him. He took out his phone and tapped the bank's icon - six digits - it opened. He tapped the "money in" icon, and there it was, like promised £2000 deposited forty four minutes ago. He laughed. She must have put it in before they sat down. *Confident bitch*, he thought, then realised she wasn't paying for weekends. He was then interrupted by...

'Will you be eating with us, sir?' asked Kelly, offering Sean a menu.

'Er ... no, I'll be leaving in a few minutes, but thank you.' He looked twice at the young girl.

'I will leave you with a menu. Sir, in case you have a change of heart and prefer something *hot*.' Kelly emphasised the word "hot" using her lips. The eighteen, maybe 19-year-old, blonde knew how to walk.

Not quite sure about what had just taken place, Sean reached for his coffee to finish off the last drops. Looking out of place, protruding from the bottom of the laminated menu was a torn piece of paper. "Outside, ten minutes, near the bins. I am your lunch". She had signed the note with an imprint of her lips. *Why not?* he thought and looked at his watch.

Outside, he saw a different doorman standing where Chalky was earlier.

'I'm looking into the security of the hotel. Could you show me how to get around to the back where the bins are stored?' he asked.

'That alleyway, there, sir.' The man pointed to a three-foot gap at the end of the building. It didn't take Sean long to find the bins.

'You fancied something hot then?' said Kelly, as she undid her blouse buttons slowly, one at a time, revealing her black lace bra and smooth white skin.

'Is this, how you pic...'

'Don't talk, fuck!' She dived straight in and kissed him, her lips firm on his, her hand pressed hard against his jeans, her fingers working with experience on the top button.

Down on her knees, she nibbled at his bulge, his zip down, her mouth soon full. Sean moaned, placing his hands on her head, then he caught a peripheral glimpse of the Welshman coming towards him.

'Good night, prick.' Sean heard as the baseball bat hit his

head. The ex-Welsh Guard and his mate set to, kicking the fuck out of Doyle. Kelly was pushed over hard, her head collided with the bin.

'Stop it! Stop it!' she screamed as loud as possible, then shouted at the thugs 'You said he was a pick-pocket and had stolen from Lady De Pen Court. And you were going to arrest him.' She ran still screaming, blouse wide open, through the alleyway she fell twice scrapping her knees, up on her feet she managed to get to the front of the hotel. Chalky was there waiting for Lance.

'This way! Now! They're beating up that man. They'll kill him! Quickly, his head is bleeding,' she begged him.

'What?' replied Chalky, and ran after her.

'Oi, Taffy!' shouted Chalky, wading in. Powerful punches hitting the pair of them. Lance arrived and joined in on Sean's side. The scrap continued until the police turned up. They had no alternative but to use a taser on Chalky. One officer described him as a Tasmanian devil. An ambulance was called for Doyle - his head had received several blows requiring stitches. Everybody was arrested but freed later that same day, released on bail. All the remaining charges were dropped the next morning, after a tall grey-haired barrister wearing pinstripes, accompanied by his posse of four similar individuals visited the police station. The Welshman and friend no longer worked for Lady De Pen Court after that day. Several times she visited the hospital only to find Doyle remained in a coma. One night, she spotted Tank, talking away to Doyle, fearful of his condition. She watched from the wings as the gigantic biker supported a close friend.

A week later, Barchards and Ward funeral parlour

'Mr Doyle, how are you feeling after your stay in hospital?' asked Lady De Pen Court.

'Better thanks. I think I was out for a couple of days, not sure how long. Still a bit sore.' Sean ran his fingers over the bandages.

Four days, Emma said to herself. Then her voice was shared again, 'Have you managed to look into my predicament with regard to my son, Henry? Sorry to be a nuisance, but it is playing on my mind.'

'I have La...' Cut short again.

'Emma, please, I don't want to stand on ceremony. You are doing a very personal job for me; I don't see you as just an employee.' As she was talking, her hand turned over the pages in the police file, titled: Henry Allister De Pen Court, underneath this with a line through, John Doe.

'I have, Emma, and I can understand why you'd like a second person on the case. The plod, as we imagined, haven't really given it much time, in fact, from the little I've managed to find out, no time at all has been allocated to the investigation, sadly. It's clear they have him down as a homeless junky, and that puts your son at the bottom of their long list.' Sean stirred his coffee, his mobile pressed tight to his ear, his shoulder raised, keeping it in place. The stainless-steel toaster popped. *Golden brown*, he thought, placing the two slices on the paper plate before applying the butter.

'Does that mean you will be happy to assist with this matter?' She waited, but she was confident. The question to her was a formality, but she was aware he actually hadn't agreed to take the position as yet.

'I'm already on it ... Lady ... Emma. I'm going to visit the shanty town later this evening. Get a feel for his life, see what turns up. Somebody must have known him, of that I'm certain. Once I have a starting point, we can set a plan in place.'

'Shanty town?' Emma rebounded.

'Yeah, or like the press call it, Cardboard City. It's down by the Thames, a part of London you won't find on the holiday brochures. By day, it's a cut through for the wealthy city workers, brings them out near to the bridge. By night, it's the hub of the homeless world. From eight onwards, the supermarket trolleys arrive, their owners clad in the heaviest coats man can tailor, but they don't cross the bridge. It makes you think, Emma. People can have all their life in a stainless-steel cage on wheels.' Sean took the first mouthful of the *Nescafe*, followed quickly by the first bite of the toast smothered in *Lurpack*.

'Sounds to me like you have had a similar experience, to these people,' she enquired, surprised by his insight.

'You could say, but I had a rucksack and dressed in green. But for certain, I don't see the need for all the trappings people seem to acquire in their lives, just for the sake of acquiring and trying in some form to be a chieftain on the block.' He paused, taking a second mouthful of coffee, his teeth crunched into the toast. 'I'll be in touch, Emma, as soon I have something concrete.'

'Thank you, again, Mr Doyle, I am sure you will. I remain in London until Wednesday, late evening if you require further contact with me.'

Damn, thought Sean, just after the conversation ended. He had meant to ask for some photographs of Henry. He crunched into the still warm toast and pressed re-dial.

'That was quick, you have something for me already?' she teased.

'No, sorry.' He laughed around a mouthful of food. 'I'm hoping you have something for me? I forgot to ask, do you have any recent pictures of your son?' there was a fair silence, before he got his reply.

'I'm afraid not,' was her sad response. 'Actually, come to think of it, I may be able to get hold of one. Allow me a few minutes and I will make some calls. How do I get it to you?' she asked.

Sean's first response was for her to text it to his phone, but her sad reply made him suggest, 'You can give it to me over lunch, my shout. One thirty?'

She looked at her Cartier before confirming. 'Yes, that gives me three hours. Where would you like to meet up?' she enquired, quite taken aback by his directness.

'I'll send you the address.' Sean ended the call and placed the half-eaten slice of toast between his teeth and typed, "Joe's, Pennington Rd", followed by, "look for the big red canopy, you won't miss it".

The text arrived on Emma's phone just as she dialled another number.

'Tanya,' said Lady De Pen Court, as the line connected.

'Emma, nice to hear from you. How are you?' then she covered the speaker on the phone and told someone to give her five minutes, and close the door.

'I am seeking yet another favour from you, I'm afraid. I am such a nuisance, sorry.'

'Not at all, Emma, happy to help. What can I do?'

'Would you possibly have a photo of my dear Henry? A recent one that is. I have an album full, but unfortunately all of them are ten years old.'

'No, not off the bat, Emma, I don't recall us holding any, if I'm honest but give me an hour or so. I will try and get hold of one for you. I do have one idea that may bear fruit.' Tanya started typing a password on the keys of her keyboard.

'You are such a dear. I will remember your kindness. And be assured it will be repaid.' The lines disconnected.

Two hours and ten minutes of time had elapsed. Sean was still sitting in the old office of the funeral parlour, sketching away on the back of a cornflake's box, busy detailing some ideas for the house he wanted to build. As he wrote the final measurements down, Lady De Pen Court's phone received a picture text.

On opening the message, she simultaneously felt both sadness and joy. The picture Tanya had sent was just a head shot, the background shaded out in white. And there was something strange about Henry's complexion. She smiled and cried; and for a second, had to look away. Her hand covered her mouth while staring hard at the young man's image. Like any mother, her first thoughts were, *"he needs a good meal"*. The joy subsided as the memories came back to her, her hand was again pressed firm to her mouth in an attempt to dull the sound of real crying. She began to contemplate as the realisation of his death hit home. The driver wasn't sure what to do, he'd seen her upset before, but not to this extremity and never, never tears. He lowered the glass divider 'Ma'am is there anything I can do to help? Ma'am?' The lady that was always beautiful, calm, confident and strong was a mess. 'Ma'am.' He offered her a couple of paper napkins,

Emma said nothing but relieved him of the napkins, she gulped in then blew her nose, snivelled twice, the second stronger than the first, 'forgive me, Lance you should not have to had witnessed my weakness,' several smaller sniffles came, he gave her a couple more napkins, she thanked him by curling her lips, 'Where are these from? They are strong.'

'McDonalds, ma'am,' he uttered. She smiled again and thanked him for his discretion. Lance was pleased to see the tears were over as he couldn't deal with them, but then came her wrath.

'My Henry, my little boy is dead and so will every single person who had anything to do with my son's death. Until the day I perish, wither into the earth, I will see them all suffer. Each will regret the day they interfered in his life. I will discover who instigated and who carried out his killing.' This was said out loud, as the driver turned into Pennington Road. He had heard all and recognised it more so than the tears.

'We're here, ma'am,' he bravely told her at the same time he slowed the Bentley and stopped virtually opposite the tatty façade, of Joe's café. In his head he was saying, *that is a big red canopy.* Emma had vented and allowed out a lot of pain, Lance caught a glimpse of her eyes in the mirror, he recognised his real boss.

'Are you sure we are in the correct place? Lance,' she asked, looking at her surroundings. She collapsed the lid of the make-up container.

'Yes, ma'am, well we are according to the sat nav,' A second car pulled up opposite them parked near the green. Four men remained in this second vehicle.

'There's Mr Doyle now, ma'am.' Lance pointed out the windscreen as the wipers gave visibility. Sean was less than 20-feet from Joe's, dressed in light well-worn jeans and a hooded sweatshirt with some small embroidered insignia on the left chest. The hood was up his hands in the pockets of the hoodie. His head slightly facing down, oblivious to the world.

'Is he playing some sort of practical joke, Lance? Surely, he cannot be expecting me to eat in there, CAN HE?' She mused out loud, but she was really asking herself, plus, Lance had no intention of commenting. Once more to herself she reiterated that this Mr Doyle was a very interesting character indeed.

'Would you like me to go in for you, ma'am, I could make your excuses?' offered Lance, reading the gobsmacked expression via the mirror.

'No, no of course not, but thank you, you are a dear,' she replied. Lance exited the car and went around to her door.

'This shouldn't take long,' Emma remarked as she took hold of the umbrella offered. 'Have you and the men eaten?'

'Only breakfast, Ma'am,' Emma nodded as a reply and set off. Lance looked across the road at the other vehicle, giving a nod. Emma strolled along the dirty pavement until safely under the pull-out canvas. Its wide red stripes bellied in the centre as the rain fell and fell and yet there was no escape for the water. She wanted to stamp her feet, but she felt this was inappropriate, instead she settled for collapsing the brolly down. He had been correct with his instructions: it was big. The door was held open by an overweight postman exiting the café.

'Thank you, sir,' said Emma. She entered and was greeted by wolf whistles professionally orchestrated by the builders, scaffolders and wheeler dealers as they looked her way.

'Okay, boys, settle down, settle down! That's enough!' shouted Joe, waving a T- towel.

'You found it ok then?' Sean made his way over to her. 'I took the liberty of ordering the food. I hope you don't mind.' He pulled out a chair for her. Joe was soon over, wiping down the table's plastic cloth. 'Nice to see a real lady in my establishment, I'm honoured.' He smiled at her, not in the slightest bit bothered by the egg, fat and beans covering the front of his white T-shirt. This to him was the same accolade as an 18th century barber's apron.

'Let me introduce you, Lady De Pen Court.' Doyle pointed to her. 'Emma, this is Joe. A good friend of mine.' He pointed to him.

'Really nice to meet you, your ladyship.' said Joe, using Fagan's accent. He wiped his hand, back and front, on his top and held it out. Emma smiled and willingly shook it.

'My pleasure, Joe, and a fine establishment you run here, it is full with customers a very good indication your food will be delightful. I am looking forward to sampling the cuisine,' she replied, her hand still encased within Joe's. She couldn't help but notice the disfigured fingers and swollen knuckles, her stare was captured by a big gold ring on his wedding finger, barely visible as the skin had grown around it.

'Well ... er ... thank you, ma'am, th ... that means a lot, a real lot,' he replied, his head nodding, showing he was fully engaged. He released her hand then continued. 'I'll be right back with your food, m'lady.' His tone changed as he turned to Sean. 'You mind your manners now, young Doyle' you ee'r.' He clipped Sean on the back of the head as he turned. His voice raised yet again, 'And what you lot staring at? Ave yah not seen a member of the royals before?' Joe told the café, as one. He walked back to the kitchen, head held high, chest puffed out.

Sean laughed covertly.

'What are you laughing at, Mr Doyle? He seems a really nice man.'

'Oh, that he is, for sure. I've known him a lot of years, and you wouldn't believe it by looking at him, but he loves the royal family, tells everyone he has blue blood.' Sean kept on laughing softly, not really at Joe, more at the whole situation.

True to his word Joe returned just after these words were shouted out.

'Two full English with extra black pud. Table six,' came from the kitchen.

Joe received the massive oval plates. After a few steps, they were placed with pride in front of the two diners. Emma's eyes widened.

'Forgive me for taking the liberty, Emma, but this is my world,' said Sean.

'Touché,' she replied, acknowledging Sean's home run. And if truth beknown she was enjoying herself.

'Did you manage to get hold of a picture?' Sean remarked, picking up his knife and fork.

Two white pint mugs of milky tea with several rounds of toast were placed on the table next to them, Sean's toast, whole, on a small plate, Emma's sliced at an angle and stood upright in a silver rack.

'Thank you again, Joe.' She acknowledged the latest course to arrive at the banquet. Joe backed away from the table. 'Enjoy,' he said before leaving them to their meal.

'Yes, I managed to acquire one. It isn't the greatest portrait of him, although it is an accurate likeness, and I am sure it will help with your investigation. I have also arranged for several more to be sent from my home all of Henry between the ages of 16 and 18.' She pulled out her phone and pressed a button. 'You should have received it.' She put her phone away.

Doyle's phone pinged. 'Yes, that will be a help. Good looking lad, he has the look of you,' kindly said Sean. He knew instantly that it was a mug shot from when he must have been arrested at some point, the give-away sign, was the man's hands were up and shut, he took from this he would have been holding a card facing out wards, but this had been removed with some Tipex. The white pen had also scribbled out the lines for telling the persons height.

'No need to try and appease my feelings of guilt, Mr Doyle. I deserve to carry them 'til I go to my grave, and I will do so, as my penance.'

Her fork stabbed hard into the fat Cumberland. Lifting the full sausage to her mouth, she took several bites: half of it was soon gone. 'I may just have to visit here on a regular basis.' She smiled, as her hand took hold of the large mug, all of her fingers comfortably inside the handle.

The conversation continued with Emma delving into the history of the café and how Sean knew Joe, a deliberate distraction from her thoughts but it worked well she was captivated by the whole scene.

'Joe?' she spoke as he walked by holding a mop, 'Could I be a bother and ask a favour?'

'Anything, M'lady, you could never be a bother, not to me.'

'I have some men with me, five of them and I wondered, ... could you feed them? Take some food out to the cars, I will pay extra for the inconvenience, of course,' she finished the sentence with her eyes.

'No problem, I'll nip and see what they want, but first a little job,' and Joe was out the door, 'He is a lovely man that J...' Sean's eyes grew. She turned quickly to look through the window, there was Joe pushing the mop up, causing tones of water to come of the sides of the canopy, a man walking his dog got washed, Joe was virtually attacking them with the mop as he cursed at him and the dog barked.

Sean pointed to the wall behind him: it was wallpapered with photos and framed newspaper cuttings and old posters.

'Can you spot Joe?' he asked.

She stared above him, squinting slightly. She rose to get a closer view. 'I cannot.' She continued to stare, moving even closer, determined to find the chef. It was like a hard game of, *Where's Wally?* She pointed.

'Nooooo,' said Sean, in a clear voice.

'Too late.' The inhabitants of the café all spoke together, then started clapping. Sean was shaking his head. Emma turned to see Joe making his way to the wall, carrying something under his arm. 'I couldn't help notice that you took an interest in "the Wall" Ma'am,' announced Joe, pulling up a chair. 'I have a few more pics in here, if you'd like to peruse.' He didn't wait for her to answer, the largest photo album she had ever seen dropped on the table. The café's inhabitants stopped clapping and started saying, 'Jackanory! Jackanory!'

They were a few pages in when Joe coughed out the words, 'And this skinny thing here, is this brute.' He pointed with his thumb to Sean and his finger on his other hand pointed to a young man in the photo. Doyle was holding up over his head, a boxing belt. Clear was his eye, which appeared to have a red plum above it; his lips were full. Sean was left out of the conversation for another twenty minutes.

'Have you some washing-up to be doing, Joe?' asked Sean, in an attempt to stop the slaughter of his teenage years. It didn't work. So, he changed tactics. His finger pointed to a stocky individual dressed like a Mafioso don, including the oiled back Italian hair. Emma spent a couple of seconds looking at the faded picture. 'That isn't you, Joe? Very handsome indeed.' Sean then pointed out several more pictures that had the five-foot ten Italian stallion on and this o...' he was cut off sharply, but then too was Joe, '...'

Lady De Pen Court spoke, 'That is Manhattan, the old Madison Arena, is it not?' she asked. She wasn't wrong.

'And that's you again, Joe. What's the belt for?' Emma was referring to Joe holding a gigantic leather belt above his head. It held a dozen medals; his face also resembled leather that had been worked, and worked hard.

Joe didn't reply, so Sean stepped in. 'That's Joe alright. Twenty-two plus a day he was then, and you can thank Muhammad Ali for the redecoration of his face.'

Joe added, 'I'm just an old man with a fucked-up face and some glory years behind him, that's all, M'lady. Like many a man, you make your way best you can.' Joe quietly wrapped up the conversation and closed the album. He loved boxing, but not with the spotlight shining on him. 'Sorry to have taken up so much of your time.' Joe got to his feet. The café was virtually empty; it had officially closed twenty minutes earlier.

'Please, Joe, don't you dare apologise. I have enjoyed this time immensely. I only wish I had more of it to sit and chat, and you shouldn't be so introverted with regard to your past, I would like to wager it is a very interesting past. In fact, how would you like to be a guest speaker at one of my dinners? There will be some royals in attendance, for real,' she enticed.

Joe's head was nodding; the brightness in his eyes told her he was on cloud nine and the answer was going to be a clear yes. He left the table, snarling at the last of the locals who had started taking the piss. Yet every one of them would have agreed with Emma's speech, and yes, she was right, he was a very interesting character, but it wasn't the boxing alone that had fucked up his face or hands.

'Well, Mr Doyle, thank you, I'm truly full.' She pushed the plate a couple of inches away.

'I'm impressed. You've done well,' said Sean, mopping up the remainder of the bean and tomato juice with the last piece of toast. 'Can I get you a doggy bag?' was shouted from the counter.

'No, no, but thank you, Joe. I actually really enjoyed that. I will pay for the five bacon sandwiches and five coffees. If that's ok?' Her eyes returned to Sean. 'I must be on my way. I have a fixed appointment for four which I cannot escape from.' She gave the Cartier a glance; her eyebrows raised as she saw it was half past three. Lance was entering the café carrying the plates and cups, Joe relieved him of the crockery. Lance held the door, Joe returned to the counter, Sean wanted to stand and ...,

'Thank you for a very interesting lunch, Mr Do... Sean, I am indeed in your world, and for the fascinating company.' She looked to the counter, smiled as she rose from her chair. Lance was still holding the door

'Oh, I almost forgot, your first bonus, Mr Doyle.' She opened her designer bag and slid over an A4 envelope.

Lady De Pen Court exited the café. Outside she was met by some of her men, one of them being Chalky. Sean acknowledged, a good mate, a good man, and he now had a job worthy of him. Emma gave a final glance to Doyle. Lance held the rear door open for her.

'You're mixing with a better class of people these days, young Doyle, I approve,' commented the bald man, wiping clean the plastic table cloth again. He coughed, and coughed some more, but he didn't take the cigarette out of his mouth.

'I guess you could say that, Joe, but I'm only doing some work for her.' He grabbed the pint mug before it was swept away.

To a lot, Joe would have come across as a dirty overweight back-street café owner. Sean saw a decent man who had saved him and lots more kids, when he was a boxing trainer alongside Danny. The world had given Joe a lot of anguish, more than most could handle. On top of this came the bottle, and unfortunately, he couldn't put it down, but there were reasons for that. Sean looked at his old role model and wondered. In some respects, he was as strong as they came, yet in others he couldn't handle life.

'Thanks, Joe, you should see a doc about that cough, it doesn't sound good. Sean put a couple of twenties on the wet but clean countertop.

'You don't have to pay, Sean.'

'I want to pay, you're not a charity, Joe, and I'm not a little kid any more, let people help you.' Joe took the twenties and was thankful of them, but it was still awkward.

'Take it easy, and don't be a stranger, you hear?' And he clipped Doyle on the back of the head once more. Sean was stopped at the door by these words, words which Joe couldn't say close to him, even though he wanted to, and he would have liked to hug him while he spoke them. 'I'm very sorry about Mary, young Doyle, she was a good woman, a bloody good woman, who will be missed.' Joe walked off. Sean pulled the door shut, his hands back in the soft pockets, the hoodie in place. Leaving the back-street café he realised that he had a few hours to kill before the night's information gathering. Phone out, he dialled an old school friend. He had meant to do this for the last couple of weeks since he'd been back. He'd been given the number by another old mate, but he felt awkward dialling it. These two had been really close as kids growing up, except Sean just upped and left, joined the army at sixteen without saying anything. Kev thought his friend was going away for a weekend, another test before he joined! Sean never came back. He kept telling himself he would write and explain, but his time was filled with mindless military bullshit during his basic training.

'Kev, its Sean,' he said, as if he had never been away and they had chatted the day before.

'Bloody hell! Where you been for the last ten years?'

'In the army, mate. How are you? You still welding and shit?'

'Yeah, I work offshore now, on the gas rigs, two weeks on and two off. How did you get my number? How long you bin back? Are you back home? Not that I'm bothered. Glad you called though, and glad you're alive,' Kev asked, as he was cautious, bordering on being paranoid, and rambling.

'I'm home and met with Spike, that's where your number came from. You okay? You sound on the offensive, but maybe I deserve it?'

'Spike? As in John Nash? He's a big player in the property world now, and I mean big, he was involved with the Olympic stadium, you know. Surprised he had my number,' mused Kev, his voice lowering towards the end of the sentence.

'Still belittling yourself, I see, Spike spoke very highly of you, didn't you advise him on some lintels and a special butter, or something. Apparently, what you said worked and made a design of his possible. Even the architects had been impressed, you made it possible for an extra floor. Then he tried to encourage you to go to university to be an architect, but you never got back to him.' Sean was just talking to an old friend as if he'd never stopped. It was strange and at the same time felt good.

'I'm not that clever, Sean. I didn't want to embarrass Spike in front of his new people. It was only a flying buttress. I just split the support element, made it flatter with a beehive shape, but still strong enough to help keep hold of the false ceiling he wanted, that's all, nothing really. Steel is my thing.'

'Well, if you're not going to uni, I may have some work for you, if you're interested?'

'Car failed its MOT, hey, Sean?'

'No mate, I'm building a house using a couple of steel containers and other shit I have in the yard.'

'Cool! I'm in, that's what I've always wanted to do. When do we start?' Kev was eager, the lapse in communication over.

'Come round, see what you think first. It might not be possible, just pie in the sky at the minute, but there's loads of shit in the yard and outbuildings we could use, hopefully.'

'When?' asked Kev.

'What you doing now?'

'Now ... this minute ... nothing. Where are you?' Kev's voice was still full of enthusiasm.

'At the funeral home. Come round the back on the river front. The steel gates are locked, but just push the left one forward, you'll be able to get through the mesh.'

'See you in forty, Sean. And don't worry about tools or any of that stuff, I have all the gear we'll need to build another Eiffel Tower.' Phones switched off, Kev felt as if he'd won the lottery - his best friend was home - out the blue. And his passion had been given an outlet. Kev may have said he wasn't clever enough, and he did feel that way. He was without a doubt an introvert, with some nerd features tossed into the pot. John Nash had offered to help him, like Sean had said with an offer of a job, but this came with the pressure of going to university. All Kev knew was he hurt inside, hurt to the point of he needed to design and build. So, Sean's offer was pure karma, given from the universe. He sat down at the desk and pulled open the drawer. Hidden under the dozens of pens, scissors, staplers and rulers, was a notebook. On the front cover was the title, 'Dream it, Believe it, Achieve it'. On the first page was a sketch design of a house built from a container; the drawing was dated and signed by Kev seven years earlier.

12

CARDBOARD CITY

Sean's wrist turned: it was1940 hours. He went to the fridge, but closed the door not having taken any food out. His plan tonight was to spend most of the evening with the less fortunate, in a place a lot would call home. But you wouldn't find one fixed kitchen appliance. So, having a meal right now somehow to him felt like cheating.

Twenty-five to eight and Sean was walking along the Thames flood barrier, hands in the wide pockets of an old rain Mac. He didn't know who it belonged to, but for the last five weeks he had noticed it had been hanging on a hook on the back of the office door, at the funeral home. He laughed to himself remembering that Tony, his stepdad, years ago loved to watch *Colombo*. Now, here he was wearing a similar Mac and investigating.

'Spare some change, sir?' asked an old lady. She had no trolley, only a heavy-duty bin-liner and tatty holdall with handles fashioned from a belt. 'Thank you, guvnor,' she said, receiving the deep-sea diver from him. He said nothing as the reality of the place fell on him. Her well-worn, toothless, face smiled, resembling a gurn. He had earlier intentionally filled his pocket with dozens of the blue notes. Eight-thirty and he found himself sat on a cast iron bollard, unwittingly staring at a tall man, bearded with long messy hair, but still with some style to it. The gent's clothes, although it was clear he was homeless, had been crudely washed and flattened with the intent of maintaining some sort of a crease. A large canvas holdall sat close to him, touching the man's leg for reassurance. Again, no trolley, he was laying down a large piece of black plastic. On top of this was laid the first piece of cardboard, then the second sheet of plastic. Sean continued staring throughout this process. It was difficult to stop looking.

'Do you want a picture?' asked the man, not angry but in a tone that was hard for Sean to explain. A self-anger that had turned into disappointment and back again maybe, but he wasn't Freud.

'Sorry, mate, didn't mean to stare.' But Sean continued looking on and off, just not as obvious. He knew this man, but he couldn't recall from where, which for him was unusual: his memory rarely failed him.

'Danny, would you like some soup and a bun, its oxtail tonight?' asked the cute Salvation Army girl.

His connection was completed. 'Danny Rhodes, Officer Rhodes.' Sean couldn't believe it. He was looking at the very man who was responsible for him staying out of court and more than likely jail a decade and a half ago. He remembered it was Danny who planted the army seed in his mad young head. He even helped him join, swat for the test, everything that comes with becoming a young soldier, and not just Sean. Like Joe, Danny helped with many more lads, whose lives would have been very different today if it wasn't for this man, who was now sat in front of him on plastic and well-worn cardboard. 'PC Rhodes,' he muttered.

The homeless guy stopped blowing on the beaker and looked up. 'You say something, son?' The beaker swapped hands.

'PC Rhodes,' said Sean again, this time clear and intended to be heard.

'I was, but not no more, just in case you had any ideas that I was undercover.' Danny laughed, but it took effort, and it didn't last. Sean opened his mouth to ask why, but Danny beat him to it. It wasn't the first time someone had known him in that other life and wondered what had happened.

Danny, in his first life was a guy who had everything. He had his shit together; that's how Joe used to explain it when he regularly offered Danny up as a role model to the young gym rats. 'Good job, stunning bird, powerful car, and a fucking brilliant right hand,' were his exact words. Doyle replicated them all, apart from the bird, no long term relationships for him.

'Why? You are about to ask, why? Circumstances, I guess.' Danny began to sip the hot soup, blowing on the liquid. Not just enjoying the soup, but the actual experience of a warm drink. A silly, simple pleasure that most take for granted.

'Sean Doyle, Mr Rhodes. Do you remember me?' Doyle put his hand out.

'You've grown, lad, and filled out. What you doing down here? Last I heard, you were still in the armed forces, hanging out with the special boys, no less. Not that I was surprised, you always had that "grit" about yeh. I knew you would achieve, I just hoped it would have been in the ring. You could have hit top billing.'

'I was, sort of, still am. Don't know about special, stupid sometimes, that I can guarantee. As for the fighting, done my fair share. I'm down here looking for information about someone who may have lived here recently.'

'You got a name then, son?' spoke Danny, sounding less angry, interested even.

'Henry, Mr Rhodes, I believe he spoke with a posh accent, lots of tattoos, even on his hands, stood a good six-foot, with a skinny build, that's all I got on him.' Sean had the picture from Emma in his inside pocket, but somehow showing people on the last steps of humanity a prison photo seemed cruel.

'I may have seen him around, but I haven't been here long, and I tend to keep myself to myself. You don't know who to trust on the streets.' He sipped the oxtail soup and his eyes looked over the cup, towards the Salvation Army girl, not wanting to be noticed by her again, or anyone. Sean watched his mentor become reclusive in seconds.

'I'll keep asking around, Mr Rhodes,' said Sean. He fished in his Mac pocket for a few of the blue notes, but he hesitated. Were a few fivers enough for what this person had done for him? Did he have enough in his pocket? Did he have enough in his bank?

He flashed back ten years to Danny driving him to Kent, to the training camp in Folkstone. Mary cried all the way there in the back of Danny's Mustang. He had to pay him back.

A couple of notes, get a meal, he thought for now. *Surely, that wouldn't hurt, would it?*

'Molly Malone, she'll know him, if anyone does. I don't recall such a character myself, but Mo is like the go-to around here, so I'm told. But it's only my second week here,' added Danny, with one eye cautiously fixed in the direction of the young Salvation Army girl. He was speaking again, yet the tone in which the words flowed was still reclusive, his brain acting like an East German citizen.

Sean pushed himself off the bollard and handed Danny four fives. Feeling he was interfering, yet somehow, he couldn't believe he was looking at his ex-mentor.

'I don't want your charity, son. I'm here because, well, let's just say it's my punishment, and I deserve it.' Danny turned away.

Sean didn't know what to do or say. He walked off. It was too hard to watch one of the people who had helped make him who he was, suffer like this. He just didn't know what to say.

From a dozen feet away, the young Salvation Army girl approached him. 'You can donate the money if you like, sir, it will be put to good use, I promise.'

Sean didn't say anything, he gave her the notes and walked off, then waited five metres away for the young girl to finish her rounds and catch up with him.

'Do you know where I can find a Molly Malone?' asked Sean.

'Molly! Yes of course, but she's not here at present, if she was, you'd hear her, believe me.' The girl laughed but then became self-conscious of her giggle, which had allowed her braces to become visible.

Sean gave a neutral expression and maintained it, while the girl spoke to him again. Her lips re-covered the silver and gold band. 'She will be down the High Street at this time, getting herself thrown out of the bingo hall, amusement arcades, and other places.'

Sean's expression changed to one of misunderstanding, his brows furrowed. The girl took the frown as a question,

'She goes in the buildings, hangs around, and then the

staff pay her or give her food to leave. Only a couple of pounds at a time or sandwiches close to their end date. But it gets Molly her supper, and she always returns back here with stuff for the others. Our very own Mother Teresa she is that one, the heart that pumps for the community.' She gave a shiver that was unnoticeable to most, due to her Parka being two sizes too big.

'Why do they make her leave? Does she cause trouble?' Sean asked, curious.

She moved closer to him; reaching up on her toes she whispered into his ear. 'Body odour.' She fell back onto her feet, falling to the left slightly. Sean steadied her. 'Thank you, I can get a bit dizzy on nights, low sugar, you'd be amazed how many miles I walk around here.'

'You look a bit young to be down here on your own.' His arm was still on her shoulder.

'I'm not on my own, silly, look around you.' She pointed to all the homeless men and women who surrounded them both.

'I didn't mean it li...' He removed his arm.

'I know. People who are homeless, to many they're invisible, or they have a bad reputation. And some are bad, yes, and they deserve that title, but some doctors, some police and some teachers are bad, are they not?' She uncrumpled a bag of jelly babies. One went into her mouth then the packet was offered to Sean. 'No, no, thanks.' The bag was returned into her pocket.

'Come back a bit later, around ten-ish. Molly will be back by then, but I can't guarantee she will be sober, or even that she'll speak with you. Our Molly is our Molly, and she does what Molly wants, you'll see. Oh, and thanks again for the donation it will be put to good use.'

'Thank you for your help.' Sean set off back to the

funeral parlour to attend a meeting with Ann, and strangely tonight's events had helped make his mind up about a few things. To a lot of people, when they first met Sean, they would say selfish, distant, direct, hard, strong, maybe a touch of arrogance about him. This man was far from that, but his life had produced a self-resilience that equated in a solid outer shell.

The door to the parlour slammed. 'Is that you, Sean?' Words floated down the stairs.

'Yeah.' He removed the Colombo disguise and draped it over his arm.

'We're up here, in the office.'

"*We*", thought Sean, climbing the two-hundred-year-old steep steps. He pushed the door open and five out of the parlour's six staff were present. There were only three chairs in the office so the others perched on the available flat surfaces.

'Sorry to spring this on you but everyone is so worried Sean, darling,' said Ann, desperate to apologise, but knew this had to be done.

'Worried! About what?' he answered. No one else said anything, they didn't know Sean as well as Ann.

'Tell me, what is everyone worried about? Come on, feel free to speak up.' Sean gave everyone eye contact.

'Rumours, Sean, are you selling this place off for development?' one asked, the first to take the plunge.

'How the hell did that come about?' he replied, laughing to himself.

'Don't deny it, you were seen talking and having a meeting with John Nash, the big property developer. He's known for turning old buildings like this one into posh apartments,' said another.

Sean started to laugh and laugh. The staff in the office

weren't sure how to take his attitude and began to look to Ann for reassurance. But she wasn't hundred percent sure what was going on either.

'It's not a laughing matter, Sean. You must see how worried we all are. Most of us have worked here for years, it's not just a job to us,' she said, averting her gaze.

'Forgive me, please, don't take it personally. I wasn't laughing at the situation, or at any of you, but at the rumour, that's all. I know John Nash, I used to run with him at school and we boxed together at Danny's for a good couple of years. We were only catching up over a coffee. Yes, he did make me an offer on the parlour, but he also told me if I wanted any help, he was there. Believe it or not he likes the fact that this place has been here for centuries. He isn't the monster you all think he is. If it wasn't for his developments a lot of the old buildings would have been demolished, and levelled, he extends them a second life. Times have changed, sometimes businesses can't continue the way they used to, whether we like it or not. But no, I'm not selling out to John.'

The staff started laughing; the relief was clear on their faces as they smiled.

'Any other interesting things happening to this place that I'm not aware about yet?' he asked the audience.

'Yes, that you may be selling out to Lamington's on the High Street,' stated Harold.

'Now there is some substance behind that one. The old man was a good friend of Tony's which I'm sure you all know, he asked me if I was going to sell-up, would I give them first refusal.' Sean walked over to the coffee machine.

'I'll say one thing to you all and then I would like to have a meeting with just myself and Ann.' He poured the coffee; the room murmured quietly and looked at each other. Sean found the last flat space and perched on the corner of the worktop.

'I have no immediate intention of selling this place, nor am I developing with John, at least not with the intention of selling, so you can all sleep easy for now. There are going to be some changes, but these will be made as and when, and only if they are necessary to keep the place running, yes there are some financial restraints on the business, but we should be able to work around these. I will inform you all before any plans are made permanent, you have my word on that. And while I have you all together, I would like to say a big thanks to all of you for being loyal to Mary while I wasn't here. I know how much she appreciated it, as do I.'

The chatter followed the four staff out the door and it was closed behind them.

'Sorry to have sprung that on you, Sean, but they all insisted, and they have been really worried. Mary was much more than a boss to us all, you must realise that.' Ann was speaking quietly after bringing Mary's name back into the conversation.

'No problem, I understand. Would you like a coffee?' Sean was well aware of Mary's legacy and her big shoes he had to fill.

'Oh no, way too late for me, but thanks. No caffeine after 12 noon, not unless I want to be awake all night.'

'Down to business then,' said Sean, sitting down behind the teak desk. It was two centuries old and brand spanking new when the funeral parlour first opened.

'I'll be honest from the beginning, but I won't be as people-skilled as Mary was, that's just me.' He sipped the brown stuff. 'I intend to make some changes around here, some big changes, starting with me putting in a manager. I know nothing about the funeral game, and at the present moment I feel as if I need to follow a different path. There are things I need to resolve before I can settle.'

'Whatever you say, I'm sure you know best, you're in charge now.' said Ann, surprised at Sean's manager idea.

'Do you still have a hand in running the charity shop?' asked Sean, both hands now on the large coffee mug.

'No not really, not these days, it was taken over by that big national charity and they're only interested in large salaries for the top management.' She shuffled in her seat and then gave more of an explanation. 'It wasn't a community led operation anymore, I left I couldn't stomach the false ideals they spouted. It really got me mad.' Ann answered openly, even though she had no idea why he was enquiring about the charity shop, especially at this moment.

'Could you run and organise a charity from scratch?' he asked, sipping the hot drink.

'Me? Er ... wel ... yes, I guess I could, depending on the set up, and I would have to believe in it. Why all these questions about charities, Sean. What is going on?'

'I was downtown earlier looking around Cardboard City and I bumped into Danny Rhodes. Do you remember him? From the bo...'

'Yes, of course I do, but I haven't seen him for a year or so, not since the crash. He just vanished after that.'

'What crash?' asked Sean, leaning forward on the desk.

'Eighteen months ago, the community had a fundraiser to send Danny with his wife and disabled three-year-old daughter to Disney World.'

'Danny had a daughter?' interrupted Sean.

'Yes, she was such a cute little thing, Kerry. He had given so much over the years to the town and people, with the gym; in fact, now that I remember, your friend John Nash also refitted out the gym while Danny was on holiday. On the way back from Heathrow a drunk driver smashed head-on into their vehicle. Helen and Kerry were both killed outright on the spot.' Ann dropped her head down, going quiet for a moment before continuing. 'Danny was devastated, as anyone would be, but I swear he lost something that day, and not just his family. People tried to help him. He returned to work but got suspended and eventually the police finished him; then the gym fell apart.' Ann took another breather. 'I think I will have that coffee after all.' She went to the machine, looked at Sean as if to say, refill?

'Yes, top us up.' She poured some more of the black stuff into Sean's mug before sitting back down. 'I guess he blames himself. It explains how he ended up down there in Cardboard City. Poor man.' She drank some coffee. 'What you thinking, lad? I can see your brain ticking over. I remember that look from Mary.'

'Something strange happened to me tonight, ... while I was down there, all these questions and thoughts were flying around my head. My life changing overnight, the loss of Mary, being back here in the funeral parlour.' Sean looked around the place 'This and that, suddenly everything fell into place.'

'Why are you asking about a charity though? To get some help for Danny?' asked Ann.

'Something along those lines, yeh. The old saddler's shop at the end of the funeral home and the land behind it, it's been rebuilt so I want to open that as a boxing gym, run it as a separate entity, a charity, put Danny in there and get him back to what he was. The help he needs is to help others.'

'Good idea, will the new manager be running that as well?' Ann was asking two questions in one.

'I would hope so, I trust her to, and she's good enough.'

'The staff will be on edge around a new manager, you do realise this, don't you?' she fished.

'No, they'll be fine, don't worry. If Danny wants to come on board, I would also like him to move into the granny annex above the workshops.' Sean knew Ann was becoming anxious, even her cup had begun to shake.

'What? Did you say the granny flat, I live there, have you forgotten?' Ann was annoyed, feeling rejected and about to walk out.

'But not for much longer,' answered Sean sipping the coffee, continuing the ruse.

Ann shot up out the wheeled captain's chair. 'Is this how I get treated after thirty years of loyal service?' She was hurt rather than angry.

'Mary's flat comes with the new manager's position,' announced Sean, with his cheeky grin.

'So? Good for the bloody new manager, I hope they feel at home there. Where am I supposed to move to, at my time of life? I don't have a lot of savings. I loaned a lot to Mary.'

'Mary's flat, with your husband. And I know Mary owes you fourteen grand.' Sean ended the torment.

'I'm not understanding you, Sean. And the business can't afford to pay back that fourteen thousand, I do the books, remember!'

'Let me make it simple. You are the new manager with a new flat and a pay rise, who else I would I trust? And we will work on the loan being paid back, that I promise, as Mary would want you to have your money. Oh and what about your John, I know he doesn't like where he is now, what about if we made our own coffins, here, I know Mary was looking into that.'

Ann sat in stunned silence. She looked at Sean, tears

welling up. She was overwhelmed by his little speech. Mary, money, manager, parlour, bigger flat, and John would be overwhelmed, he'd solved everything.

'Don't you want the manager's job?'

'I ... I ... I, well, ... well I'm not sure Sean, not sure if I could do it.'

'You've been doing it for years. Mary often sang your praises, and this is a little payback from me.' The cheeky smile was still visible, but it had humbled.

'Payback, what for? You don't owe me anything, do you?' she asked him, genuinely unaware of what he was talking about.

'I do. I owe you a great debt. You remember when I first arrived here, all them years ago.'

'Of course, how could I forget, a little scrawny lad who didn't say a word for weeks.' The memory brought comfort to Ann. Sean may not have realised it, but he brought a new energy with him when he arrived back then, an energy that filled the parlour and the people in residence.

'Remember when I used to be sent to the chapel of rest to collect things for Tony, and I would be standing outside, too scared to go in on my own, but upset because I didn't want to disappoint Tony.'

'I remember now, I held your hand and went inside with you.' She smiled, aided by a precious memory.

'Yes, you did, Ann, on several occasions over a few months until I could do it myself. You never let go of my hand until I was ready. I've never forgotten that.' His eyes filled with emotion: a rare event.

'It's perfectly normal to be scared of dead bodies, especially as a young child.' She started to well up herself.

'It wasn't the bodies I was scared of, it was all the crosses and church clobber, it reminded me too much of the care home and the nuns. I was terrified they would come back and take me away.'

'Bless yeh.' Ann grabbed Sean and hugged him, broke away, then slapped him on the arm for teasing her about the flat and job. 'You're a rum lad, you are, but one I'm glad to have in my life right now.' Then she brushed down his shoulder where she had slapped, then hugged him some more, even tighter than the first time.

'I'm not ten no more, Ann.'

But she didn't stop hugging. 'You're never too old for a good hug. And you'll get another slap if you wind me up like that again.' She broke the embrace. 'The manager's job though, really, Sean, I'm not sure if I'm capable. I don't want to be the one who closes the place down after nearly 220 years, serving the community, I would feel awful.'

'How about then, if we share the job? You run the place day to day, and I'll check anything you're not hundred percent on. So, the buck stops with me.'

'Yes, yes, I can do that, but I don't need my pay raised, and the 14,000 can wait, the flat is enough, thank you, Sean. But where will you live? Mary and Tony would want you here. You're not leaving, are you?'

'I'm going to fence the yard off at the end, the old shipping containers, I'll convert them into something. I haven't lived in a conventional house for a long time.'

'You can't live in a tin can, lad, it's not good for your health, and it will be cold.'

'I'll feel at home. I need some alone time, with you running this place and Danny in the stables I can leave this for a while, not having to worry. John has given me some design drawings and tells me Kev is one hell of a fabricator and shouldn't have a problem building what I want. You remember Kev? He's going to help build the house.'

Sean sounded stuck on the idea, so Ann didn't push it.

'We'll talk more towards the end of the week. If you get a moment, look into setting up the gym as a charity, do some figures, see what we'll need, tomorrow I'm over at the bank, it's time I restructured the loans and overdrafts, they've milked this place long enough. Nash is accompanying me. And you're to tell me if things get too much for you?'

'I will, I look forward to it, it will be good, but could we make it a general gym for girls as well, and there will be room in the old shop for a café, people can talk, eat and mix?' she asked.

'Brilliant idea.' Sean loved the way she answered, it showed her ownership of the project. 'Regards my John, and the fourteen thousand, John has been wanting to go self-employed, so why don't we put a little more in, and take over the back of the workshop?'

'Yeh, sounds good to me, we'll buy the coffins off of John, he won't want them, nor will we, and the poor buggers who do need them, they'll never know about it.' He poured more coffee.

'I'm off back down to Cardboard City, see if I can catch up with someone called Molly Malone.'

'Molly! Is she still alive?'

'Apparently, why do you know her?' he asked, not expecting she would have known Molly.

'She used to be a West End singer, very good in her day. Then she suffered some sort of breakdown, ended up in the funny farm, the one on Claxton Hill. And in the '70s the doctors were frying people's brains, with electricity straight to the head. Then she disappeared for years.'

Sean was brought from his deep thought. 'Tell you what, Ann, it really does make you look a little deeper into the homeless people. Anyone could virtually overnight, find themselves there, especially ex-forces.'

'She knew Mary as well, did Molly, really well in fact, for a good few years, before her breakdown that is. Mary tried to help, but Molly left the area after she got out the big round house. She never talked about what happened to her in that dreadful place. Man can be so cruel at times. I know it's supposed to be for the greater good, but I don't understand how anything that hurts or kills even one single person intentionally, how can that be the "greater good"?'

Twenty past ten, Sean tap-danced down the six concrete steps; his eyes caught the image in front of him. Now he really knew why this place was named Cardboard City.

Nearly a couple of hours had passed since his visit earlier this evening. The camp had grown to well over a hundred and sixty people, all gathered around a couple of dozen or more 45-gallon drums. These basic heat sources shared the warmth through hammer head holes smashed in the sides; the patina was toasted, red rust, glowing in the dark.

'SUPPER! SUPPER! - plenty for all.' Was heard in a slurred Irish accent.

Doyle followed the audience walking, turning up the collar on the *Colombo* Mac, he watched the grey-haired woman hand out multiple items of food. What Ann had said about her being an entertainer, well she still was, and playing to a packed-out crowd was still part of her life. The food and rhymes stopped coming. Her audience had been fed and began to disperse, joyful about receiving the simplest of gifts and human banter.

'Mrs Malone?'

'Sorry, lad, I haven't anything left to give you, it's always a rush. First come first served, I'm afraid, come a bit earlier tomorrow,' answered Molly, automatically.

'I'm not here to ask for any food,' replied Sean, with a sudden complex about his attire.

'I would like to ask you some questions, Mrs Malone, if you could spare the time, that is?'

'Questions, sounds very interesting, but what could you possibly want to ask me, a lonely old woman?' Molly was no longer facing him.

'Henry,' he simply said, loud and clear.

'I'm sorry, I don't know anyone who goes by the name of Henry. It's past my bedtime, so if you have no objection, I'll bid you a good night, lad and leave you pondering.' The old woman turned her back and began entering a cross between a tepee and a bonfire.

'My name is Sean Doyle, Molly.' Sean spoke clearly, aiming his surname at her inquisitive side. It didn't work. She was nearly in the large hedgehog house.

'You turned your back once on Mary, you going to do the same to me?' He knew that what he had just said was unfair, a low blow even, but he had a bit between his teeth, and he wasn't giving it up.

'That was low, was it not, Mr Doyle?'

'Yes, it was, I apologise, I needed to get your attention.' Sean noticed she sounded different, no longer drunk, no jovial tone in her voice. She came closer and he realised what the cute Salvation Army girl meant: the stench was pretty potent.

'How is Mary these days, well I trust?' She looked Sean up and down.

'She ... passed ... a couple of months ago.'

'I am sorry to hear that, genuinely, we were close once, very close, in fact like sisters we were, well we couldn't be separated. But it was many years ago, well before she was able to get you back.' Molly paused for a moment. 'I can see her in you, especially the eyes. Powerful and determined.' Sean heard the words and the sincerity behind them; he didn't have the heart to say he wasn't related.

'Are you a reporter?' asked Molly.

'Everybody keeps asking me that. No, just looking into something for a friend.'

'Maybe because you are after information, wearing a 20-year-old rain Mac, and from the jungle drums, I hear someone was giving away five-pound notes, that you, lad?' She looked semi-impressed; it was mirrored by Sean. He liked her, she had gumption, said it as it was, no butter on the bread.

'You have her cheeky smile as well. If you are going to grill me, lad, then the least you could do is treat me to a meal.' Her eyebrows raised, and she waited for an answer.

Sean consumed yet another breath of B.O. Molly excused herself, re-entering her nomadic home, reappearing in only a few minutes, hair tied back, no big overcoat. She was now wearing a light-blue sweatshirt, two sizes two big, a baseball cap advertising Coca-Cola and a pair of blue dazzling glasses, again two sizes too big. The stench had substantially lessened; he guessed the big coat was the true source of the smell. Sean took in the new Molly.

'I can be a lady when I want.' She laughed, noticing his stare. 'So, you shouting for dinner then?' Her eyebrows went up again.

'Do you have a preference where to eat? I haven't been

around here for a good while. And my palate is varied,' sarcastically answered Sean.

'You're Mary's son alright. She'd have answered the same way.' Her eyebrows reached a new height. 'The Bistro on the High Street, they do a mean pie and chips, with a scrumptious gravy. Good home cooked food, none of your warmed-up muck you're served at these chains.'

Fifteen minutes, at a slow pace, it took the odd couple to arrive at their place of choice, a pace which Sean found hard to maintain, aside from the dodgy hip. Molly was clearly a regular, a part of the crowd at The Bistro, or Ken's, as most called it, including the second sign above the door. The joint was full when they walked through the doors. A dark-haired waiter approached and showed the couple to a table, then waited on them. Sean felt sorry for the young lad, the way Molly was suggesting. The meal was eaten in virtual silence, which suited Doyle, as she was right about the meat pie and gravy. Evening rush over, only three tables were now occupied. Approaching theirs, was a man.

'Mo, was the pie to your standard?' asked the owner/cook/cleaner/delivery driver. The only job he didn't carry out was waiter; not because he couldn't, but because he would talk and talk.

'Divine as ever, Ken dear, your pastry is second to no one's. Larry would be proud, and how is he?' She blew him a well exaggerated kiss.

'My Larry's still with me, I tell myself anyway. I was just saying to him the other day, when you left the stage, Molly, something in both of us died. One of the last great performers you are, you had the ability to hold the audience in the palm of your hand and play with them.' The camp owner appeared genuinely upset as he looked at the hundreds of framed signed photos hanging all over the walls.

'You haven't changed a bit, my dear.' He was staring at one photo in particular, a younger version of him and Molly and another guy much older. Two more customers entered the establishment.

'I will love and leave you both now.' He spoke flamboyantly to Molly and then twirled on the spot, as if a switch had been pulled and he was back in character. 'How are you, my dears? Very hungry, I do hope. Come this way, please, come this way. I have a table with your names on it.' And he was gone. With the young couple following.

'Never mind me being theatrical, he hasn't lost any of his talent as he?' she jested whilst tidying the table, to the level of being autistic. 'But I do feel for him. Larry, his partner, passed away two years ago last week, to be accurate. He just can't accept it, such a shame, a wonderful man.' She swapped the salt and pepper pots around twice more. Sean's eyes watched, as she flicked a couple of bits off the table on to the floor.

'You seem to be a regular here, Molly. When was you last on the stage?' asked Sean, who noticed Ken pointing to the pictures on the wall and then over to Molly, showing the couple that had just arrived. They looked over as well, the female waving with half a hand.

'I made an appearance or two, twenty years plus ago. Ken is one of those people who are permanently fixed within an era and sadly stays there, emotionally.

Right, lad, ask your questions, but bear in mind my memory isn't what it used to be.' Her arms folded, she looked forward as if ready to take part in a quiz. Sean noticed the two scars on either side of her head, right where the temples are. Burn marks. He thought of what Ann had told him earlier, but this topic wasn't going to be on the list of questions.

'First one, an observation really, you appear to have sobered up very quickly.' He tried not to re-look at the scars. She had attempted to cover them with foundation, but the skin itself was crinkled.

'You're referring to my performance earlier at supper time. One does what one must to get by, lad, next question.' Her forearms fell on the table, hands crossed; she never removed her stare from Sean.

'When was the last time you saw Henry?' He threw a curve ball.

'Is that Lisa?' came from Molly. She got up and passed Ken at speed, asking if she could use the back door.

'Yes, of course, Molly darling, you know where it is.' She didn't stop. The question had been purely a courtesy. She was gone. Sean, still sitting, turned around.

'Hello, Mr Doyle, nice to see you again. I didn't know you hung out around here.'

'Hi.' Sean looked up at the sweet Salvation Army girl and the boy band look-a-like on her arm.

'This is Luke.' She introduced the young man with a hair style that was related to a peacock.

'Are you eating with us tonight, Lisa?' asked Ken.

'No, I'm just showing my cousin around,' she replied. Sean felt stupid but he was relieved when she had said the word "cousin".

'Any of the crowd been in for a meal today? Do I owe you any money, Mr Lucas?' asked Lisa, clumsily fishing in her shoulder bag.

'Only Green Mile over there, he's been here since ten-ish, he was late today.' Ken glanced over his shoulder. 'He's had his usual half dozen coffees, and I gave him some pie and mash. Oh, Helen and Clare came in for sandwiches.'

'I'll pay you for his tea and the ladies' sandwiches, Mr Lucas. How much will that be?' asked Lisa, purse in her hand.

'No you will not, young lady, put that purse away. To be honest, I like having him here, he's like a resident doorman. And I often talk to him when the place is not so full, although he never answers, well not with words per se. And if I can't give a couple of sandwiches away, then what's the world coming to?' replied Ken, then turned his attention and shouted, 'Ready for another cuppa, GM?' As if he was underlining what was just said.

Sean glanced at the man and agreed. Green Mile was the right name for him, a big lad he was. 'Did you meet our Molly, Mr Doyle?' enquired Lisa.

'Ye ...' Ken cut in and stared at Sean with meaning. Sean caught on very quickly.

'But only for a moment, she felt tired and I was to come back another time when she was more hospitable.' Sean had just lied, he didn't know why, but it felt right somehow. Lisa may look like butter wouldn't melt in her mouth, but he knew better than most that looks mean nothing. Not judging a book and all that, was a stance he adhered to at least until he was sure. And apart from Mary and Tony, he'd never really been sure, he had been close with his SAS comrades, but this was different.

'I wish you well with her, and don't worry about her foul language, she means no harm, salt of the earth she is that one. Right, we're off, will see you all sooooon.' And a smile took over Lisa's face. Sean saw the silver and gold again.

'Lisa.' He got up and made his way to her as she was about to leave.

'Yes, Mr Doyle.' His height made her raise her head.

'Could I meet up with you sometime, take you for a drink?'

'To talk about the homeless people, you mean?' the sweet girl enquired.

'Er, yes, talk about the homeless, that's it, you seem to have a lot of knowledge of their world.'

'Ring me tomorrow, make it late though, after lunch. I'll be sleeping in you see, we will be out and about late tonight.' She took hold of his big hand and wrote her mobile number on his wrist. She left the place and Sean returned to the bar.

'What was all that about... not saying Molly was here?'

'You sweet on Lisa then?' came back.

'Don't be dodging the question,' countered Sean.

'Not fully sure myself, but Molly doesn't want Lisa to know about her alter-ego, and well, only gossip mind, but I have heard some folk say Lisa may not be as sweet as y..., well, you get the gist.' Ken was in his element with a little gossip on his lips, he enjoyed sharing it too, but a secret he could keep if someone special asked him to.

'Why? She seems a great girl, doing all the charity stuff,' commented Sean.

'She is, unlike her twin sister, the pair are identical in looks but Alishia is motivated by greed, a different kettle of fish altogether, bit of a bitch. Lisa doesn't have that ability to see harm in people, like I said a sweet girl, but that will be her downfall. But no one has ever seen the pair together and they didn't grow up around here, from Manchester, I think.' Ken, for some reason, wanted to change the subject, and quickly, he wasn't comfortably any longer.

'Will Molly be back tonight, would like to chat some more?'

'No, we won't see her again this evening. Do you want another drink, on the house, naturally?'

'May as well, a lager, cheers, Ken,' said Sean, as he looked again at Green Mile.

'What's his story? The big lad.' he asked, taking the beer.

'Well to be perfectly honest, no one really knows. He is in his 30s, we think, but black doesn't crack, dear, so he may be older.' Ken looked to Green Mile then continued. 'I've known him at least a year, not had more than a broken please and thank you from him. I've tried to give him a job here as a pot washer. Told him he could live in the rooms outside. I know it's not The Ritz but much better than the streets, I'd have thought. I furnished it for him, showed it to him. All he did was look around, nod his head and grin at me.' Ken pushed a glass under the optic, and came back around to Sean. 'But every night I lock up at eleven, he just smiles and leaves. I open up at nine in the morning, he's there outside, waiting. Smiling again, he walks in, sits there, the only time he moves is to use the little boys' room. Or if I have a delivery then he helps bring it in, shows me his teeth and passes me his cup for a refill. I guess it's his way of paying.' Ken emptied the glass and re-visited the optic. 'One thing that does puzzle me, he has a lot of old hacking wounds on his wrists and forearms and what looks like some sort of cattle branding on his neck, going all the way up to his ear. Looks horrific, whatever caused them had to be brutal. I shudder at the thought of it.' Ken had a cup of hot tea in his hand.

'Is that his refill?' asked Sean, with his hand out.

'Yes, I'm just about to take it over. Why?'

'Do you mind if I?' Sean took the cup off Ken and set off towards Green Mile's table. Sitting down opposite the big man, he slid the drink over, a smile and a broken English

"Tank ya" came back. Sean offered his hand out as a friendship gesture. It was received, yet Sean couldn't remember the last time his hand had been dwarfed by another. They were held there a few seconds before the shake took place.

Sean looked at the scars on man's wrists. 'Nice to have met you,' he said slowly with miming lips, subconsciously believing going slow would maybe help.

'Tank ya.' Green Mile responded again and passed the empty cup over.

Sean placed the mug on the bar, saying nothing. He then walked outside, scrolling through his contacts list.

'Tanya Howlet speaking.'

'I need a favour.'

'Hello to you as well, Sean, and yes, I am well, thank you for asking. And you have changed your number, why?' she sarcastically responded. She was pleased to be speaking to him, but she wasn't going to admit it, not out right.

'Cut the crap, Tanya, you owe me, remember? Any time - any place?'

'You are so articulate, Sean Doyle, but bef...'

'You can speak Swahili, can't you?'

'Some, yes, why do you ask that?' Genuinely perplexed, she forgot about being cut off and Sean's lack of words.

He quickly gave an explanation regards the man called Green Mile and all the scars on his wrists, arms, and the branding on his neck and cheek.

'Whereabouts are you? I will be right over.' She was intrigued.

The address was given verbally; she arrived half an hour later. 'Thanks for coming, Tan, hope I haven't spoilt your night,' said Sean.

'Who's the well-dressed lady?' asked Ken, as Tanya

walked straight to the table where Green Mile was drinking his tea. And smart she was, Doyle had caught her leaving the US embassy.

She didn't waste any time. 'Hello, ni jinsi gani?' greeted Tanya.

The big man looked at her, his eyes open wide. 'Mimi ni mzuri,' he happily replied.

'Inaweza I kujiunga nawe,' she said next.

'Ndiyo yesu pesa,' he replied.

'Asante.' She nodded and sat down opposite him.

'Jina lako nani?' asked Tanya.

'Shyaka.' A smile was exchanged.

'WHAT'S HAPPENING?' questioned an astonished Ken, emotional tears forming in his eyes.

'He speaks Swahili, they're having a conversation,' answered Doyle. Ken turned to him and stared; his mouth open. Sean continued. 'From Rwanda, he has scars that I took a guess at being caused in the genocide in '94, then with what you estimated his age to be, two and two together, he speaks Swahili, simple?' replied Sean, drinking his beer casually leaning backwards elbows on the bar, boot backwards on the foot bar.

Ken looked back to the table then back to Sean. 'Then you just produced a woman who happens to speak fluent, swaarlee, whatever it's called. Who are you? Where you from? Am I asleep?' As Ken was talking, or questioning Doyle, Tanya and Shyaka came over to join them.

Tanya spoke first. 'Shyaka would like to say something to you if that's okay.'

'He ... ye ... good, course.' Ken poured himself a shot, a large one, he didn't expect any of this today.

'Asante kwa wema wako wote,' said Shyaka.

'Thank you very much for all the kindness you have

shown me every day. I enjoy visiting your place,' translated Tanya.

'Ninafuri sana kwa kuniingiza kwangu kukaa hapa ninafurahia mahali hapa kama mimi ni chef kutoka kijiji change.'

'I am very grateful for you allowing me to sit and rest here in your wonderful establishment. I enjoy this place as I am a chef also. Back in my country I cook for the rich people in Byumba,' advised Tanya.

'Please tell him he's ... s... so welcome, in in fact - he's more than welcome. I have offered him a job and a room here ... here, several times, its ready for him now in the back - look - come - look. I like him, he can stay. You can sense good ... people can't you ... the offer is still open. Tell him - tell him now. Tell him now,' Ken had a spout of the verbal shits caused by all the excitement of being able to communicate with this man, after all this time. His words came flying out, no brain brake engaged. The two men embraced. Ken was a big cockney but in the bear hug of Green Mile, "Shyaka", Ken was like a child. Tanya felt warm inside, watching a strange friendship flourish. It was already there, but it began to blossom in front of her eyes.

'Thanks, Sean for calling me this has been a joy, really glad to be a part of it.' She turned. Doyle was gone, nowhere to be seen, half a pint left in the glass. The bistro's door had already closed.

Tanya stayed and translated for the men for a further few hours and arranged to have a translator contact them in the morning, with a view to helping them learn to communicate, and also discover why Shyaka had come to this country. Green Mile took up the offer of employment and of the room. He stayed there that night.

Sean had been spot-on with his hunch: the scars had

been cut into him in 1994 and Shyaka no longer had family or friends in his own country. In fear for his life, he had made his way to the UK to seek asylum. As Tanya began to say her goodbyes to her two new friends, Shyaka opened his carrier bag and gave her an old tatty folder. About to open it, Green Mile placed his massive digits on the torn cover. 'Baadae,' he said. Tanya nodded and left the bistro, sending a message to Sean's mobile.

It took her half an hour to get back to her apartment, door closed, keys in the glass bowl, tatty folder dropped on the desk, answer machine pressed. She listened to several messages and deleted all but one. The hour was late, she curled up on the sofa, legs tucked in, glass in one hand, the other about to open the old folder. Page two had her in tears, halfway down she had to re-read the powerful words that she knew were the truth, even though here in the West we would have trouble believing. She re-read slowly as she sipped the wine, with the hope, it would numb the words she was digesting.

'Nilianguka, mikono yangu na miguu ilikuwa ikiteleza kwenye mashimo yenye mvua, joto la joto, nikawa na hofu ya mita nilikuwa nimefanya kazi na mashimo bado yalibaki, nilikosa usingizi, harufu ikaniamsha masaa kadhaa baadaye kama jua la joto, alinionyesha nimelala kati ya maelfu ya watu waliokatwa vipande vipande. Unata damu yao huboa asili yao ya asili na ya mwanadamu ilinifanya nikashindwa, h...' After reading the rest of the file, and a second glass of white was required, she emailed a journalist friend and addressed the folder to him. Four days later, what Tanya had read was shared with a few million people.

The Guardian

Johnathon Bishop

Memories, Old Memories

We, today and rightly so, try hard to remember the fallen. 'Lest we forget' is what we all say once a year in November on Remembrance Day. This is where the horrific acts committed on others by the Nazi party are brought forth. However, for the remaining 364 days, our busy lives overtake the fundamentals of our mind. Four days ago, I received an email from a good friend of mine. There was no name or reference on the email, which was unusual for them, only a few words written before the attachment. Here is what she wrote, talk about a grab ... *Please read, Johnathon. I cried before the end of page two.* Reading those honest words, what journalist would not open the attachment.

The old file had been carefully translated, painfully every word was twisted into a second language with the intent of losing no emotion.

'I was 12 years old, walking home from school on a Wednesday afternoon, trying hard not to dirty my school clothes, as I didn't want to give my mama any extra labour. My younger brother and his friend passed me at speed.

Each taking turns at whipping the tyre with a stick, then chasing it in the hot sun.

People came out from their homes. The wheel fell over when the whipping ceased.

Everyone looked behind me to the dust cloud. Time itself appeared to stand still, the heat from the sun became hotter, or that's how it felt. Nothing but the cloud of dust was there, all breathed slow, then appearing out from the dry whirlwind were four open top lorries. Out the cloud they came and drove into our village. I ran to grab my little brother. We were hit by things blood ran from us. We kept running and hid inside one of the offal barrels to the side of the butchers.

The screaming started and didn't stop for hours and hours. The darkness had arrived before the cries had completely ended. The trucks had left, and it was another hour before I dared to escape the tiny tin shelter, we were hidden in. It was so dark now I couldn't see. I put my four-year-old brother onto my back. My arms and legs slid into the hollows as I crawled along, they were wet and warm and deeper than my elbows. It was so hard to move, I struggled to travel a few meters. And still my hands slipped into the many hollows. I collapsed and fell asleep – so, so tired. The sweet sickly scent awoke me, the warm sun showed me the full horror of the previous day. I was on the road yet I couldn't see it, because of the hundreds of bodies that had been macheted into pieces, there was so much blood I didn't know I was cut. The crevices and wounds were the deep hollows, were my hands and sunk. No longer wet, the blood had baked. No one was left to see or hear my cry's, not even my younger brother, I saw my mother strung up, she was hanging upside down from the telegraph pole, and yet I still could not produce any tears. A Western journalist called Tom encouraged me to come off the road. He dressed my wounds and smuggled me out of the village. To this day I still haven't shed a tear. I remember the day the lorries came, but I don't believe it was true, or I don't wish it to be.

The page was titled 'My Genocide'

Not ashamed to admit it, I also cried before the end of the second page. These dark memories will be published in full later this month with the permission of the author.

'Lest we forget.' Should this not be applied to the world not just us? Why, when there is a disaster or war, does the news report the death count then report which country they were nationals of? We are all one, or am I wrong? People are so busy, they live their lives today, which is good, but the majority leave a footprint which supersedes their needs. Just look at the individual persons aggression in some parts of the world, an anger to other people with a different coloured skin, or different colour hair. Hatred to people that demonstrate a different sexuality, even from some of the planets so called biggest religions. They way we treat females. People that are overweight, not attractive, it seems any difference, is all it takes to cause attacks. When will we change?

Jonathon Bishop
Investigative Journalist
The Guardian newspaper

13

FRANKENSTEIN

The cleaner polished for the sake of polishing. Every three hours she buffed the high gloss walls, floor and ceiling. The corridor was a gallery displaying eleven locked doors, five on each side and a slightly wider one at the end; none of these had keys, swipe card entry only. The cleaner held the entrance door open for the doctor.

'Thank you, Susan. You're doing a great job.'

He walked to number ten and swiped the shiny card in front of the small box.

'Good morning, Louisa, how are we today?' he asked, so condescending.

'Aw, aw, aw.' She couldn't speak back because of the gag. Her head was going side to side, eyes popping.

'If I remove it, will you be civil for me, Louisa?' asked the supercilious doctor, bending over her bed, his face only inches from hers, his breath burning the inside of her nostrils.

She nodded to acknowledge his request. He stood away. 'Remove the mask, nurse,' he instructed.

'A ... rrrr, she bit me, the bitch, it's bleeding!' hissed the nurse, holding her finger.

'What, oh what, are we to do with you my dear Louisa, what are we to do with you?' said the doctor as the door opened behind him.

'Leave the mask in place and prepare the patient please, nurse,' instructed the doctor, turning to greet the two surgeons.

Louise tried to sit up as the nurse connected another drip.

Do you have it with you?' asked the doctor.

One of the surgeons held up a stainless-steel container, the size and shape of a regular tea flask. The nurse pulled on thick heavy-duty gloves, then relieved him of the container. She placed it on the side, put a pair of safety glasses and a face shield on, before she began to slowly unscrew the lid. After the hiss, came the cloud of dry ice. Lou's legs were opened, bent into shape then secured in the stirrups. The dark-skinned surgeon positioned the multi angled lamps. The doctor passed a very thin fibre-optic cable to the surgeon. This clinical snake was fed into Lou's vagina followed one by one, with microscopic tools fixed to cables.

'We ready?' asked the surgeon, looking at everyone in the room.

'Do not drop that, nurse,' warned the doctor as he watched her turn and pass over the genetic material, carried in a miss-shaped syringe. Three hours later, the sweat was wiped from the surgeon's brow for the last time.

'Has it been successful?' eagerly asked the doctor.

'Only time will tell, I'm afraid, but I do believe they have fused because there has been no crackling of the two DNA substances, which if the host was rejecting the implant, this would occur within minutes. I've seen it so many times, but the mix you created doctor, it does appear to be uncongealed, you did a good job, sir. You would be able to clearly see the lines spreading on the screen. The host's antibodies eat the new DNA. The outcome, literally does resemble pork crackling.' Both doctor and nurse looked automatically at the monitor. What they saw was the perfectly shaped human foetus. The only difference was a pulsating line of illuminated fluid moving slowly around the body of the brand-new life. The liquid was illuminating the veins and arteries; as it did so the medical couple were satisfied with their achievements.

The surgeon removed his gloves. 'I don't wish to appear callous, but what about our payment? We must be able to fly back to the states tonight. Our flight is at 2100 hrs from your Heathrow. Don't forget this is a new procedure and you aren't the only people wanting to have a designer baby,' added the white surgeon.

The doctor pointed with his arm; the black surgeon made his way to the table in the far corner of the room. Stopping, he clicked the two locks simultaneously. The lid popped, he tilted the case, the white surgeon nodded. 'Dollars, not sterling, very thoughtful of you, sir, and much appreciated too, do I have to count it?' he asked, shaking the hand of the doctor.

'You can by all means but I assure you that there isn't a dollar missing, one hundred thousand, like we agreed.' The handshake stopped no counting happened. The white surgeon winked at the young assistant.

Both surgeons then left, accompanied by two guards waiting outside the room. The young assistant patted her pocket.

'Will you call her now or wait until tonight is over?' asked the nurse.

'I'll wait, yes, I ... I'll ... wait yes, until the morning. And if all appears well with the embryo after an inspection, and the fusion takes hold fully, I can then implement the ageing process, then I'll call her. She really is a scary person, a real bitch, believe me. I don't want to disappoint her. I wouldn't like to guess at what she is capable of, and I know she has never put a timescale on this project, but when we last spoke she seemed edgy, and to date she has invested tens of thousands of pounds into my lab, which has advanced my research by at least a decade. I know I created that thing for her, but that was a couple of years back.' He looked at his young assistant. 'What's wrong?' he asked, noticing her pale skin.

'Sorry, doctor, I have already mixed the ageing solution in with the DNA injection,' said the young assistant.

'You did WHAT! Why? What were you thinking, stupid girl?' The doctor left the girl, going straight back to the monitor.

'That was the procedure with both the rats and the cats in the first stage trials.'

'Yes, I know, I am aware of that I designed the fucking trials, didn't I? But with the complexities of the human foetus, we could not risk a double infusion. I told you that, did I not. If this goes wrong, both you and me and her will be killed.' His hands flew up to his face.

'She will understand, she's a lady of standing,' pleaded the young assistant.

'You have no idea what she is like. I met her; I was terrified - she took ten years off my life. I was petrified when they kidnapped me, then flew me to the fucking Outer Hebrides. And I am aware of the advances we have made, but I still signed an agreement with the devil. I pray this child lives, or we won't! I'm not joking when I say she's a BITCH!' The doctor was physically shaking. Worked up to the point of tears, he stared hard at the monitor, his hands clasped together as he asked any god listening for help, then was forced to run to the sink where he vomited.

'The baby is doing just fine, look at it. The line is nearly complete, and there are no signs of this pork scratching, the American told you was the warning sign. And he complimented you on the formulation of the mixture. Let's not worry about her, come on we should go and celebrate,' reassured the older nurse. Leaning over to kiss the doctor, she waved at the young assistant to leave the room, not wanting her to receive any further wrath.

'Yes, yes, I agree, I'm becoming neurotic, I'm tired. You're right as usual, my sweet thing, we have reached a milestone here today. The field of human cloning has moved forward. If my fusion is even in part successful, I will go down in history.'

She wiped his eyes using both her thumbs and kissed the end of his nose. 'You taste all salty.' She rubbed his shoulder.

Four hours later, the doctor was sipping his fourth glass of pink champagne in one of the city's most exclusive restaurants. Nurse Fuller sat opposite him, slowly sliding her shoeless foot along the inside of his inner thigh. A very smart waiter approached the table, he coughed quietly then began to speak to the doctor. The nurse smiled wickedly as her toes massaged the doctor's penis. The waiter was well aware of the under-table hanky-panky taking place. He stood silent and offered the doctor a vintage looking telephone, resting on a silver tray.

'Thank you, Morris.' The waiter bowed and backed away

after leaving the tray on the table.

'Hello,' he answered.

'Doctor, you better come back here right away, something is happening to your patient, the foetus monitor has gone off. That fluid line appears to be leaking from some sort of a crack, which has appeared in the last few moments. I've never seen anything like it in any of the trials so far, not even in the orangutans.' The assistant was frantic.

'Call the crash team and keep her stable. Do not do anything with the child until I arrive. Do you understand?'

'Yes, doctor, I understand.' The assistant placed the receiver down and left the clinical room in a hurry. It took her ten minutes to leave the building; she had no intention of coming back.

'Call me a taxi,' instructed the doctor to the waiter.

'We have one outside now, sir, waiting for a different client; however, I'm sure they would not mind you taking it, not if it's for a medical emergency.'

'Thank you, Morris. Come on, Clare, I knew we shouldn't have left.' Her feet were fishing blindly for her shoes.

'What's occurred?' asked the nurse getting into the cab.

'The new homeless hostel in the docklands, and quickly,' directed the doctor.

'You're the boss. The Waterfront it is, sir.' The cab shot off.

'DOCTOR, AT LAST YOU'RE HERE!' shouted the tall skinny man, his blue shirt covered by the ultra-thin plastic apron.

The three of them rushed to the third floor.

'Bring me up to speed,' demanded the doctor as they entered the elevator.

Nurse Fuller took care of the buttons as the tall man started spieling.

'Everything was normal, all signs giving no clue as to what was about to begin. The patient began to fit five minutes before I called you. Then her breathing became so erratic, never seen anything like it, followed by her temperature spiking; at one point we recorded 43.2. We then implemented all the cooling down procedures, but this had no effect whatsoever, then we lost her, end of life happened literally a couple of minutes previous to your arrival, and she is at present on life support systems, with her body packed in ice. But clinically she's certainly dead.'

'The child, what about the child, you stupid man? I don't care about some beggar off the streets,' shouted the doctor.

'That's the weird thing, nothing has changed with the foetus, its stats have never altered, if anything it appears the child has grown, well it has for sure and quite a lot as well, you will see for yourselves. I don't have the words to articulate the growth spurt.'

The lift stopped. The smooth female computerised voice announced the floor they were on. The doors opened, they moved out together their shoulders bumping preventing egress. 'Get out of the way man?' The doctor ran down the corridor. 'Come on, get the door open,' he demanded. The skinny man had caught up and slid in the card.

'Prep her for theatre. And where has that silly little girl gone? She's dead when I see her!'

At the same time as the doctor questioned his staff, the "silly little girl" was driving over London Bridge to the safety of her brother. She stopped the car and pulled on the handbrake outside the Cock and Pussy. She ran to the solid door, banging it with her fists, shouting, 'TANK!'

The three and a half month old foetus was now the size

of a one-year-old infant. The new mammal was literally splitting its mother apart. Louisa had bled out from a rupture, ultimately causing her death. The bright tangerine-coloured illuminating fluid, had also infused with her blood, resulting in the record temperatures being recorded. The child was cut out of its warm womb and placed in a gel-filled incubator, which had hundreds of wires attached. The early human suspended in the dense fluid was on display, glowing like a rare Damien Hirst exhibit.

'The temperature! Look at the monitor, have you seen the figures?' Clare pointed to the side of the incubator where a digital reading of 48.6 was displayed.

'It must be faulty, surely, that can't be real, can it?' said the skinny man as he placed a manual probe to the glass.

'Look at the child, it's growing in front of our eyes. Look at the temperature, it's raised again now, it's at 49.7.' All three were mesmerised; they couldn't keep from staring. The foetus had also expanded again by half its current size, the gel being forced through the air holes cut into the lid. With the growth came development, its eyes opened, appearing to stare straight at the doctor.

He was both shocked and disturbed by the intense light blue eyes, it was as if this freak of nature, had diamonds for eyes. He saw Lady De Pen Court looking back at him. He lost it, there and then - falling to the floor, jabbering like a burnt-out theoretical physicist.

'Are you alright?' asked Clare as she witnessed the doctor wetting himself. He remained oblivious to the fact urine was leaking out from his trousers. Her response was to drag him up, then she slapped him hard across the face. It worked in a fashion. 'We have to save the child. If it dies, we'll be killed and probably all who are involved the full clinic.' The doctor stared at Clare as she took charge. He was frightened. She started disconnecting some wires from the glass incubator and from the foetus. 'Don't just stand there, do something.'

'I'll go fetch a larger incubator.' The skinny man exited the room. 'Out the way!' he shouted at the cleaner buffing the floor, he managed to stay on his feet as he tripped over the polishing machine. The cleaner remained with her back on the wall listening to the loud voices coming from the only room where she didn't clean.

'Clear the room of the mother's body, and will someone take care of this blood,' instructed the doc, reaching for the phone fixed to the wall. All in the room were sliding their feet so as not to slip. The phone was answered, just as the cleaner looked in the room, on the far side she saw what was once sweet Louisa, now there was a female's body split in two from the anus to the breast, its insides were now a mess on the floor. She fainted; the doctor spoke into the phone. 'Lock down the building, no one in or out, get me the security manager. Find me that new assistant, do you understand? She has sabotaged this child! I want to know why she would do this? She has injected more growth serum. Why?' shouted the doctor as he spun round.

'My God look, look at the cra...,' said the nurse.

'We need to get the thing out of there now and an external fan set up.' The doctor couldn't move. He watched as this man-made bag of DNA enlarged by one millimetre per second, and its cranium was growing at three times that rate. 'It looks like an alien,' said the security manager, entering the room. His left arm flew up, his right grabbing the nurse's shoulder to prevent his fall. She grabbed hold of him, 'Do you not see all the blood? There's enough of it.' Her eyes went to the floor.

Across town the solid door opened, Stella threw her arms around Tank.

'What up sis?'

In her hand she held a brown holdall that contained ten thousand dollars and a used syringe. Stella didn't answer she sobbed. Tank looked around he saw nothing, the door was closed.

A private American plane landed at Heathrow airport. The second the engines were cut, the aircraft was surrounded by police vehicles and airport security, all of them armed. Half the police team, with the security, were setting up a cordon around the jet, the other half marching at speed toward the aircraft, crouching slightly in double file, the front two held their weapons high, each officer behind had their hand on the the the one in front, weapons down by their sides, slung on their shoulders, hands on the grips, ready to flip up. On board the Boeing, the all-American crew became anxious, frightened, unaware of the reason for what was occurring outside the tiny windows. They had made this same stopover dozens of times before, and never had there been a greeting like todays.

'OPEN THE DOORS AND VACATE THE AIRCRAFT - SLOWLY! HANDS ABOVE YOUR HEAD, FINGERS INTERLOCKED!' instructed the police inspector, his volume aided by the use of a megaphone.

All the aircraft staff were soon standing at the base of the steps. 'Get down, get down, on your knees, keep your hands on your heads,' shouted the officers, approaching the staff coming down the steps, the officers in hard-targeting mode with nine-millimetre machine guns all held high and pressed into their shoulders, at least a dozen red laser dots rapidly changing targets. Two officers approached the staff individually and laid them down face first. The inspector accompanied by an escort walked up the steps and entered the Boeing as if nothing unusual was happening below him.

'We are here to search the air conditioning system. We believe you are carrying some form of contraband,' informed the inspector, as he handed over a sheet of paper.

'Carry on, sir, she's all yours, let me know if I can be of any assistance,' replied the pilot in a calm tone. As he finished speaking, several men had arrived at the top of the steps.

'In, you go, lads, record every section you touch,' instructed the police commander. Six men and a Golden Labrador walked by him, all the men wearing police coveralls, carrying tool bags and wearing body cameras. 'Remain in your seat, please, captain, or you will have to join your crew on the tarmac.'

The pilot looked down from the doorway. He took a deep breath, seeing his people lying on their bellies, legs and hands crossed and tied behind their backs. All seven of his colleagues looked in discomfort.

'As you say, inspector.' He began to retreat. 'Do you really have to treat my crew like terrorists?'

Before the inspector had the chance to reply. 'It's clean, sir, nothing suspicious located,' notified the commander of the workers.

'Okay, sergeant, and thank you for your assistance. Gather your men and vacate the plane. I will still require the formalities completing and the twenty minutes camera footage downloading. And emailed over, if nothing else it will be good for training.'

'Yes, sir, of course, before we sign off.' The sergeant spoke into the radio. 'Exit the bald eagle.' Was the signal to end the operation.

'Thank you for your co-operation, sir,' said the inspector as he offered out his hand to the pilot. Just as the pair were shaking, a man appeared from the rear of the plane.

'What are you still doing aboard?' asked the inspector.

'Sorry, sir, call of nature,' replied the officer, as he scurried up to the two leaders.

'Join your squad, officer.' The man passed the inspector; the pilot stared at him. The man winked as he left.

'Don't worry, inspector, I understand that you are only doing your job, security is after all, in all our interests. Can I call my crew back aboard, we have jobs to complete before we take off again?' The pilot once again looking down at the tarmac.

'Yes, yes, of course you may. I will leave you alone to complete your work. Thanks again for understanding, and unfortunately protocol requires that we apprehend potential threats in that manner. I just showed you a courtesy, due to your rank.' The inspector placed on, and adjusted his flat hat, a nod was given before descending down the steps. His thoughts had turned to the tip-off he'd received, which had brought them to this situation.

'Let the crew go, sergeant, and be gentle,' shouted the inspector, with some feelings of guilt. The runway was dark yet illuminated in parts with a number of different forms of lighting: blue beacons, orange work lights and tall flood lights. He reached for his mobile phone, as he walked away to be alone.

'Sir, nothing was discovered. It must have been a false

lead. My men searched the aircraft thoroughly, especially the air con system, just as you suggested. I will forward you a copy of my report in the morning.' The inspector waited for a reply.

'It looks that way, Stewart, and I do apologise for wasting your time. I am aware of how busy you are,' said Shoebridge.

Not a waste of time, sir, it was a good opportunity for us to test out our new systems related to situations like this one, rehearsing is good practice and installs movement. But a call to duty really tests the team, for that it was good.'

'Excellent, glad then that I have been of some service. Goodnight, inspector, and thank you again for your rapid response. I was very impressed, and certain ears will hear of this, rest assured.'

'Goodnight to you, sir.' The phones both went cold, but Shoebridge's was instantly hot again.

'It has been completed, sir,' said the anonymous voice. Shoebridge didn't reply. He switched off the phone. Sat back in his office chair, he dialled another number.

'Load up the cargo when you're ready.' He turned his phone off again, then he immediately dialled another number.

'It has been arranged, and make sure to remember we chose these particular sixteen items, not just any sixteen. Ensure that you give them the sickness tablets with their meals, well before the landing is due.' Shoebridge again promptly ended the call. Still in the chair, there was a knock on the door. 'Come in,' he ordered.

'Your afternoon tea and refreshments, sir.'

'Just leave them on the table, and then close the door on your way out.' He didn't even look at the tray bearer.

Several miles downriver from the Parliament building, on the opposite side of the Thames, the foyer of the

Waterfront homeless centre had become packed with excited people. The tall man dressed in blue put down the telephone receiver and began calling names off the clip board. 'Sally Body, Alex Chum, John Cassy, Louisa Long. With the mention of Louisa, the female stood next to him whispered. 'She won't be on the trip. She has left us.' She stood back.

'Charlie! I guess it's your lucky day, we need a sub, are you in or out?' The young man started hugging his friend. 'I'm going, I'm going, yes, I'll come.' The excitement was clear to all. He continued the list of names.

'Right, that's it, all of you who has had their names called can you make your way to the white coach outside.' The man quickly took a step back, anticipating the rush. 'And remember, people, NO alcohol, NO smoking and definitely NO drugs, am I heard and understood?' added the female attendant. The stampede began. Within an hour and a half, the homeless were off the coach and climbing the same steps the police had stormed earlier that same day. 'Okay, okay, I know everyone is excited, but please, we have to board slowly and with some degree of order,' said the captain.

'Get us a drink,' shouted one of the passengers.

'That's enough, any more noise and the plane will be emptied.' The female flight attendant was only small, but she carried the order off with enforcement.

Everyone was now seated; the volume of the conversations became acceptable. The hostess began her in-flight safety routine as the mega-tonne flying machine began to move. Screams came from passengers, some from genuine terror, others from all the excitement they felt. And who could blame them as the luxurious 747 finished taxiing and become a ballistic missile, shooting down the runway at a speed of around 200 miles an hour. Minutes later the plane was cruising at 40,000 feet, the air was thin, ensuring the Boeing jet had reached its optimum height for its fuel consumption. Levelling off, it maintained cruising without any complications. The people on board had relaxed; all the TVs were playing films. The male and female hostesses had been busy preparing food trollies.

'Your meal, sir, chicken served with a salad, and if my memory serves me well, I have you down to take altitude sickness capsules.' She offered him a small glass of water and a yellow and red capsule held in a thin paper cup.

'Your dinner will follow shortly, sir.' She moved off, scratching a thin red line through the man's name. He was number thirteen on her list, only three left to dispense.

DING was heard loud and clear. 'This is your captain speaking. I would like to on behalf of the crew and myself, welcome you all onboard this beautiful plane. We are currently cruising around the 40,000 feet mark. No problems are foreseen, so please enjoy the meals being served and relax for the next few hours. There are plenty of options for on-board entertainment. Enjoy, and feel free to call for assistance if you are unable to enjoy these facilities, we're here to assist you. Alcohol is available and it is free of charge, but I do ask you to be sensible with the amount you consume. We do have a no tolerance approach during the flight. I am sure you have all seen our current flight marshal sitting in aisle 32. Say hi, Yumi,' said the captain. Everyone looked behind. A male the size of George Foreman raised his arm.

14

THIRD TRIMESTER

'Miss Howlett, sorry to call out of the blue, but another body has been found in the early hours of this morning, and again by the river. The same place as the last, at Hangman's Wharf. This one is female who had recently given birth or possibly miscarried late in her third trimester and a real mess was her pelvic region. She has also been decapitated and had her hands removed. Making this the same MO, we guess, as the last. The difference in this case she had, had all her blood drained somehow.' A breath was taken. 'The coroner the took time to describe in detail how the female had literally been split in two, from the top of the rib cage - this was broken front and rear.' There was another pause while the page was turned over. He continued, 'As if the baby was full-term, yet every biological sign suggested a term of no more than two months gestation. The victim was also chained, just like Henry,' read the officer.

'Excuse my bluntness, but how is it connected to us? Is it just purely the location and the mutilation? And who informed you I may be interested?' asked Tanya with her sergeant's voice.

'I apologise, sergeant, I should have said, I was working with Cathy before she took extended leave, I'm unable to contact her, so I had your name from the report. The location, yes, and she also has a tramp stamp on her lower back, the name "HENRY". Written in old English and encapsulated in the shape of a heart. The coroner estimates her age at mid - to late - 20s. Again, he made the point to say she was very under nourished; however, the last couple of weeks of life, she had been force fed or suddenly given a very fat rich diet, which produced a subcutaneous fat layer.' The officer's eyes remained on the page, skimming through to ensure he hadn't missed anything.

'Could I see the file, it has a lot of cross overs? I would like to put my eyes over it?'

'Already being couriered over to your office as we speak, ma'am.'

'Thank you, officer ...?'

'Simon, Simon Gummer, ma'am.'

'I will keep you posted after I have a chance to peruse the documents.' Tanya ended the call with Simon, then used her intercom to inform the front reception she was expecting an important package.

'It's just arrived, I've signed for it, Miss Howlett, shall I bring it up to your office?' asked the very familiar voice.

'No, I'll come down Debbie, an excuse to stretch my legs.' Before leaving the office, she made a call on the phone once more.

'Emma, its Tanya. I have some more information for you.'

'Regarding Henry?' she eagerly enquired.

'Are you aware he may have had a girlfriend?'

'I am ashamed to say I don't know, Tanya, but I hope he did. Really hope that he did, and that they were happy together, but sadly I can't shed any light on the question factually.' She felt sad, genuinely sad, but the thought of him in love warmed her, what was this girl like she imagined.

'I believe he may have been in a relationship, and it's possible that she was pregnant with Henry's child.'

'Wow! ... Tanya, ...this is all a bit too much for ... me to take in right now. Can I ask how you came about this information? And in your opinion, how worthy do you believe it to be?' Lady De Pen Court's tone was energised and emotional.

'A good source of mine has passed me a file, containing the coroner's report of a dead female w...'

'She's dead, ... dead? Gone and t... the baby? Tanya, the child, tell me my grandchild is alive, please?' gasped Emma, her hopes raised, a hairline between the answers.

'Sadly yes, she is dead. It appears that the child, we do not know of its whereabouts as of this moment, but the pathologist makes a note saying the estimated age of the child, when the mother was killed, would result in death outside of the womb, in hours.' A silence was next. Tanya allowed for this as it was grave news she was passing over.

'Could you possibly forward me this file or a copy of it, dear?'

'Yes of course, Emma, if you believe it will help. Please don't get your hopes up, this is not in the report; however, my source, who was present at the autopsy, told me that the coroner made a mental note of the amount of care and the time taken to remove the unborn child. And it was clear to her that whoever removed the unborn, had a good knowledge of surgery. Gruesome as it may sound, the mother had been sliced into two halves, but this gives some real substance to the child actually still being alive. The coroner made a second point. There is a real possibility that the perpetrators of this unthinkable act did so intending to keep the child alive, for whatever reason that was their purpose.' Tanya sat back.

'I will give the report to your Mr Doyle, and say a prayer for my grandchild. I do hope this is what occurred, I truly do.'

'Did he agree to work for you then?' Tanya sat forward.

'Yes, he did, not immediately, but it's just a case of finding a man's price, that's all, dear. They all have one, of that I can assure you,' replied Emma.

Tanya was taken aback slightly, as the Sean Doyle she knew was more concerned about the person who he worked for, rather than the number of zeroes on the cheque, if he had wanted to and it was money he sought, he could have earned tens of thousands in the private sector. Then she remembered that he was broke; beggars don't always have the luxury of choice, she assumed.

'Men are just like our children, Tanya. They're greedy, self-centred and easily manipulated, with the right sweets of course,' said Emma in a matter of fact way.

'I guess you're right,' answered Tanya quietly, as she said goodbye. Her impression of Emma had changed slightly, or was she misreading a well-known feminist's opinion, that could have been mistaken as the opinion of a bitch? The conversation ended.

'Are you okay, Miss Howlett? You do look pale,' asked the sweet, caring voice.

'I'm fine, maybe working a bit too much, but thank you for your concern. Would you please copy this file for me, and send the duplicate to the address on the back of this card, via a secure courier, please?'

'Of course, no problem, right away, Miss Howlett.' Debbie turned and set about her task in hand.

Tanya wasn't fine as she had just claimed, and she became paler before she collapsed on the stairs.

'Get a first-aider,' shouted Debbie, then she rushed to the curved stairwell, to Tanya's aid.

'Miss Howlett, Tanya, Miss Howlett, can you hear me?' Tanya tried to talk but she was so weak, nothing materialised. A couple of men arrived; they carried her to the long couch. 'Can someone get her some water, please!' As this request was shouted, Charles came in through the door.

'Brigadier, brigadier, over here, she's just collapsed, after going really pale just a minute ago. She said she felt tired then she collapsed onto the floor.' Debbie was worried trying to get her brief over amidst a panic: Tanya was her boss but also her fantasy partner.

'Ring for an ambulance. NOW!' ordered Charles, unbuttoning his jacket.

'Yes, sir.' Debbie quickly pressed the three nines.

'Has anyone got any anti-inflammatory tablets?' shouted the brigadier.

Three people rushed to him with ibuprofen and naproxen.

'Hold her head!' Charles started to feed the tablets into Tanya's mouth, washing them down with water. 'More water, fetch me more water.' Seven tablets in total were swallowed in less than the equivalent minutes, when one of the girls felt the need to say. 'You'll kill her, sir, stop it, please she'll overdose.' This didn't deter Charles in the slightest, he continued on and force fed a further six tablets before the paramedics arrived on scene. They entered through the office double doors, and it was clear where the incident was taking place: at least a dozen people were standing around the sofa. The ambulance is here, sir,' said one of the staff.

'My daughter is having a massive lupus attack.' Charles informed the medic.

～

'Mr Doyle, thank you for getting back to me so promptly.'

'Your message said urgent, Emma, what's up, what's changed?'

'I have just received some further information from a reliable source of mine. We may need to up our game. It appears I still have a grandchild alive, just not sure where.'

'What? Great news.' Doyle was surprised.

'I have it from a good source, Mr Doyle. If I didn't feel this was valuable, I wouldn't pass it on. I also have a possible address where Henry may have been staying for a few weeks, with the mother of my grandchild. I'll fax it all over to you and a copy of the police report. Shall I still send it to the funeral home?'

'Yes, I'll collect it from there later today,' confirmed Sean.

'Later? Please, Mr Doyle, will you give this matter some urgency? I can't explain with any number of words, the joy that a grandchild would bring into my life right now. If you find the grandchild alive and it is brought to me, you can have anything you desire, anything in my possession.'

'No need for the extra motivation, the possibility of a small kid out there alone is motivation enough. I'll get straight on it, fax over the material now.'

'Thank you, oh and I nearly forgot to ask, did you find the information in the envelope interesting?'

'Very, Emma, it appears that I am of Irish descent.'

'To-be-sure, to-be-sure. And there is more to come,'

laughed Emma. She had also dropped in a small amount of Sean's "price".

Doyle turned off his iPhone and continued with his workout for a few more moments. He wanted another half an hour, at least, but just couldn't shake the thought of a small child somewhere out there with no parents or protector. Sixty-six, and he dropped from the chin up bar. Sweating, he stretched and completed his warm down. A shower and he was out through the temporary door fixed to the container. He was only 130 feet from the office, but in his wisdom and quest for total independence, he'd had the yard fenced off, so a walk of several hundred metres was required.

'That's for me, Ann,' he said entering the office. Ann was next to the bulky machine which was regurgitating the information onto clean sheets.

'Who's sending you faxes, Sean?' Ann put together the 12 sheets of paper, and without a glance, she expertly stapled the corner then passed them over.

'Are you well? You look pale and a bit tired. Are you losing weight?' she asked, as a substitute mother.

'Thanks, and yes, I'm trying to get a bit fitter and want to shed a couple of pounds. It's been hard to be fully mobile, but now the hip's feeling better I'm getting stuck in.' He gave the sheets a glance as he grabbed them.

'Pass me an envelope, Ann.'

Nothing.

'Pass me an envelo.....'

Ann's head dipped to one side. Still nothing.

The penny dropped. 'Please,' asked Sean.

'That was easy, you also need a good home cooked meal, lad, that's what you need, are you listening to me? Why don't you come over to the flat for tea one night? Tonight even,' Ann half demanded.

'Sorry, but I'm busy and will be for a few days, but I'll come towards the end of the week.' Sean left the office, beginning the descent of the stairs.

'Tonight, Sean, eight! And don't you be late! You listening?' Ann ensured he heard her. The bottom of the stairs was upon him. 'Hello, Mr Doyle,' said the young receptionist. Sean half smiled and raised his eyebrow. It made her day.

Outside he began looking for a taxi when he heard his name being shouted.

'Sean, Sean, wait up.' He turned to see a man coming towards him.

'Danny, how are yeh?'

'Good thanks. I've been asked if I want to re-start the boxing gym in that building over there.' He faced forward, but his arm was pointing in the direction of the old stables.

'Good, good, you interested then?'

'Maybe, would this be anything to do with you, by any chance, young Doyle?' he asked, sounding like he was back in his old profession.

'Let's just say you changed my life once, remember? And now I'm able to return the favour, that's all, plus there are a lot more kids like me who could do with your influence,' answered Sean. He patted Danny on the back.

'But t...' Danny was cut short as a car pulled up.

'I have to be somewhere, Danny, sorry, speak later. Ann will give you a key, go and look around, see what you think could be done, and remember what you told me once, "pride before a fall".'

The back door of the cab opened; Sean turned, window down. 'Danny! Don't be a macho fool, let people help, there are a lot that want to.' Sean nodded, the window went back up.

'Stoneferry Green, please, mate,' he asked, looking in the rear-view mirror.

'Which end, guv?' came back.

'Are there some empty buildings there? Squats, I think. That's what I've been told.'

'You'll want the docks end then, sir, but I believe they have emptied them recently. It's due for demolition next week. You still want to go?' The cab driver looked through the extra-large rear-view mirror.

'I do, mate.' Sean pulled the seat belt on. His mind was on the conversation earlier with Emma and the possibility of this missing grandchild. The journey was long; there had been no real conversation as Sean was busy reading through the report.

'Will this do yah, guv?' The car had come to a stop.

'Great, thanks,' he replied, exiting the cab. In front of him stood a row of old offices, three stories high with tall arched windows, protruding stone sills, and beautiful words carved in the local stone doorway: "Stoneferry Pumping Station". Underneath was written "1884". Back in the day, these Victorian buildings would have been something special. Today, however, they were scarred with graffiti and tell-tale signs of entropy, boarded up, discarded and decorated with fresh flyers pasted everywhere, warning people of the building's execution to come. "Demolition arranged for Thursday 9th November at eleven am. Viewing is available from dedicated sites, tickets purchased from City Hall".

The area had been labelled for redevelopment by his mate John Nash, no less. For years, this place had been home for the druggies, dossers, and prostitutes who were too old to work the main areas of the city. They made good use of the deep, darkened doorways of this dwelling to carry out their business. Three quid got you a shake, a deep-sea diver and you got blown. No pussy available, biology and gravity had put a stop to that.

Sean made his way around to the rear of the building, tucked the report in his trousers then started looking hard for an entry. At one point he slipped over a jar filled with raw liver. It took him several minutes to pull off the recently nailed board. 'Hey, stop!' shouted Sean, as he fell through the window into the building. A figure rapidly scurried away as he got back on to his feet.

'I only want to ask you some questions.' He heard the figure running up some steps. He gave chase. At the top of the stairs three bodies separated, running in different directions, aiming to confuse the possible predator chasing them. The middle one, was his choice. 'Easy now, I don't want to hurt anyone,' he said cornering the young woman, or was it a man?

'Why can't you just leave us alone? We'll be out before Thursday,' shouted a male voice from his left. 'Or we will be blown-up, so you win both ways,' shouted a female voice from his right. The cornered, unidentified gender remained silent.

'I'm not here to get you out, I'm trying to find out some information, on a couple of people, they may have lived here a few weeks ago, maybe longer.'

'Leave us alone, you bully,' shouted the female voice, now from behind him.

'What the fuck!' said Sean as an empty tin can was thrown at him, cutting his chin.

'Get out before you awaken the spirits, then you'll be sorry,' said the male voice.

'I could do with some spirits now! Look...' He sort of, laughed to himself. 'I'm only here for some information, it's your choice to believe it or not. I'll pay you for it, if that's what it takes.' His hand delved into the Mac's deep pocket, backing up the gesture of payment.

The cornered female stroke male ran past him to join the other two.

'Okay, I can see I'm wasting my time here, be safe and I'll bid you a farewell.' Sean turned, playing the "who will crack first game?". Eight seconds passed his foot about to hit the stairs.

'Wait, wait, we're hungry, we need the money. What do you want to know?' The three dishevelled individuals cracked first; they began whispering amongst each other.

'How much then?'

'How much what?' sarcastically asked Doyle.

'You said you'll pay for the information. How much have you got on ya?' The middle one who had thrown the tin can, became the spokesman.

'Let's see what you know first, you may be bluffing and know fuck all.'

'Let's see your money first. How do we know you have any?' said the middleman.

Sean fished again in the mac's pocket. 'Will this buy me anything?' He showed them fifteen pounds.

'Is that all you have? You can't want a lot of information,'

'What you doing now, robbing me?'

'What do you want to know? Let's get this over with,' interjected the female.

'Henry and a possible girlfriend lived here. Henry was posh speaking, skinny with a lot of tattoos, including all over his hands. Sound familiar?' He held out the money. 'Ring any bells?'

'Why are you looking for them? Have they done anything? Where are they? You the law?'

'I'm not the law, just trying to find out who killed Henry and his partner. I'm, shall we say, working on behalf of an interested party,' said Sean, again he held the money in their direction.

'Henry and Louisa are dead? You're lying. You really think we're that stupid? You're from that charity, trying to scare us again. Tell that devil we're not going back there, not to that place, we'd sooner kill ourselves. And that developer doesn't care, we saw him talking to the devil, laughing with him then making explosive gestures.' The middleman opened his arms in a pseudo attempt to shield the other two. All three of them moved back several paces, feet sliding instead of being lifted.

'I'm working for Henry's mother, Lady Emma De Pen Court,' explained Sean, in an attempt to distance himself from this devil character, they kept mentioning.

'He had no family, and nor did Louisa. He told us he was an orphan. Why would he lie about that, especially if his mother was titled, and he had no money? You're lying again,' stated the spokesman.

'Your pants are on fire,' shouted the female / male figure.

Sean wasn't interested in tittle tattle about who said, she said, he said.

'Can you confirm if his girlfriend was pregnant or not? That is all I need to know and I'm out of here, and I'll leave you alone, you have my word.' Sean added another tenner to the fifteen already in his hand. 'This jog yah memory?' ARM OUT FUTHER.

'No, she would have told me. I was friends with her, good friends. I can't believe that she's gone. She wouldn't hurt a fly, not Louisa, so kind and would help anyone, she would. It was the devil and that developer.' The man stroke woman who Sean had originally cornered began to cry. She was a woman, with a weight of no more than five stone and a haircut fashioned in the German concentration camps of the Second World War. Her clothes too, would have not been out of place there. Sean heard some banging on the downstairs doors. The three people in front of him changed drastically. The last time he saw humans in this state, with such fear portrayed on their faces, was in one of Assad's death camps in Syria.

'They are here to take us back, you lied, you have been a decoy, you have sentenced us to death.' The middleman pointed his thin arm at Sean. 'This is your doing, be it on your soul for life, they will kill us now.' The middle female put her hands over her ears and started repeating nursery rhymes, words at first, but these turned into a beautiful song. The other two fled into the loft space. The banging became louder and louder, as did the nursery rhymes. Shouting began originating from the ground floor, and from more than one person.

'We know you're all in here, make it easy on yourselves, come out now.' A few seconds break followed. 'Come out now and we won't hurt you.' A few more seconds. 'You have 30 seconds to show yourselves!' It went quiet; the counting started. 'One... two... three...' It continued.

Sean stepped back into the shadows, hidden behind the broken door. The counting continued. He listened to the deep male voices and their movements, trying to determine how many people were down there. Three moving, plus the one counting.

'Twenty-seven ... twenty-eight ... that's enough, go get 'em, lads,' ordered the man, and the counting was replaced with heavy footsteps. Sean looked at the frightened female, her eyes so tightly closed, her sweet, very worn face was distorted. Her hands held her satchel, as if holding on for dear life. He couldn't let her get hurt, she was so tiny, so in need of help. The footsteps came closer.

'We're coming to get you and we will burn you alive. Like the witches you are.' Two men laughed out loud. Sean slowed his breathing. The nursery rhymes became louder. The poor creature had reverted back to being a small child before the age of three. She believed if she couldn't see or hear the bad things, they couldn't see or hurt her. How wrong was she!

'Look at this? A bit of pussy, waiting for us to play with before the bonfire.' The laughter came again from the men in unison this time.

The rags the girl wore were ripped off her homeless bones. He dropped the cloth to the floor, bent down and licked her flat chest. 'Are you wet and ready for me little girl?' the creep asked as his hand slipped between her legs. 'Want some, Jimmy?' He turned; Jimmy was on the floor, neck bruised, face blue, he didn't have long to think. Doyle's hand flattened, with two fingers bent, a rabbit punch pushed the man's Adam's apple through to his spine.

'Shush.' Sean whispered to the girl, who was still reciting nursery rhymes with her eyes squeezed even tighter, unaware of the full horror around.

'What's going on up there? Stop fucking about, get them lowlifes down here now, and don't cut them, he doesn't want them bleeding, we have to empty them first.' Next to his foot was a box of blood bags, 'I'll get the tyres and petrol ready.' This came from the same person who had failed to complete the countdown. Steps again began ascending the stairs, much slower this time, at least two seconds between the legs being moved. Clearly this one was expecting trouble after no answer had come from the other two. Doyle returned back into the shadows, leaving the naked girl standing there as bait for his next victim.

'Fuck! Cleaver, get up here.' He shouted when his eyes laid on the bodies.

Doyle watched as an arm held out right and holding a pistol, came into his vision.

'Pssssst,' Doyle whispered. The man's arm moved. 'Pssssst.' Doyle did again. The man moved.

'Okay fucker, where are you? Come to daddy if you want to play. Don't hide like a coward?' The pistol was aimed around the room, the dim light an advantage for Doyle.

'Pssssst, here, over here.' Doyle showed himself to the man and the arm came around at speed. Like something from an Arnold Schwarzenegger movie, Doyle's hands moved like lightning, his left grabbed the barrel, his right slapped the man's hand. He now had hold of the pistol; with the handle he cracked his forehead. 'Cleaver, up here, you're the last one,' enticed a cocky Doyle. The response was the sound of running, then a loud bang as the board covering the window bounced back, clattering against the frame, after Cleaver's eager exit.

'Just can't get the staff.' He laughed to himself.

'Come out, it's clear now.' He bent down to pick up the girl's rags off the floor.

Sean told the others to come out, it was safe now. The nursery rhymes had stopped; she opened her eyes. 'They didn't see me, did they?' And a genuine smile appeared on her happy face. Doyle saw the damage lying within and behind this creature's eyes, they shone but looked empty as if she was high on something.

But if she had taken any drugs it would have killed her. Being so undernourished, her liver would have packed up.

The lack of hydration meant the drugs would have cracked her brain. The other two slipped from out of the ceiling cavity.

'When was the last time any of you lot saw daylight?' he asked the pale mammals.

'We only go out at night, and that's if we dare, they've been after us for weeks now. It's because of our blood,' said the spokesman without any malice or distrust, but this was the reason they were in this trouble.

'Why? What's going on? Why would they want you three? What do you mean, yah blood?' Sean stood back and looked at the girl. 'Have you any more clothes for her?' his arm still pointing,

'No, we've nothing, everything we had was stolen by the BONES people. They caught five of us, two we think got away, but only us left here now,' said the female. Sean came back. He removed his Mac and hung it on the door. His arms went up in front of his face and bent over his head. He pulled off his sweatshirt and passed it over to the tiny female. Her friend put a hat on her after the sweatshirt. Sean reminisced, as she resembled a Michael Bentine puppet. He replaced his Mac. The second female hugged her. 'You look really pretty, Lucy, we will have to do your hair.' And she kissed the young girl's forehead.

'How old is she?' enquired Sean.

'Twenty-one.' A second kiss was placed on her head.

Sean drew in his lips; dimples appeared. 'What is it, you're all so scared of? Have you nowhere else to go, no family, friends, away from here?' He was surprised at her age, her frame resembled a young teenager. He looked at all three of them: they were like skeletons.

'It looks nice from the outside, but its pure evil within. We escaped, but they won't allow us to live, in case we talk.

When they had us in that place, for two weeks they syphoned our blood, we were fed nothing but a gruel mixture, every three hours and iron tablets which made us feel sick, because there wasn't enough solids in the belly. But even if we told people what we saw, they wouldn't believe us, they just wouldn't believe what was going on in there. I still think it's a nightmare myself,' said the spokesman, he turned his arms outwards to aid the words. Each arm held more than a dozen holes. And on each upper bicep was tattooed a couple of numbers, below this was a bar code.

'Talk to me, let's see if I can help. Where is this place?' asked Sean.

'Twelve of us had been chosen, one minute we were eating lunch, talking and laughing, we couldn't believe our luck getting accepted in. The next we had been rounded up, corralled in the small back room, we were drugged and kept in a coma, our bodies sealed into vacuumed bags, with only our arms hanging out, we were sources of rare bloods.' The female stopped talking, she looked to the male.

'What was that?' screamed the spokesman. 'They're back, why, why us?' He lost all hope in humanity.

'This waaaay, now!' shouted Doyle watching, as behind the three of them, the walls and floor fell away, literally collapsing into nothing - an abyss of dust, rubble and contaminated air. Two of the party turned, they panicked, froze and fell prey to the moving void, appearing to be consumed by the dust cloud. The girl several feet in front started to recite her nursery rhymes again, eyes tight shut once more to make herself invisible. Sean lunged forward. Unable to save all three, he grabbed his sweatshirt with one hand and pulled the human bag of bones to safety. He chucked the young poet over his shoulder, grabbing her tight across the back of her legs. He pounded down the stairs, oblivion chasing and gaining ground on them. On his recce earlier he had spotted a flat door in the kitchen floor. One arm yanked it free; up it came. The dust about to swallow the pair, he dropped Lucy down. Joining her, but jumping to the left, the rubble flying past closed the door. Four minutes passed, the noise vanished, and dust had begun to settle. 'How many were in here, Cleaver?' A deep voice sounded.

'At least two, plus our three, sir,' coughed Cleaver, covering his mouth with a handkerchief and blinking fast to prevent the grit entering his eyes. The loud demanding voice bent down and pulled some rubble from one of bodies. 'Who the fuck could have snapped his neck like this? It wasn't any of the homeless blood rats, that's for certain. What's this?' he bent once more, picking up the file folder or part of it. 'Looks like someone may be taking an interest in us?' He began to read.

'Over here, boss, take a look, two more bodies,' a distant voice said, coughing as he finished his sentence.

The man bent again his fingers placed on a neck. 'How could any of them have killed Hoskins? I don't know of any person, any one, that could have murdered him. Fifteen minutes men and we are away, no bodies or any signs that we were here to be left behind. Do I make myself clear?' He walked out of the collapsed building as his men went to work, first off removing their dead. A passer-by with a big dog spoke. 'I guess it wasn't safe then, like they said on the news,' he declared with humour, his head aimed towards the rubble.

'No, it wasn't, you're correct about that, good sir. The homeless who had been living here, they had burnt all the wood. The floors have given in, under the weight of the walls, causing it all to collapse. We have arrived to flatten the rest and ensure it's safe for the tax paying public.' He looked towards the JCB, as if he needed confirmation, then there it was, a big yellow machine in the middle of the rubble, levelling the fallen building, flashing lights and all.

'Shame really, it was a beautiful place back in the day, should have been declared a place of interest, a museum maybe.' The dog-walker moved on towards the long body of water.

'Five minutes and we're out of here, come on.' The boss shouted then left them to it, he set of walking at a good pace by the canal. The dog walker turned, about to say something, there was a crack, followed by a splash.

Two pickups drove away, followed by the digger. The swirling orange work-light faded as the excavator turned the corner. Leaving the dust settling on the warm rubble, the site above ground was now vacant. Below, the only sounds were coming from the cellar. 'Humpty Dumpty sat on a wall, Humpty Dumpty had a great fall, all the king's horses and all the king's men couldn't put my sweet Humpty together again.' Lucy sat close to an unconscious Sean Doyle, her bent knees firmly pressed into his chest as she softly stroked his face. Just as if he was her doll, the soft touching continued as did the reciting of the old nursery rhyme, "Humpty Dumpty".

'Fuck, that's gonna hurt later.' His hand pushed through his hair; he felt the wetness. 'How long have I been out? You ok?' Sean sat up and dusted himself off as he came around, but he got no reply from the girl, all he heard was more embellished nursery rhymes.

'A ring, a ring of roses, a pocket full of posies, a tissue a tissue, we all fall down. A ring, a ring of syringes, a pocket full of doses, a tissue a tissue, and we all fall down. Picked up and squeezed into bags,' She began to repeat the same line over and over. The girl hadn't moved her knees, they remained tucked into Sean's chest, she hadn't even realised he was awake. Her legs were still, her upper body rocking to the rhythm of her own acapella rhymes.

'Hey, hey, come on, look at me. Can you tell me what's frightening you?' Doyle had hold of her shoulders.

'A RING, A RING OF ROSES, A POCKET FULL O...' Her head spun round at speed, freakishly staring at Sean, her bright eyes eating in to him, the singing was louder, her eyes still firmly fixed. She started again, but this was like no rhyme Doyle had ever heard.

'The big, big, bad man is coming to get us, he will, he will share us out, he has sharp knives and cuts, and cuts and cuts, then laughs while his eyes sparkle. We will live in hell together forever, with the big, big, bad man. A ring a ring of roses, a pocket full of posies.' The girl still didn't move, her eyes now closed, she no longer held Sean's soul.

Doyle pushed himself up off the floor. 'Fuck, I'm going to have some bruises.' He grabbed the young girl, standing her up with him. Sean had spent a hell of a lot of time in the forces, but this was stranger than anything that came before. He had known people lose a few marbles, and even break down to melting point. However, this creature's mind had gone to another place, a dark evil place, but it had come back in a different way, but to him she was an angel, worthy of saving, he'd taken so many there in the past, to bring one back would redeem part of him.

'What's wrong with you?' he demanded, shaking her firmly by the shoulders. He stopped quickly, remembering how tiny and thin she was.

He was frustrated by her lack of clear speech, and more than likely he had a bit of concussion, which may have impaired his judgment. Her eyes re-opened and stared into his, but hers were totally empty, gone was the sparkle, they didn't engage because they couldn't, she was, for want of a better word, "broken".

'The big, big, bad man will take us all away, he will eat us, if we are not good boys and girls, all of our arms and legs, hearts and lungs he will sell on the market stall, the rest he will mince and feed us more. Please sir can I have some more, fed with a drip but the fluid the wrong way. A ring, a ring of roses, a pocket full of posies, a tissue a tissue, we all shall pay.'

She pushed herself away from him and started to scream uncontrollably, her pitch so high as loud and sharp as a banshee. Sean had no choice but to gag her. He didn't know where they were, or who was around still, he only knew that whoever was responsible for all this, had some fucking power and a lot of leverage, an enemy to be scared of, whoever you were.

'Sh ... sh ... shush.' She nibbled at the inside of his fingers; he pressed harder on her lips. The ceiling shook again and again, making the cracks between the floorboards release yet another heavy cloud of dust. Sean instinctively pulled her into him, shielding his angel from any potential harm. He began to cough. She started the strange rhymes once more, mumbling away. He felt the words' vibrating on his skin.

'A ring, a ring of roses, a pocket full of posies, I hear the giant's footsteps, a ring, a ring of roses. We'll be dead, a ring a r...' The girl was muted into Sean's chest. Hand over his own mouth, dulling the dry cough, he looked up. Whether it was a giant or not, she was right about the footsteps, each one releasing more suffocating dust, in turn temporarily cutting off the light coming through the cracks. It was all he could do to stop himself from giving away their location. He desperately released small amounts of air through his nostrils, his lungs wanting to burst, holding in the cough. The steps stopped in one place; the feet shuffled as if taking root. Rubble was tossed across the room for a good couple of minutes.

Dozens of small and large pieces of masonry flew in all directions, every one of them forcing more dust down into the cellar. Sean had stripped off, covering his and the girl's head with his Mac. The trap door was slowly pulled upwards.

'Any one down there, hello? Can I help?' said the voice, followed by a dog barking.

'QUIET, Sherry, quiet! I can't hear anything with you trying to talk.'

'Bark!' was received as if Sherry gave an answer.

The man rubbed the dog's head with his free hand, then tried again. 'Anyone down there? I'm going to call the fire brigade.'

'Down here, mate.' said Sean, coming from under the coat, but leaving her there.

'Thank God! Are you alright? Are you alone? Anyone with you?' came back, followed by another bark.

'On my own, just cuts and bruises, I think.' replied Sean. He didn't know who was up there, and his instincts told him to protect his "mark" the poet.

'Wait, wait there, I'll go fetch a rope from the canal's life ring.' The dog started barking again as the man walked off. Both he and the dog returned in quick time.

'Got it, tie the end off, I'll climb up,' said Sean, his voice directed upwards.

The man was busy thinking, he gave his answer in the form of a nod, but Sean didn't know that. Spotting a brass water inlet, three times he wound the rope around, finishing it off with a reef knot; the only one he knew. 'Ready,' he shouted.

Sean lifted his jacket for a minute, 'I'll pull you up when I'm out, we're safe now, do you understand me?' He locked his eyes with the female. No response, she still displayed the face of a poor, Bedlam inmate.

'Thanks,' were Doyle's first words as he came clear, still on his knees, but out of the cellar. The area was dark, Doyle remained on his knees falling forward, the man was taken aback with the size of him. Sean was naked on the top, not ripped like an obsessive body builder, but all the slabs of meat were in the correct places, and in abundance, he pressed down with his hands to come up, the muscles changed form.

'Any time, just glad you're alive. I saw all the building give way and came running to help,' replied the rescuer.

'There's two of us, a girl, she's still down there,' Doyle informed the dog walker. He didn't resemble the big bad man that the girl was terrified of, if such a person existed in reality, and he was no threat to him.

On his feet, he turned and pulled on the rope. One moment, the line was a fisherman's delight, taut as he had tied the other end around the girl, he pulled; then he hit the wall as the rope went slack. The two men returned to the trap door and heard.

'A ring, a ring of roses, a pocket full of posies, I will die, I will die down here in hell not through the false gates and clean rooms, you try to take me to. I will burn you can't have me like you want to, my syrup is mine - it's not for sale.' She was rocking away.

'Stop! Look at me, tie the rope around your middle, so I can pull you up. Do you understand?' Sean didn't know if she understood a word he said. The dog began to bark and leap in the air.

'A ring, a ring of roses, a poc...' She sat rocking on the floor as he watched helplessly at the top of the cellar. 'I'm going back down for her; I'll lift her up you grab her hands.'

'You can't, I can smell gas,' said the man, sniffing the air. Sherry barked more as if in agreement.

'Come to the rope, please, come to the rope. I'll get you some help.' His head and face were inside the opening to the cellar. The darkness and dust prevented his vision exploring more than a few feet.

'Here.' And the man passed him a small torch.

'What yeh doing?' Sean shouted down.

'Come on, let's get some help, leave her. If the gas ignites, we all die. Leave her, it's too dangerous,' encouraged the man. Tugging at Doyle's arm, he tried to pull him away.

'You go, I'm not leaving without her. I've lost enough people in my life, she's not going on the reel.' He'd spotted the girl sat up in the far corner next to the large brass tap. He watched her thumb trying to spin the serrated wheel of the Zippo, his regimental ZIPPO, with two small wings, and the words "who dares wins" she must have pinched it out of his pocket when he was out of it. The smell of gas became stronger, but he'd accepted the responsibility for her life, no contract no verbal instruction, just Doyle's morals.

'I can't just leave her down there, she's a person, she needs help.' Sean began shouting louder, trying to get Lucy to respond.

The dog stopped barking. The man stared at the girl; her eyes were drawn towards his. She switched her gaze to Sean and gave a smile. Again, as if in a recording studio, she began to sing the next song, her voice so calm and majestic her tiny hand up on her ears.

'London's burning, London's burning, fetch the engines, fetch the engines. London's burning. Goodnight my Mr Doyle, forgive my exit, I no longer wish to dwell in this hell.' She looked again at the man next to Sean, her sweet smile left the pretty face, then down the gaze went, back to the winged Zippo, now coupled in both her hands. Her thumb went to work as she flicked the lighter once more. The dog, its owner and Sean were propelled up and over by the blast.

'NOOOO! Nooooo, no?' cried out Sean stumbling to his feet, unsuccessfully staying up, falling left then right, deaf and disorientated from the explosion, he tried to stand once more determined to get to her, again falling left, then right on the piles of rubble, immediately getting back up desperate to find Lucy. Coughing, holding his ribs and trying to spit, it felt to him as if he had no fluid in his body, let alone in his mouth. Pain shot from his lower back to his shoulder, his breath became short, then virtually nothing. He saw his Mac on the rubble a few feet away. Darkness appeared, taking away his vision, and his legs gave way underneath, like a paper weight he lay on his Mac.

'Emergency operator, which service do you require?' asked the female.

'Fire, fire, ambulance, the building, it's ... it's ... iit... gone,' said the dog walker.

'Can you give me some information, please, sir. Is anyone trapped in this building? And the address of the building, please, sir.'

'Yes, no, ... I think she's dead, the building has gone. The Old Pumping station on the canal. A man is here as well, who is injured, but I can't see him, and I might be bleeding, there's so much dust, I can't see him.' He felt drips of something from his head onto his open neck. He talked as he looked for Sean. Visibility still low, the cloud of dust had yet to settle.

'The fire service is on the way, sir, ambulances and police will attend your location also. Please remain on the scene in a safe location away from any further danger. The rescue services will be with you very shortly. Could I take your name, and will you remain on the line for me? Are you hurt, sir?'

The phone connection ended. The dog walker called a different number.

'Where are you, you're late?' His tone was nothing like it was when he spoke with the emergency operator or Doyle.

'Two minutes away, sir.'

'Get here now.' Phone down. The dog was barking. *CRACK!* the .22 bullet stopped the barking instantly. The fur covered carcass was dragged by the hind legs onto the remains of the burning building. Blue flames ignited as the heat digested the long black and tan fur.

'You're cutting it fine. Go!' The black Merc pulled away literally as the emergency circus arrived. 'Mission successful, sir?' Came from the front.

'Yes, but I had to deal with it myself. All three are no longer living, including Hoskins but there was a stranger there, a Mr Boyle, I think that's what the crazy girl called him, just a passer-by who became involved, a big lad he's probably dead. I saw him fall near to the fire, nothing to worry about, in fact it will be good if he is alive, he will give a statement about a dog walker helping. But make it a priority to find out what has happened to him, and some background. Tick the boxes. Okay?'

'Will do, I'll get Laurence to enter the Met's computer. Where to now, sir?'

'The club of course, I am in need of refreshments. I

believe I have earned a large malt, don't you?' Shoebridge pressed the button; the glass divider sealed off the front from the rear. He dropped the cover of the chair and pulled out a first-aid kit.

Eight minutes later two more large red engines rolled up to the demolished building, followed by another ambulance and squad car. A crowd had gathered, called by the towering flames and sporadic explosions. Sean bent over, his right arm pressing against his ribs. He had grabbed his beloved Mac and left the scene via the canal side a few moments before the engine's arrival. He needed help, but with all that had gone on this evening, he no longer felt safe. Whoever was behind all this shit had means, money and fucking motive and a lot of knowledge, which confirmed his earlier thoughts, as he put two and two together.

To be continued in Grave Trade

PART TWO - THE CONCLUSION

Thank you for reading one of my books, join Sean Doyle
Grave Trade

Printed in Great Britain
by Amazon

17780529R00174